"So na?" he ar.

Like she'd tell him that! "Hunting? What makes you think I was?"

"You're not ready to hear what I think, little girl." His smile continued to taunt her.

"I'm not a little girl." Especially the way he was making her feel at the moment. Oh yeah, she really needed to put some distance between the two of them.

She was about to tell him so when she realized that his eyes had become fixed on her mouth as he slowly leaned in close enough that his warm breath teased her skin. What was he doing? Please tell her he wasn't going to kiss her! She should be outraged, but instead she was . . . intrigued.

Dear God, her world rocked on its axis the second his lips settled over hers. As her ability to think short-circuited, she grabbed on to the first thing she could find to anchor herself as the alley seemed to rock and roll: Sandor himself. Her fingers clutched his arms, the buttery-soft leather of his duster doing little to disguise his muscular strength.

This had to stop!

This title is also available as an eBook.

REDEEMED IN DARKNESS

"Captivating, compelling, and totally hot! Don't miss this series!"

—Alyssa Day, *USA Today* bestselling author of *Atlantis Unleashed*

IN DARKNESS REBORN

"Utterly compelling. I love these hunky, sexy, heroic guys! Great sexual tension and action. Really terrific and totally unique."

—Katherine Stone, author of *Caroline's Journal*

DARK PROTECTOR

"An innovative story line, passionate protective champions, and lots of surprising twists. . . . Don't be left out—pick up a copy, settle in, and enjoy."

—*Romance Reviews Today*

"A complex paranormal fantasy that pulls readers in from the first page and doesn't let them go."

—*Paranormal Romance Writers*

DARK DEFENDER

"Tons of suspense and drama. Morgan proves that she's . . . here to stay."

—*Romantic Times*

"An intense plot with twists and turns and wonderful surprises."

—*Paranormal Romance Writers*

Also by Alexis Morgan

THE PALADIN SERIES

Darkness Unknown
Redeemed in Darkness
In Darkness Reborn
Dark Defender
Dark Protector

THE TALION SERIES

Dark Warrior Unleashed

Dark Warrior
UNBROKEN

ALEXIS MORGAN

Pocket **Star** Books
New York London Toronto Sydney

Pocket Star Books
A Division of Simon & Schuster, Inc.
1230 Avenue of the Americas
New York, NY 10020

This book is a work of fiction. Names, characters, places, and incidents either are products of the author's imagination or are used fictitiously. Any resemblance to actual events or locales or persons, living or dead, is entirely coincidental.

First Pocket Star Books paperback edition August 2009

POCKET STAR BOOKS and colophon are registered trademarks of Simon & Schuster, Inc.

For information about special discounts for bulk purchases, please contact Simon & Schuster Special Sales at 1-866-506-1949 or business@simonandschuster.com

The Simon & Schuster Speakers Bureau can bring authors to your live event. For more information or to book an event contact the Simon & Schuster Speakers Bureau at 1-866-248-3049 or visit our website at www.simonspeakers.com.

Cover design by Lisa Litwack. Illustration by Craig White.

Manufactured in the United States of America

10 9 8 7 6 5 4 3 2 1

ISBN 978-1-4165-6344-0
ISBN 978-1-4165-6396-9 (ebook)

Meredith, this one is for you. Since the day you were born, I've had so much fun watching to see what you'd accomplish next. Thanks for being my daughter. I couldn't imagine a better one.

Acknowledgments

Writing a book is never a solo effort. It takes the help of a lot of talented people to take a story all the way from concept to publication. I'd like to thank everyone who made my story even better.

To my fabulous agent, Michelle Grajkowski, bless you for all of your encouragement and support. You help keep me sane, and you make me laugh. It always helps to know that you're just a phone call away.

To my incredibly talented editor, Micki Nuding, I so appreciate how you make my best writing even better. I've learned so much from you, and your encouragement and support mean so much.

And finally, to everybody at Pocket who contributes so much to the success of my books. You might be behind the scenes, but I know you're there and how hard you work. Thank you, thank you, thank you.

Dark Warrior
UNBROKEN

Chapter 1

*L*ena Wilson was a woman with regrets. Her shoulders sagged as the day's heat and her high heels made the short walk even harder than expected. She'd worn dress clothes out of respect, but her usual jeans and boots might have been a smarter choice. Lord knows, the person she was going to see wouldn't have cared.

Pausing at the top of a rise, she pulled out the simple map the caretaker had given her. She was almost there.

"One, two, three . . ."

She counted off the headstones to alleviate the oppressive silence, her footsteps slowing as she approached the end of the row, her goal but a few feet away. She crossed that last painful distance and sank to her knees on the cool grass.

Her hand reached out to trace the inscription on the polished granite marker: a name, a couple of dates, a Bible verse, a fireman's badge. Not nearly enough to define the man who was buried there. Maynard Cooper had been her friend, her father figure, her conscience.

At long last the tears came, flowing down her cheeks in hot streaks.

"Coop, I'm so sorry."

Her throat closed, damming up the flood of apologies she owed to the man who'd been laid to rest on the pastoral hillside overlooking his beloved city. As the tears tapered off and her breathing eased, peace slowly stole over her. Coop had never judged her as harshly as she judged herself, but the self-forgiveness she needed would have to be earned.

That she'd missed his funeral hadn't been her fault, but missing out on the chance to heal the breach between them was. She placed her palm over his name, needing that small connection as she contemplated her next step.

If she couldn't make peace with her old friend, she would do the one thing no one else had been able to: avenge his death.

With a new sense of purpose, Lena rose to her feet and walked away, making plans. Somewhere in this city there was a killer with Maynard Cooper's blood on his hands. She wouldn't rest until the bastard was brought to justice.

The shrill ringing of a phone was Sandor Kearn's least favorite way to wake up, especially when he'd been up late. He didn't know which half of his job he hated more: the frustrating search for the Grand Dame's lost relatives, or his new role as chief enforcer for the Talion warriors Kerry commanded. He covered his eyes with his forearm to block out the sunshine and groped for the phone with his other hand.

When he finally found it, he growled "What?" into the receiver.

Kerry's voice was a mixture of good humor and business. "Sorry, Sandor, did I wake you up?"

"Yeah, you did. Put your husband on the line so I can take my bad mood out on him. When I'm able to be civil, Ranulf can give the phone back to you."

His Dame giggled. He was tempted to point out how undignified that was for the ruler of their people, but that would only encourage her.

"If it's not an emergency, can I call you back in a few?" he said instead. "Right now I won't remember anything you tell me."

"Please tell me you weren't up half the night working again. We've talked about that before,

Sandor. You're my Talion, not my slave." She sounded reproachful.

"All right, I won't tell you."

She sighed. "Get up and eat breakfast. Make that lunch—it's almost noon. When you're feeling human again, come see me."

"Okay. See you in an hour or so." He yawned loudly. "And by the way, I'm *not* human, and neither are you."

"I'll try to remember that. And an hour will be fine."

When she disconnected the call, he tossed his phone at the table. As it bounced onto the floor, he threw back the covers, then went into the bathroom and cranked the shower on hot. Leaning against the cool tile wall, he let the water pour over him, clearing out the cobwebs better than a cup of coffee.

Kerry knew that he already had a lot on his plate, so whatever was worrying her had to be serious. Well, he'd find out soon enough what it was.

He pulled on jeans and a casual sports shirt, then threw together a sandwich and grabbed a cola to drink on the way. After tossing his briefcase onto the passenger seat, he reached for his sunglasses.

Traffic was light, and he soon reached the gates to her driveway. He punched in his security number, waited as they swung open, then pulled into his usual parking space, alongside an unfamiliar car. Hughes, the butler, opened the front door before Sandor reached the top step. Inside, he headed for the living room, then stopped. Kerry hadn't mentioned the fact that anyone else would be there, so the unfamiliar woman was probably another Kyth who had dropped in to meet the new Dame.

Sandor waited impatiently in the foyer for the visitor to leave. Who was she anyway? He would have remembered meeting someone built like that—honey blond hair, long legs, narrow waist, and all the right curves. If she was anywhere near as stunning from the front, he might just start drooling. When she finally turned to leave, her piercing blue eyes swept past him, then snapped back to stare into his.

And time stood still.

All of his Talion instincts surged full force, making him want to stop her, to learn her truth before letting her walk out that door. He didn't recognize her as Kyth, but he could have been wrong.

He forced himself to nod politely as she passed. When the door closed behind her, he had the strangest feeling that their paths would cross again and soon.

Kerry was walking out of the other side of the living room as he walked in, leaving only Ranulf waiting to talk to him. The Viking looked hesitant, not an expression Sandor had ever seen on his face before.

"If there's something you want to say, Viking, spit it out. I'm not in the mood for games."

Ranulf's mouth quirked up in a small grin. "What put a burr up your backside?"

"No sleep. No progress on anything." Gods above, he sounded whiny. "Sorry."

"Don't sweat it." Ranulf turned to stare out the window. "Sometimes things close in on you, especially here in the city. I'm long overdue for some downtime on the mountain, alone with my wife."

"So why don't you and Kerry head up there for a few days? I can hold down the fort."

"She won't go. She worries about you," Ranulf grumbled.

"Damn it, I'm fine." He wasn't and they both knew it. But it was his problem, not theirs.

Ramulf let out a deep breath. "Kerry asked you here about a new problem that's popped up. She needed to make a call but should be off the phone by now."

They found Kerry sitting at the dining room table, immersed in paperwork. She didn't look any happier than Ranulf did.

"Damn it, Kerry, you promised to eat lunch before starting in on that stuff." Ranulf picked up a plate of food and set it directly in front of her. "Now eat or I'll burn those files."

She looked up from the report to glare at him. Her refusal to be intimidated by her warrior husband was one of the many things Sandor liked about the new Dame. Most people took one look at Ranulf and had the good sense to be a little afraid. But Kerry knew she had the man wrapped around her little finger. Ranulf would die before hurting her.

So would Sandor, even though she'd never looked at him as anything but a friend. He sometimes wondered about her taste in men, but he couldn't question the depth of her feelings for Ranulf, or his for her. Their relationship had been tempered in the heat of battle, a life-and-death struggle that had come close to destroying all three of them.

As she dutifully picked up the sandwich, she asked, "Did you already eat, Sandor?"

"Yes." He sat in his usual chair and reached for the coffeepot. "Some caffeine would be good, though. Can I top yours off?"

She held out her cup. "Sorry to have disturbed your beauty sleep."

"It's my job to be at your beck and call." He softened the comment with a smile. "Finish your lunch and we'll talk."

She gave him the same disgusted look she'd given her husband. Like many Kyth who'd grown up unaware of their true heritage, Kerry had been a loner before fate had catapulted her from graphic artist to ruler of their kind in a matter of days. She wasn't used to having people fuss over her, much less bearing responsibility for an entire race. It was a wonder she was coping as well as she was.

Ranulf had left the room, and now returned with his own sandwich and a plate of cookies. Sandor snagged a couple for himself. The Viking wasn't the only one with a sweet tooth.

When Hughes checked in a few minutes later to see if they needed anything else, Kerry dropped the rest of her sandwich on the plate and handed it to him. "Thank you. That hit the spot."

It was clear that Ranulf thought she should've eaten more, but she shot him a look that said she'd had enough of his hovering.

It was time to get down to business. "So what's up, Kerry? Ranulf said you had something to talk to me about."

"Actually, a couple of things now. That woman who just left has the potential of becoming a problem for us."

"Why? Who is she?"

"Her name is Lena Wilson, and she was a friend of Maynard Cooper's. She said she's investigating his death and wanted to talk to us about it. She's looking for his killer."

That wasn't good. "Why would she think you were involved?"

They hadn't had anything to do with the fire investigator's death. But the three of them *had* combined forces to execute his murderer, a renegade Talion warrior and Sandor's lifelong friend.

"I don't know that she did," Kerry said. "I think she was on a fishing expedition."

Ranulf looked at his wife. "She tried to read my thoughts while she was here. I suspect she did the same to you."

"What? You didn't tell me that!"

"I figured you could tell."

"Well, you figured wrong. Need I remind you that I've only recently learned something like that was even possible?" She looked more disgusted than upset. "If she did try to read me, she couldn't have gotten far. I'm a lot better at keeping my shields up. If they'd been breached, I think I'd know."

"If it's any comfort, her efforts were pretty clumsy. I doubt she's had any training."

"She's Kyth?" Sandor hadn't sensed any indication that she was, but their encounter had been brief.

Ranulf shook his head. "Couldn't really tell. If she is, the connection is pretty weak."

"Let me know if she becomes a problem." He

wouldn't mind interrogating her thoroughly. "So what else is up, boss?"

Kerry picked up a file folder and shuffled through a stack of newspaper clippings. "I noticed the first of these reports a couple of weeks ago. If it was the only one, I wouldn't think anything about it. But I've found several more incidents mentioned from all over the area, so they're probably not random."

Sandor flipped through the clippings quickly, glancing at the headlines and dates before going back to read through them more carefully. She was right to be concerned. Even if the various police departments hadn't yet connected the dots, a new gang was clearly operating in the Seattle area.

Unlike with most gang-related violence, drugs didn't seem to be involved. On the surface, the victims had little in common other than being mugged. The amount of cash taken had varied from a few bucks to a couple of hundred. Both men and women had been attacked, their ages running from late teens to elderly. The time of the attacks seemed to be limited to afternoon through late evening, although there were exceptions.

None of that would have drawn the attention of the Dame or her Talion enforcer. Petty crime had been around since the dawn of time. What made this crime spree different was the victims' physical condition after they'd been robbed.

The police described them as dizzy, vague, confused, weak, stumbling, exhausted, and so on. To anyone outside the Kyth, the symptoms would probably be written off as shock from being robbed, but they made Sandor's blood run cold and then hot. He lifted his eyes to meet his Dame's worried gaze.

A renegade Kyth—it had to be. There was no other explanation that made sense. Worse, it could be more than one, since the victims' descriptions varied too much for the same person to be behind all the attacks. Sandor spread out the clippings and reached for a lined tablet to write on, dimly aware of Kerry and Ranulf leaving. Once he had the facts organized, he'd turn to his computer to delve deeper. With luck, he'd have a handle on what was going on and a plan of action to present by the end of the day.

For violent crimes against humanity, the Kyth justice system had only one punishment—death. And it was his job to carry out that sentence. He was still haunted by memories of his first execution, a renegade he'd once called friend. The darkness he'd drawn into his soul that night still prowled inside him, reminding Sandor what he was capable of.

Though they'd had no choice but to execute

Bradan, the price Sandor had paid had been very high.

As a job description, *executioner* pretty much sucked. But if more Kyth had gone rogue, he would kill the bastards. Rolling his shoulders to get the kinks out, Sandor started writing again.

Lena tossed her half-eaten pizza slice in the trash and put the box with the remainder in the small hotel fridge. Lately, nothing had much taste. Coop's death had cast a pall over her world, dimming even the simplest pleasures.

She was battling depression mixed with an obsession, and neither problem would go away until Coop's killer was behind bars. Talking to a shrink wouldn't solve these problems, and her body's reaction to medications was too unpredictable, usually making her sicker than the ailment they were supposed to cure.

Lena got out her spiral notebook to record her findings so far. She'd already gone over the details of the dance club fire Coop had been investigating. After leaving the cemetery, she'd gone directly to see Kerry Thorsen, the chief witness at the fire.

The interview had netted mixed results. Kerry had seemed genuine in her sorrow over Coop's death, but confirmed that their acquaintance had been short and strictly professional. Kerry's grim-faced behemoth of a husband, Ranulf Thorsen, had loomed beside his wife as both denied any knowledge of Maynard Cooper's murder.

They were lying. Maybe neither had had a direct hand in Coop's death, but her gut told her they'd known more than they were telling her. Desperate to learn those secrets, she'd dropped her inner shields and tried to reach past their surface thoughts to delve deeper into their minds.

All she'd gotten from Kerry was an affirmation that the woman had liked Coop very much and had truly regretted his death. Her husband had immediately blocked Lena's efforts to probe his thoughts, leaving her feeling as if she'd been slammed against a brick wall. A gleam in his eyes had suggested that he had not only been aware of her efforts but found them amusing.

The experience had left her badly shaken. She'd broken her personal vow to never use her gift again, since doing so had cost her so much the last time. And not only had she failed to garner any answers but she'd also brought herself to the attention of someone whose powers obviously eclipsed her own.

Before she'd been able to figure out her next step, a handsome, dark-haired man had appeared in the doorway behind her. Relieved at the opportunity to make her escape, Lena had quickly thanked her hosts for their time and followed their butler toward the door. What kind of people had a butler, anyway?

The new arrival had briefly held her gaze before silently walking past her. During that brief connection, she'd sensed a power in him that had sent high-octane energy bubbling through her veins. The sensation hadn't been totally pleasant, and left a taint of darkness in its wake. It seemed she wasn't the only hunter in the crowd.

Who *was* he? Hours later, she still couldn't get him out of her mind. Once she exhausted her other leads, maybe he'd be worth checking out. The finely honed instincts that made Lena such a good investigator were telling her she hadn't seen the last of the handsome stranger.

She began taking off her good clothes, and sighed with relief to shed her panty hose. Her next stop was the ruins of the fire, and she wasn't about to wear a skirt and heels to rummage around in ashes and debris. After dressing in her rattiest jeans and a chambray work shirt, she pulled on her steel-toed boots. Normally she would've worn a hard hat, but there hadn't been room for one in her suitcase.

Picking up her clipboard, she tucked her room key and a digital camera into her shirt pocket. The dance club was within easy walking distance and the exercise would do her good. Then she headed out to learn what she could of her friend's violent death, dreading facing the gruesome site.

Though the ashes had been cold for weeks, her well-trained nose picked up their scent from a block away. Good. She'd been worried that the owners would have already hired a contractor to start the rebuilding process. In fact, it was odd that they hadn't. Although the cause of the fire had been arson, nothing indicated that the owners had been involved. She added that anomaly to the list of things that needed checking into.

From where she stood, the remnants of the fire looked undisturbed. The area was cordoned off with rope and signs warning off trespassers, but nothing was going to stop her from seeing where Coop had died. If anyone came along, she had her badge with her. It was for a fire department three thousand miles away, but hopefully no one would notice.

Ducking under the rope, she made her approach cautiously, taking in general impressions before focusing on any details. The fire had definitely burned bright and hot. Considering how little was left of the building, it was hard to believe that no one had died in the fire that night. There had been only a few minor treat-and-release injuries and one woman hurt badly enough to require hospitalization. That was nothing short of a miracle in a blaze this size.

According to the reports a friend at the fire department had slipped her, the person most responsible for getting everyone out safely was Kerry Thorsen. Not only had she kept a cool head—a hard thing to do even for experienced firefighters—but she'd actually carried a couple of people out herself. Given her petite size, how was that even possible? Lena would have been tempted to write the report off as an exaggeration, but there had been too many witnesses.

One puzzle after another.

The fire had started at the front of the club and burned toward the back, driving the trapped customers and employees before its fury. If the arsonist had blocked the rear exit, the death toll would have numbered in the dozens. Lena shuddered. During her career, she'd seen her share of horrific sights, but nothing this bad. Not yet.

Circling around to the back, she studied the parking lot, noting the alley from which the arsonist was purported to have watched the fire. Not only was Kerry Thorsen the heroine that night;

she'd also been the one to spot the alleged arsonist. Coincidence? Maybe, but Lena didn't buy it. Kerry definitely knew more about the fire than she was letting on.

It was time to step inside the burned-out shell of the building. Ordinarily Lena wouldn't hesitate to cross the threshold to learn the fire's story, but this crime scene was different. She ruthlessly shut down her secret abilities, determined to evaluate the scene through the five senses she shared with the rest of humanity. She started by taking a deep breath.

Scent: the smells of charred wood and other chemicals had faded, but they were still pungent enough to clog her sinuses. That was normal.

Sound: nothing helpful there, not without dropping her guard, but she wasn't ready to do that yet.

Touch: nothing noteworthy. Again, she'd need her more specialized senses to learn much from a cold scene like this one.

Taste: there was a faint chemical flavor to the air, which was to be expected. The flames had devoured plastics, wood, metal, paper, and cloth. The resulting hodgepodge of smoke and ash was bound to stain the atmosphere for some time to come.

Sight: her fireman's eyes took in the details, reading the fire department's attack on the blaze as if it were a motion picture playing out before her. Other than the cause of the fire, there was nothing to distinguish the scene from a hundred others she'd investigated.

Using the graph paper she always carried on her clipboard, she sketched the layout of the club as she took measurements, making notes of anything of potential interest. There wasn't much, especially since she wasn't even sure what she was looking for. Something about this fire had been worth a man's life, but nothing stood out.

After she was satisfied with her notes, she took a photo survey of the building, inside and out. She'd stop at the local drugstore later and make enlarged prints to study.

As she finished with the routine stuff, it was time to bring out the big guns, though the thought made her queasy. Her secret abilities had been at the root of the breach between her and Coop, and she'd sworn off using them ever again. Now, for the second time in one day, she would break that promise.

She picked the cleanest stretch of wall she could find to lean against, hoping it would help ground her as she stripped away her mental protections. When she opened her eyes, colors were brighter, scents were more pungent, and the air felt heavy on her skin. For a few seconds she savored the experience, the sensations making her feel more alive than she had in ages.

God, she'd forgotten how good it felt—and that was the danger. Over time, it had become way too easy to depend on the extra sight, letting her mind fill in the blank spots rather than doing the grunt work of investigating. And innocent people had paid the price for her hubris.

She squashed the bitter memories, not wanting the past to taint the present. Concentrating on the immediate area, she began to reconstruct the fire through the images burned into the parts of the club still standing. Her mind recoiled at the cacophony of screams laced with the pounding beat of the music. Pain had etched its own special flavor in the air, and fear tasted dark and foul.

Slowly the sights and sounds began playing out for her like a macabre movie, sometimes showing long, detailed scenes, and sometimes a burst of images that faded too rapidly to see clearly. She absorbed the suffering, panic, and the relief as the escaping dancers filled their lungs with fresh air once they reached the safety of the back parking lot.

Through the fog-thick smoke that made picking out details difficult, she recognized Kerry Thorsen helping a man twice her size toward the exit at the back of the club. She shoved him toward a larger man who'd appeared out of nowhere. Something about the newcomer looked familiar, but the image faded too quickly. Maybe it would come to her later.

As the echo of the smoke continued to thicken, she followed the path the people had taken out of the club and back outside to watch the predictable chaos that was part of any major fire. Fire trucks and aid cars jockeyed for position. Cops directed traffic, shouting for passersby to keep moving along. The injured were assessed and transported—all of it tragically normal in her world.

She finally spotted Kerry Thorsen again. The image flickered in and out as Kerry stepped out of the back door of the club carrying a larger woman with apparent ease. How had she managed that?

After surrendering her burden, Kerry stopped to look around, obviously searching for someone. Who? Lena wondered. There was no way to tell. She could see images and hear muted sounds, but reading the thoughts of specters was beyond her weird abilities.

Then Lena's heart lurched as she recognized the man headed straight for Kerry. It was Coop! She called out his name before she could help herself. As lifelike as her old friend might look, he wasn't really there. Or anywhere, for that matter. A razor-sharp pain cut through her chest as she watched him fade away.

Chapter 2

*L*ena's extra senses abruptly shut down, giving her a respite from the violent scenes from the fire, and she waited for her pulse to slow to normal. The worst was yet to come. As strong as the memories of the fire were, they wouldn't hold a candle to the aura left behind by Coop's murder.

Turning away from the parking lot, Lena headed toward the second set of crime scene tapes inside.

Her stomach knotted as she walked toward their corner. She jump-started her powers, and between one heartbeat and the next, she was back in the clutches of her heightened senses. This time the thick scent of smoke was overlaid with the coppery smell of freshly spilled blood. As she stared at the corner, the outlines of two men slowly came

into focus. It hurt to look at Coop, so she concentrated on the other one. He was oddly out of focus,
making it impossible to see him clearly.

He was well above average in height, with an
athletic build. His clothes were casual but expensive looking. The images flickered and faded before she could get a clear look at his face. When
they returned a few seconds later, Coop was already on the ground, his expression agonized
as his blood pumped out onto the ground. The
other man leaned over him, his intense interest in
Coop's suffering obvious and repulsive.

Coop struggled to breathe as he bled out. The
other man picked up Coop's briefcase and computer and calmly walked away, leaving his victim
to die alone in the dirt.

"Bastard! Filthy, dirty *bastard*!" Lena hissed.

She forced herself to abandon the image of
her friend to follow the other man. Hurrying back
through the club, she caught up with the ghostly
image as he stepped out onto the parking lot
and paused to look around. Did he have an ac-
complice? No, this felt like a one-man operation.
Groups tended to leave more clues.

When he started forward again, she forgot
he wasn't real and reached out to stop him. Her
hand passed right through his arm and she stumbled back as a wash of pure malevolence poured

through her. Whoever he was, the man had a strong love for killing and pain. Her stomach rebelled as she tried to cope with the blackness swirling in her head. Finally, she lost the rest of her lunch, retching until there was nothing left but the sour taste of bile and regret. When the last spasm died away, she looked around for her phantom companion. He'd disappeared completely in the bright sunshine. Though she needed to learn more about him, all she could feel was relief.

Having gleaned all she could from the crime site, she jotted down the last of her notes and impressions. Then, after one last good-bye to her friend's memory, she walked away.

Inside her hotel room, Lena immediately stripped off her smoke-scented clothes and jumped in the shower. As the hot water washed her skin and mind clean, she counted herself lucky. As bad as meeting the specter of Coop's killer had been, she now knew just how dangerous the man was. The fact that she didn't know what he looked like didn't matter. Thanks to her hated abilities, she knew exactly what he felt like. Or maybe *tasted* like was a better description of his black malevolence.

He might hide his truth from others, but not her, not anymore. One touch and she'd know him inside and out. The court system relied on facts to convict, and now that she'd seen how Coop had died, she could set about building a case.

She grabbed a towel to dry off. That guy she'd seen at the Thorsens' fit the general build of the killer. Maybe a little surveillance was in order.

Crawling into bed, she prayed for sleep and a better day tomorrow.

Lena studied the Thorsens' house through the ornate iron gates that guarded their driveway. She'd parked just far enough up the block that she could keep an eye on the place from her car.

Her stomach growled. Breakfast had been too many hours ago. On the way here, she'd passed a couple of fast-food joints. Ten minutes tops, and she'd be right back here staring at nothing. Next time she'd be smart enough to bring a book.

As she reached to start the car, someone stepped out on the front porch, sending her pulse into immediate overdrive. It was the man she'd seen on her first visit, the one who'd stared at her so intently before disappearing into Kerry's living room without saying a word.

Hot damn—with that dark hair and even

darker eyes, he was a handsome one. Not that that won him any bonus points in her book; she'd met too many criminals who used their looks and charm as tools of the trade.

But that didn't mean she didn't enjoy a bit of eye candy, and Lord, she loved the look of a man in a duster. The black leather suited him well, and her hormones stirred to life. She liked the way he moved, too, with a confidence that said he was king of his world.

He started down the steps, then stopped as Kerry joined him on the porch. Whatever she said to him clearly didn't make him happy. He dodged her hand when she reached out to him, then he stalked away, his anger clear in each step, to climb into a low-slung sports car. He gunned the engine as he waited impatiently for the gates to open. As he drove away, Kerry's shoulders slumped in defeat as she disappeared into the house.

Very interesting. Their heated exchange might have had nothing to do with her investigation, but tailing Mr. Dark and Dangerous would be far more interesting than staying here. As he drove past, Lena ducked down in her seat to avoid being seen.

When he was halfway down the block, she started her car and followed him. This was her first big break!

• • •

It had been a bitch of a day, and fighting with Kerry hadn't helped. Hours later, Sandor was still pissed off. The next time he had to spend hours prowling the streets on a renegade hunt, he'd remember to wear more comfortable shoes and a less noticeable coat. More than one shop owner had given him the evil eye for lurking too long near their stores. He had to find a way to blend in better, or some do-gooder would call the police on him.

He also had the strangest feeling that he wasn't alone on his quest. Someone was using the rush-hour commuter crowd as camouflage to dog his footsteps. He'd turned into a doorway a couple of times to see if he could catch anyone, but either his stalker was good at his job or Sandor was imagining things.

Definitely time to take a break. He stopped to consider the restaurants he'd passed, and the slight breeze carried the scent of tomato and basil. Italian—just the ticket. He turned back, following his nose to one of his favorite restaurants.

When there was a break in the traffic, he cut across the street midblock, to keep his behavior unpredictable. As he reached the opposite curb, the sound of screeching tires and running footsteps made him spin around, but the cars were already starting to move again. If someone had bolted out into traffic to follow him, he'd already blended back into the crowd.

That, or else Sandor had gone completely paranoid for no good reason. Rather than continue to play tag with a nonexistent pursuer, he was going to kick back and enjoy a hearty meal, and a glass of good wine.

Inside the restaurant, the waiter ushered him to a small booth in the back. Sandor slid in, facing the door so he could people-watch while he waited for his dinner.

He wished there was a simple way to draw the renegade Kyth out of hiding, but it was unlikely that they'd choose him as a victim. He could only hope to catch one of them in the act and follow the renegade back to the rest. If Sandor tried taking them out one at a time, he'd only drive the rest of the gang into running. Once he had them penned in, he'd enlist Ranulf's help in taking them all out at once.

Closing his eyes, he tried to think about something happier before he ruined his meal. Strangely, the only image that came to mind was Lena Wilson. She was another problem he might have to deal with at some point, but right now he was more interested in recalling the exact color of her too-serious eyes. Gray, maybe? No, more of a deep smoky blue, the perfect shade to go with her honey gold hair.

He admired her determination to seek justice for her friend, even if that meant trouble for him. Maybe if he got to know her better, he could find a way to share the truth about Coop's killer without betraying his people.

Sure, *that* was real likely. He could imagine her hanging on to every word as he explained that neither he nor Coop's killer was really human, and both had powers straight out of a graphic novel or superhero comic book. He could prove his claim by shooting off a few energy bolts and making his eyes glow. Once that totally freaked her out, he could explain it was his sworn duty as a Talion to execute bad guys instead of letting the civil authorities do their job.

Then, as a member of the law enforcement community, she'd instantly be on the phone for reinforcements to haul his ass into jail to stand trial for murder. No matter that it would've been a total disaster if the police had found Bradan before he and Ranulf had. Countless more innocent people would have died—but he couldn't tell Lena that. He owed his allegiance to his Dame and his people, and he wouldn't—couldn't—betray them.

The waiter appeared with his dinner and refilled his wineglass. "Will there be anything else, sir?"

"No, thank you." Sandor sipped the wine, savoring the woodsy flavor. "On second thought, leave the bottle."

"But it's *my* turn to go out hunting." Kenny shifted on the far end of the couch with his feet up on the crate that served as a coffee table. "You promised I could."

"I know, but I changed my mind." Sean looked up from counting the money from last night's haul. "We've got enough cash to last us for a few days. The police are going to get suspicious if we keep working the same area too often."

"But you promised!"

Sean gritted his teeth. Kenny had an amazing talent for getting on his nerves. At thirteen, he probably couldn't help it, with his teenage hormones kicking in and bringing on the need to rebel against someone. But why did it have to be Sean, who was barely five years older than Kenny?

"Yes, I know I promised, and I will allow you to go out on your own. Just not tonight. I'll let you know when it's safe. Until then, you'll just have to sit tight." He knew he'd made a mistake as soon as the words left his mouth. Kenny had serious issues with authority of any sort.

Crossing the room, Sean plopped down on the opposite end of the couch, not wanting to crowd him. "Look, kid, I didn't mean that the way it sounded—but we all agreed to work together on this. We've made hits three nights in a row, and so far the police haven't paid much attention. We need to keep it that way."

Kenny clearly wasn't buying it. "Fine, but I won't stay here. I'm going out."

He was up and heading for the door before Sean could stop him. Maybe it was better to let him go blow off some steam, but he hoped the kid took him seriously about laying low.

Sean leaned back against the wall and closed his eyes, exhausted. He hadn't gotten a full night's sleep since they'd taken Kenny in. It had been just him and Tara before, and they'd managed to keep their bellies full. Then he'd found Kenny hiding near the trash cans behind a couple of restaurants, and he'd coaxed him out. It took more effort to find enough for three, but they managed—most of the time. Tara was a genius at stretching their meager funds.

Sean's mind drifted back to better days, when he'd been young enough to think the world was a kinder, warmer place. The distant memory of his parents always soothed him as he slid into dreams. But before he could fall asleep, the sound of the door opening jarred him awake. Tara was back.

"How did the shopping go?" he asked.

Tara looked up from stashing the milk in the fridge, and frowned with concern as she came toward him. When her hands settled on each side of his face, familiar, sweet warmth poured through him. Sean allowed himself a few seconds, because he needed her touch so badly. Besides, if he didn't accept her gift, she'd just wait until he was asleep and force it on him. She was sneaky like that.

"Feeling better?"

He wanted to lie, but she'd see right through it. "Yeah, I do. Thanks."

"You're welcome. Don't wait so long next time. It only gets worse when you ignore it."

Neither of them understood this strange compulsion to touch other people, but they'd learned the hard way that they needed the special buzz they got from it, the way others out on the streets needed drugs. Tara was better at sharing her energy with others, especially him. Kenny was a different matter—one more reason Sean worried about him. Although the boy would accept the occasional hug from Tara, he refused to let Sean get close enough to help him.

As if picking up on his dark thoughts, Tara looked around. "What happened this time?"

"Kenny didn't like it when I told him that we couldn't go hunting again so soon. He said he had to get out for a while anyway."

"Think he'll be okay? It's getting dark out."

"If he's not back soon, I'll go looking for him. I'm afraid if we crowd him too much, he'll leave for good. Think how long it took to convince him to trust us this much."

Tara nodded, her expression grim as she put away the rest of the groceries.

"I know you'll look for him. The question is whether or not he'll let you find him."

Son of a bitch. Sean scooped the money into the box and stuck it back under the mattress. "I'll be back. No, *we'll* be back."

"Thanks, Sean." Tara followed him to the door. "I know he's been a real pain lately."

He planted a quick kiss on her cheek. "Yeah, but he's our pain."

Lena hurried down the street, hoping her quarry was still in the restaurant. When she'd peeked through the front window earlier, a waiter had just delivered her target's meal. The plate piled high with pasta and tomato sauce had made her stomach growl again, so she'd left long enough to buy a sandwich up the street. It hadn't been the first time her job had interfered with getting three squares a day.

Just as she reached the edge of the building, the door to the restaurant swung open and her mystery man walked out, stopping to put on his black leather duster. The sight made her mouth go dry. Hot damn, someone that good-looking should come with a warning label. Did he even realize how many women stopped to stare at him? Evidently not, because he looked totally unaware of all the attention.

She pretended to be involved in a cell phone call as he looked up and down the street, relaxing only after his eyes swept past her without stopping. She snapped his picture with the phone's camera, catching him in profile. What was it about him that made her pulse race when she looked at him? It had to be more than his good looks. Surely she wasn't that shallow.

When he turned to walk in the opposite direction, she waited until he was almost a block away before following. The crowds had thinned out, making it harder for her to remain hidden.

His behavior was puzzling. Ever since he'd parked his car, he'd wandered aimlessly, criss-crossing this section of downtown Seattle over and over again, stopping every so often to peer down side streets and alleys. Did he have nothing better to do? Or had he somehow picked up on her presence? She'd tailed many suspects in her job without being caught, but she had a feeling that this guy was more aware of his surroundings than he let on.

This was getting her nowhere, and the longer she trailed him, the more likely he'd catch on. She'd try again tomorrow, packing a change of jackets, a couple of hats, and another pair of sunglasses to vary her appearance.

She turned back, and when she reached the corner she looked back one last time, easily picking him out. He moved with a long-legged grace that made him stand apart from the other men. She wished she at least knew his name. A woman should know that much about the man she'd be featuring in her dreams.

The feeling of being followed had resumed as soon as Sandor left the restaurant. The guy was good at his job, because Sandor couldn't pick the bastard out of the crowd. He was about to go back down the block to catch his stalker when the sensation disappeared. Whoever had been dogging his footsteps was gone.

To top it all off, there was no sign of any gang activity, and this was the time most of the attacks had taken place. Finding the culprits would be more a matter of luck than skill, since they'd staked out a big territory for their operation. But he was reluctant to call in any Talions from out of state to aid in the search; it wouldn't say much for him as chief enforcer if he couldn't solve his first real case.

He returned to his car, flipping open his cell phone. Maybe Ranulf would be up for a workout. They both needed to keep their fighting skills honed, and he'd sleep better after taking out some frustration on someone who could fight back.

"Here—you're bleeding."

Ranulf caught the towel Sandor tossed him and wiped the corner of his mouth. He sat down on the weight bench across from Sandor with a satisfied sigh.

"Thanks. Kerry hates it when I drip blood on the furniture."

"Not as much as Judith would have." Sandor smiled as he reached for his bottled water. "She would've fried us both for doing that."

Ranulf closed his eyes briefly, his hand going to the talisman at his throat. "I miss her each and every day. There are rare times I forget she's gone, and then it hurts all over again when I remember."

The quiet confession surprised Sandor; the Viking wasn't usually one to share confidences. But ever since they'd joined forces to kill the renegade, they'd started building a friendship. The road was a rocky one, but they were making progress.

Sandor felt compelled to make his own confession. "I only served her for a few decades, but her death left a real hole in my life. You and Judith worked together for almost ten centuries. Getting over her loss won't be easy for either of us."

"Having Kerry helps." The other man's expression immediately lightened.

Sandor wasn't sure he'd ever get used to seeing Ranulf smile so easily. It was almost scary, as if some pod person had taken the real Viking's place. The man had been a legend among their kind for much of his long life: the grim, implacable arbiter of justice, a killer with no conscience.

Sandor had bought into the myth himself. But that had all changed when fate and a renegade had brought Kerry into their lives. The light in her soul balanced out the darkness that Ranulf had lived with for centuries. No wonder he looked at her with such hunger in his eyes.

It was time to go home and let Ranulf get back to his woman.

"Thanks for the workout. I needed it."

"You're welcome." Ranulf's grin turned wolfish. "I'm always up for using you for a punching bag."

Sandor arched an eyebrow. "*I'm* not the one who was bleeding."

"True, but you are developing a nice shiner." Ranulf pushed himself off the bench and started for the stairs, clapping Sandor on the shoulder as he passed by. "By morning it should be in full bloom. I hope black and blue are your favorite colors."

"Go to hell," Sandor told him with no real heat, and followed Ranulf upstairs.

Kerry was waiting for them at the top of the steps. "Are you two done pounding on each other? Hughes thought we were having an earthquake."

She reached up to touch her husband's mouth, no doubt using her healing touch on the small cut. She shouldn't waste her energy on such trivial wounds. She'd be after Sandor, too, as soon as she spotted the swelling above his eye.

As if reading his thoughts, she blocked his way when he tried to go around her. "Not so fast."

"It will heal on its own," Sandor grumbled, knowing that arguing wouldn't do any good. Kerry was a natural born healer.

"True. But do you really want to spend the next week explaining to everyone how you got it?"

He sighed. "Fine. Fix it."

He closed his eyes and absorbed the stream of warmth that flowed from Kerry's soft touch. When she was done, the new energy zinging through him made it clear that she'd given him more than it took to heal a simple bruise.

"Don't say it, Sandor," she warned. "You needed it."

"Even if I did, you had no right."

He let his anger show but resisted the urge to use his size to crowd her—barely. The Viking might pull his punches when the two of them were sparring, but all bets were off if he thought Sandor was threatening Kerry.

Time and tension hung heavily among the three of them as they waited to see who would be the first to blink. Finally, Sandor stepped back.

"It's been a long day."

It wasn't quite an apology, but it was the best he could do at the moment. He needed a shower, he needed his bed, and he needed to get a certain blonde out of his mind.

Ranulf followed Sandor out to his car. Damn it, he didn't need this. "What?" Sandor snapped, flexing his hands just in case.

Ranulf glanced back toward the house. "She meant well. She's still learning the rules."

"I know. And it doesn't help that I haven't

been exactly stable lately." Not that he wanted to talk about it. "I'd better get going while I'm still awake enough to drive."

"You've still got a room here if you want it," Ranulf reminded him.

"Thanks, but I want to get an early start tomorrow." Besides, he rather sleep in his own bed.

"Okay. Let me know if I can do anything to help. We're more caught up on things, and I could use a little action. Don't want to get rusty."

"I might need your help patrolling a couple of the areas where the attacks have taken place. Give me a couple of days to get a handle on things, and I'll let you know."

"Sounds good." Then Ranulf stepped closer, glaring at Sandor with eyes that had turned the color of polar ice. "One more thing. Don't EVER come that close to threatening my wife again. You won't like the consequences." Then he was gone.

"Did you find Kenny?" Tara asked.

"Yeah, he'll be along in his own good time." Sean flopped down on the couch. "Sorry I was gone so long, but it took me a while to find him, and then I had to wait until he was alone to make my approach."

"Was he angry?"

"When isn't he?" Sean snarled as he kicked off his shoes. Dealing with a surly teenager wasn't easy even when he was fully rested and fed.

"Sean, he's not that bad." Tara held out a plate of food as a peace offering. "Why don't you eat and then go to bed? I'll wait up for him."

Sean picked up a slice of apple and bit into it. "You shouldn't have to. He knows the rules."

She already had enough on her shoulders, but there was no arguing with her. If he ate slowly enough, Kenny might show up before Sean ran out of excuses to stay up.

He scooted over and patted the space beside him. "Sit and keep me company."

She curled up on the other end of the couch, and asked, "When do you plan on going hunting again?"

"I'd hoped to put it off for two or three days, but Kenny's likely to bolt if we don't let him try. I'm hoping he won't explode over me hovering nearby to make sure he doesn't run into any problems."

Tara stared at her hands clenched in her lap. "Me, too. It worries me knowing he's on the streets alone even when he's just hanging out. He's only thirteen, and there are far worse predators out there than us."

Sean had the same concerns, but Kenny had managed to survive for close to a year by himself after running away from his last foster home. The boy had developed good instincts—at least when his hormones and temper weren't getting in the way. Sean was about to say so when he heard a familiar noise out in the hallway.

"He's coming." He shoved his plate into Tara's hands. "Quick, so he won't think we're ganging up on him."

Tara scrambled around the corner to the kitchen while Sean dashed for his bedroom, jumped in bed, and yanked the blanket up over his shoulders with only seconds to spare. He turned to face the wall to keep Kenny from realizing that he was still awake.

Sean felt the boy hesitate outside the bedroom door long enough to see that he was in bed. When Kenny moved on to join Tara in the kitchen, the kid sounded far more in control than he had earlier. The outing had obviously done him good. Learning to live with their weird need was a bitch, but at least Kenny had the two of them to help him along. Tara especially had a knack for getting the boy to listen to sense.

Without Tara's calm, peaceful nature, Sean wasn't sure if he would've managed to hold it together this long himself. There was a gentleness about her that soothed even his roughest nights. One touch of her hand and he could gather up the ragged edges of his control again. He'd never been able to put into words how he really felt about her, but that didn't matter. He loved her, but wasn't sure what that meant.

She was far more than a friend, but they weren't blood family. She was so damned pretty that she brought out all of his protective instincts, and he occasionally dreamed of holding her in his arms all night long. Maybe someday they'd end up in bed together, but he didn't want to risk hurting her.

Pushing for more than friendship would only complicate things. Far better that they made do with the occasional hug than to lose what they already had.

For now, his family were all inside for the night and safe. He relaxed as he listened to the low murmur of Tara's and Kenny's voices, and finally, they lulled him to sleep.

Chapter 3

*I*nteresting. *Could it be?* . . . *Yes!* "Hot damn, finally some progress!"

Sandor had been at the computer for hours,
searching for information on Kerry Thorsen's
long-lost family. He'd run into one dead end after
another, but it was finally paying off. He sent
off a couple more inquiries, crossing his fingers
that they'd produce useful information. Once he
had something concrete—a name, an address,
anything—he'd tell Kerry.

Now since he didn't have to start prowling the
streets quite yet, he typed Lena Wilson's name
into the search engine. It didn't take long for
pages of possible links to pop up on his screen. He
scrolled down a few pages and finally decided to
try again, adding the words *fire* and *Cooper*.

Bingo! He clicked on an old article from a Seattle newspaper. It was about an arson case from five years before, and he sat up straighter, intrigued. Although she was only mentioned briefly, it was clear that her involvement in the investigation had been an integral part of the case. Interesting; too bad he had to leave now.

After logging off, he grabbed his hoodie and the keys to the older sedan that he kept for cold, rainy days.

He was changing his appearance today in case his tail was back again; he'd also donned a shoulder harness for his favorite Glock. A knife slid nicely into his boot, and he added a small stun gun to his pocket.

When he reached the downtown area, he chose a different parking lot from the usual one. He pulled up his hood before starting toward the area he'd patrolled the day before. Once he circled the block a time or two, he'd move north.

Yesterday, the feeling he was being stalked had kept his attention divided. Today everything seemed normal, which allowed him to concentrate on the hunt. At the next corner, he cut east. He'd found out the address where one of the most recent attacks had taken place and wanted to see if he could pick up any residual information.

His ability to read old sites wasn't as well developed as Ranulf's. The Viking had had centuries longer to hone his skills, but even time was no guarantee that Sandor would ever have much talent for it. But if he could pinpoint the exact location where the victim had been found, he'd see what he could learn. If the site was too cold for him to read, he'd call Ranulf to come check it out.

As soon as he reached the alley, he felt the darkness. Closing his eyes, he let the noise of the city fade into the background as he concentrated on the sounds and smells and energy traces in the narrow passageway. Kyth had been here, and recently. That was about all he could detect, though.

Reluctantly, he flipped open his cell and hit Ranulf's number on the speed dial. After a couple of rings, it went straight to voice mail. Sandor disconnected, shoved the phone back in his pocket, and decided to move farther north.

As he turned the second corner, his mental alarms went off again. His stalker was back. Now he really regretted not having Ranulf along. What that man didn't know about tracking wasn't worth knowing. At the very least, the Viking hunter could've hung back far enough to watch for anyone paying too much attention to Sandor. Once they had the culprit trapped, it wouldn't have taken them long to find out what was going on.

For now, all Sandor could do was keep walking and wait for an opportunity to catch the culprit himself.

It had taken Lena too long to spot him just as he'd stepped out of an alley. She was lucky she hadn't run right into him. What on earth had he been doing in there?

She didn't want to draw any attention to herself, so she watched until he turned a corner before ducking into the alley to check it out for herself. It was empty, with no sign anyone had been there recently. Other than a scattering of trash and some graffiti, there wasn't anything that distinguished it from any other alley.

Should she risk a quick check using her other senses? Yes. No. Maybe. The longer she dithered over the decision, the farther away her target got. Closing her eyes, she dropped her guard. She gagged as the pungent smells intensified, as did the noise drifting in from the street behind her. She waited a few seconds for her senses to adjust before opening her eyes. Blinking several times to focus, she studied the alley.

A few feet farther in, she could see the faint outline of a body on the ground. Oh, Lord, not again. She was reluctant to move closer, not willing to witness another death so soon after watching the replay of Coop's. But the man stretched out on the ground slowly rolled to his side before pushing himself off the ground. He winced at the effort but managed to stand up without help. Relieved, she took another few steps toward him.

The shadow of a figure looked dazed, but not really hurt. There was no sign of blood on his clothing, although it was hard to tell for sure, when she was looking at a memory. As he staggered toward the mouth of the alley, she quickly backed out of his way, even though she knew his body had no real substance. The idea of letting the specter stumble through her held no appeal.

She followed after him, but his image faded completely out in the bright sunshine, leaving her with more questions than answers. What had happened to him? And when had it happened? For all she knew, he could have been a drunk or even a druggie, but that didn't feel right. That had been fear in his pale eyes, and his face had lacked the usual ravages wrought by drugs or alcohol. Besides, her abilities seemed particularly attuned to scenes of violence—not a comfortable thought.

Her cell phone alarm buzzed, reminding her that she only had another few minutes to see what Kerry Thorsen's friend was up to before she had to leave for an appointment.

Earlier she'd called an old contact from the fire department, one of Coop's best friends. She was hoping that he might know more about Coop's activities the last few days before his death. If she hurried, maybe she could catch up with her target one last time to see if he was checking out other alleys, or wandering in a seemingly aimless pattern, as he had yesterday.

Running would only draw unwanted attention, so she pulled out her MP3 player and power-walked down the street to the newest Springsteen CD. At the corner, she paced back and forth as she waited for the light to change, using the delay to look in all four directions to catch sight of him. Finally, she saw him in the distance headed north. He was far enough away that she couldn't chase him down and still get back to her car in time.

Frustrated, she headed for the parking garage. If traffic permitted, she'd risk a drive-by to see what he was up to, since she had to go in that direction anyway.

Was she wasting all this time by following him? She had no proof that this guy was involved. It was one thing to go with her gut feeling in her investigation, but there was something more driving her interest when it came to this guy.

Considering the strength of her visceral reaction to him, she had to work extra hard to bank the heat he stirred in her. That was the last thing she needed—or wanted. Really.

Lena drove into the Starbucks parking lot and immediately spotted McCabe. When she honked her horn and waved, he stopped and waited for her to catch up with him. It had been years since she'd last seen him, and she wasn't sure of her welcome. To her relief, he swept her up in a big hug.

"Damn, girl, why'd you stay away so long? Coop missed you. We all did."

They both knew what had driven her away. If he wanted to pretend otherwise, she wasn't going to bring it up. He looked good, though, and she told him so.

McCabe patted his stomach. "Don't kid a kidder. I've put on too many pounds, and my forehead is much higher than it used to be. Not to mention that what's left of my hair has gone gray."

She batted her eyelashes at him. "What can I say, McCabe? It's a good look for you."

His booming laughter rang out as they entered the store, drawing all eyes to them. The other customers and employees turned back to their own business, smiling: people just plain felt happy around McCabe. Having him at a fire scene always lifted the spirits of his coworkers and the victims, especially children.

After they placed their orders, they headed for a table in the back corner. As she gathered her thoughts, Lena toyed with the coffee cake he'd insisted on ordering for her.

"What's on your mind, Lena?" McCabe looked at her over the top of his coffee, his bright blue eyes seeing entirely too much. "Look, I know finding out about Coop's death had to have hit you hard, but don't take this wrong. We all expected to see you at the funeral."

Her eyes burned. "I didn't hear about it until too late."

His mouth dropped open, clearly from shock. "The captain promised to contact you."

"He probably tried, but I moved to a new apartment a couple of weeks before Coop was . . ." Her throat got too tight to talk.

McCabe looked at her with sympathy, giving her the time she needed to pull herself together. She managed to choke out, "I'd sent Coop my new address and number, and asked him to give it to personnel here in case they needed it. It wasn't until someone cleared out his desk that they found my note." She looked up from the crumbly mess of her coffee cake. "I came as soon as I could make arrangements to get here."

McCabe nodded and set his cup down. "So, while I'm always glad to spend time with a beautiful woman and talk about old times, why don't you tell me the real reason you wanted to see me?"

She met his gaze head-on. "It's killing me to know that Coop's murderer is still out walking the streets. I mean to change that."

He took another long sip of his coffee before responding. His questions were to the point but not accusing. "And how do you plan to do that? What can you do that the police and our department haven't already done? We're pretty good at our jobs, you know, especially when it involves one of our own."

She nodded. "Believe me, I know that. You were the guys who trained me."

"But?" he prompted.

"No matter what happened in the past, McCabe, I'm a darn good investigator. We both know that a fresh pair of eyes can sometimes make all the difference. I'm here and I have the time. Both the department and the police have too many other cases that need their attention, but I can focus on just this one." She paused. "Coop deserves justice, McCabe. I want to find it for him if I can."

The firefighter leaned back in his chair and crossed his thick arms over his chest. His expression gave few clues to what he was thinking, but finally he nodded.

"What do you want to know?"

Relief stripped away her tension. "I've read the reports. I've already interviewed one of the key witnesses, and I plan to follow up with her again. What I need to know is if there was anything different about that fire. You know, the kind of details that stick in your mind but don't go into the official file."

He closed his eyes and pinched the bridge of his nose, as if the memories hurt. "I was there that night. Total chaos at first; you know how it is. The arsonist managed to block the front door right before the fire started. The people inside panicked when they realized they couldn't get out that way. But by the time we arrived, someone had found the rear exit. Some woman . . . what was her name?"

"Kerry Thorsen," Lena offered.

McCabe frowned. "'Kerry' sounds right, but the last name was different. Probably the same woman, though. By all reports, she not only led the charge out of the building, she went back in repeatedly to get others out before the roof caved in."

"Unusual behavior for a civilian, don't you think?"

He shrugged. "Maybe, but the bottom line was nobody died that night. I'm guessing you've already been to the site, and you know as well as I do that the chances of everybody walking away from a fire that big are almost nil."

"Anything else strange that you can remember?"

"Coop seemed to think he had a lead on a person of interest but never said how he got it. His boys took pictures of the crowd, so maybe one of them spotted something. But the bastard who killed Coop also stole his briefcase with his laptop and all of his notes and reports. We tried to piece everything back together but never got anywhere. If he was on to something, it's probably lost for good."

"He had to be, or else why would somebody kill him? It's the only thing that makes sense."

"Unless it was a random mugging. You know, wrong place, wrong time."

She knew better. Her vision had shown her that the attack on Coop had been very deliberate. This killer hadn't wanted easy money; he'd taken Coop's briefcase, not his wallet.

Not that she could tell McCabe what she'd seen. Coop might have suspected that she had a little something extra when it came to her investigative techniques, but they'd never discussed it.

"So no leads. A possible person of interest, but no hard suspects. No explanation for Coop's death." She couldn't keep the bitterness out of her voice.

McCabe sat up and leaned forward. "Listen, Lena, I know Coop was like a father to you, but he was my best friend for almost as long as you've been alive. No one—NO ONE—wants his killer brought to justice more than I do. But when you've got nothing to work with, you get nowhere fast."

He started to stand up, but Lena reached out to place her hand on his arm. "I'm sorry about how that sounded. I'm so furious over his death that I can't sleep nights—but I'm not pointing fingers at anyone except the bastard who killed him. And at myself for not being here when Coop needed me the most."

A single tear trickled down her cheek; they both ignored it. McCabe slowly leaned back in his chair.

"Sorry for blowing up like that. In a perfect world, the bad guy would be the only one who paid for his crimes. In the real world, a lot of good people get hurt."

"Were there any other fires I should be looking at? Has he struck again since the club fire?"

"The only other arson case that happened around the same time was a used bookstore. The owner lived above the store and got up in the middle of the night for the same reason I do."

McCabe winked at her, his good mood back. "When the guy smelled smoke, he ran for the steps and called it in. The place was fully involved by the time the department got there. He was alone, so no one got hurt, but he lost everything."

"Who would torch a used bookstore? Where's the profit in that?"

"Evidently he did a pretty good business in rare books. First editions, stuff like that. His total loss was a helluva lot more money than any of us expected. The insurance company did their own investigation, and they're going to pay the claim. The old man was comfortably set financially, and you could tell the business was his whole world. It's hard to believe he would've lit the match to destroy his life's work."

Lena wrote down the particulars. "Any suspects on this one?"

"Not really. The man had a stable of regular buyers, but none of them had an axe to grind. There was one customer who'd been angry about the price of some book he wanted, and they couldn't come to a compromise on it. The guy had bought things at the store before, but he always paid cash. We had nothing to go on."

"You'd think if the owner had that much money tied up in merchandise, he'd have had security cameras."

McCabe nodded. "He did, but like I said, the place burned down, cameras and all. Even if he'd kept the surveillance tapes, they were just melted plastic."

She slapped her forehead. "God, where are my brains? Was the owner able to give you any details about the guy?"

"Tall, well-dressed. Nothing useful."

The phantom she'd watched at the club fire scene fit that description too well for it to be a coincidence. She fought to hide her excitement.

"Thanks for coming today, McCabe. I appreciate it."

"It's good to see you, kiddo. But maybe you investigating this case alone isn't such a good idea. I don't know if the two cases are related or not, but either way, you're dealing with someone who doesn't give a damn that people died. If he is the one who killed Coop, it probably meant he was getting close to catching this firebug. If this guy feels cornered, he won't hesitate to kill again."

"I'll be careful."

"Promise me that if you get anything concrete, you'll let us take over—or at least let us help out. It's bad enough I lost my best friend. I don't want to lose you, too."

When was the last time she'd had to fight off tears twice in one day? The reminder of what it

felt like to have friends who worried about her
stirred emotions she'd done her best to bury.

"You won't lose me. I promise I'll call in the
cavalry."

They walked out to the parking lot together.
"Don't leave town without seeing me again, little
girl. I'd hate to have to come hunt you down."

He swept her up for a rib-cracking hug that
left her breathless and happier than she'd felt in a
long, long time.

"It's nearly sundown."

Kenny shifted from foot to foot in antsy anticipation. He'd been wired all day, pacing the floor
and whining about how slowly time was moving.
Even Tara had snapped at him.

Sean said, "I know, Kenny, I know. We'll head
out in a few minutes."

He'd rather go hunting with Tara and leave
Kenny at home. However, he'd promised to teach
the younger teenager how they worked, how they
harvested what they all needed to survive. He
worried about Kenny's lack of impulse control,
but maybe the kid would do better once he knew
how to take care of himself.

Sean and Tara had both learned the hard way
that it was easier to maintain control over their

bodies' needs if they fed in regular, small amounts. Accidents—tragic ones—were more likely if they waited until they were running on empty.

They'd only survive as long as they kept to the shadows. Sean didn't mind for his own sake, but Tara deserved more than a meager basement apartment in a run-down building. If they kept hunting so often, they'd soon have to move to a different neighborhood. And that would be more complicated, now that he had the needs of a third person to consider.

As soon as Sean stood up, Kenny charged out the door, his excitement contagious. There was enough predator in Sean to understand the heady taste of power. They might be the lowest of the low economically, but once they took to the streets, they jumped right to the top of the food chain.

Hunger for more than food smoldered in Sean's gut, ready to burst into flame. Kenny waited for him to catch up, the craving for feeding right from the source sparkling in his eyes. The shared feeling made Sean want to run through the night, howling with the joy of the hunt.

But he couldn't teach Kenny restraint if he couldn't keep a leash on himself. It had been a long time since he'd hunted without Tara's calming influence beside him; he had forgotten how it had been before they'd found each other. He stopped walking—running, really—and leaned against the building and fought for control.

Kenny planted himself in front of Sean, looking frustrated. "Tired already? If you're too weak to do this, I'll go by myself."

A smarter man would have let Kenny's taunts pass. Sean grabbed a handful of Kenny's T-shirt and shoved the boy up against the bricks hard enough to jar his teeth. A trickle of blood dribbled down Kenny's chin, probably from biting his lip. Staring into the kid's frightened eyes, Sean sent a push of energy ripping through him, holding him immobilized with sheer will. For the first time, there was fear in Kenny's eyes as he struggled to break free of Sean's hold.

Sean leaned in close, getting right in the boy's face. "Shut up, you little prick! I'm sick and tired of your mouth having no connection with your brain! Nod if you understand me."

For once, Kenny had the good sense to do as he was told. Or maybe he finally recognized Sean as a predator with far more experience in culling out the stupid and the weak.

Satisfied he had the boy's complete attention, Sean let go of him physically and stepped back a few inches to give them both room to breathe.

"Think of all those people out there as a herd of zebras or gazelles. Right now they're moving along quietly, lost in their own little world, but it doesn't take much to send them into a stampede. The last thing we want is to startle them into screaming for the police. We're like lions, watching and waiting for the right victim to pass by. Then—and *only* then—do we reveal our true nature and attack. Got that?"

Kenny slowly nodded, the mental hold Sean still had on him making it hard for him to move. Sean eased back on that as well.

"I don't look like the biggest, baddest thing on the block, Kenny, and neither does Tara. But think of that as camouflage—because even the stupidest human out there can spot danger approaching if the bad guy dresses the part. I can walk right up to my chosen victims, and they won't know what's happening until it's too late. Then it's into an alley for a quick feed that leaves them weakened and confused, but not dead."

He smiled, letting all of his teeth show as his eyes glowed bright and hot. "The first few times, you'll be tempted to finish the job—dead men carry no tales and all that shit. But if you kill somebody, even by accident, you'll bring disaster down on all of us."

He eased back his hold completely. "So our goal is to leave them dazed, not dead. Repeat that for me, Kenny. Dazed, not dead."

The kid swallowed hard. "Dazed, not dead."

"You won't get a second chance to get it right," Sean warned. "Do something that endangers me or especially Tara, and I'll take you out myself before the police even have time to arrive. All they'll find is another pitiful runaway who met a bad end. They'll think, 'How sad,' and then bury you in a lonely grave, forgotten by everyone."

Kenny slowly nodded, clearly shaken by the confrontation.

Knowing he'd made his point, Sean put an arm around Kenny's shoulders. "Okay, kid, all this talking has made me hungry for some zebra. How about you?"

Trouble was in the air, and it definitely held the taint of a Kyth gone renegade. Sandor could smell it, taste it, and his skin crawled with the sick feel of it. Now if he could just see it.

He'd never had the nose for tracking danger that Ranulf had, but he was getting better at it. The only thing he could figure was that the night he'd executed Bradan, sucking the bastard dry must have triggered some change deep inside of him. Or maybe these abilities had always been there, lying dormant until he needed them.

Sandor stalked the streets, his fingers burning with energy as he sought out a target for this powerful compulsion to protect. Keeping his fists clenched inside his sweatshirt pockets, he prowled up one street and down the next. He passed person after person; most gave him plenty of room, their eyes focused straight ahead. Odd, he'd never engendered that reaction from strangers before.

If they'd all been Kyth, he wouldn't have been so surprised. Because of the gene pool that had spawned his kind, all of the Kyth were sensitive to the predatory nature of a warrior. These were only average human beings, yet they still tried not to draw his attention as they passed by.

Their reaction disturbed him on a deep level. He wasn't the real threat walking the streets of Seattle, even if they didn't know that. Grimly, he continued on down the street, more determined than ever to find a suitable target for his aggression.

If he couldn't locate the renegade Kyth tonight, he'd cheerfully take his bad mood out on whoever had been following him. Their presence was like an unscratchable itch on the back of his neck, irritating and distracting.

He'd give it another half hour. If he didn't cross paths with either of his targets by then, he'd head back home. Once he was calmer, he'd make plans for what to do next. Because when it came to crime on the streets, there was always tomorrow.

Chapter 4

"I see we have uninvited company." Sandor moved the drape aside to let Ranulf look out to where Lena Wilson sat watching the house. For some reason, seeing her out there improved his mood.

The Viking muttered a curse. "I knew she was trouble when she came by the first time. I actually expected her back before now." Ranulf turned on the television and began flipping channels.

Sandor glanced at his irritated companion. "You think this Wilson woman didn't believe Kerry when she told her that she'd only known Coop briefly? She can't possibly think Kerry had anything to do with his death."

If there'd been any evidence that would have led the authorities to their door, they would have been there long before Lena Wilson. The simple truth was that none of them had had anything to do with Maynard Cooper's death. The not-so-simple truth was that they knew who *had* killed him, and that the killer was long dead and buried. He wished they could tell Lena the truth, since she cared so much about Coop, but loyalty to his own kind took precedence over the grief of one human, no matter how intriguing he found her.

Ranulf found the ball game on TV and began to watch it, but Sandor couldn't keep his eyes away from the window. What was it about that woman that made him want to go outside and invite her in, or better yet, go to her hotel room for some privacy?

Ranulf said, "Interesting expression you've got on your face, Sandor."

"It certainly is." Kerry entered the room. "What's going on?"

Sandor nodded toward the window. "Lena Wilson has taken up residence outside."

Kerry gave him a wide-eyed innocent look. "And that put a moonstruck expression on your face? I wasn't aware that the two of you had even spoken."

He gritted his teeth. "We haven't. Your husband was just being a jerk."

Sandor got down to business. "I wanted to catch

you up on my progress. I've patrolled downtown the last two nights and checked out the alley where one of the attacks took place. The mugger was a renegade Kyth, all right, but that's all I know. If I can't get a bead on this guy soon, I might need help reading a couple of the other locations to see if Ranulf can spot something I missed."

Ranulf nodded without looking away from the ball game. "Let me know where and when, and I'll be there."

Kerry said, "Even though no one has been permanently damaged, I'm afraid the renegade's need to feed will escalate."

Looking grim, Ranulf faced Sandor. "That's what always happens once a renegade starts feeding on the dark end of the energy spectrum. They develop a taste for the buzz and the power it gives them."

Which was why there was now an execution order on the bastard. Sandor didn't relish the role of the Grim Reaper, but that's what recent events had made him. This time, though, he'd make it quick and as painless as possible. Not like it had been with Bradan.

Sandor shifted in his chair. "There's something else. The night before last, someone was following me almost the whole time I was patrolling. Yesterday evening he was back, but for only a short time."

The other two sat up straighter. Kerry asked, "Are you sure that it was the same person both times?"

"As sure as I can be without actually seeing him. Whoever he is, he's good. I've tried to catch him out, but so far no luck."

The Viking looked thoughtful. "Maybe I should take over tonight, to see if they're after you in particular or all of us."

Sandor considered Ranulf's offer. "I'll try one more night by myself. If he's back again, I've already scouted out a place I might be able to trap him. If that doesn't work, we'll both go tomorrow night and double-team him."

"Sounds good." Ranulf settled back to watch the game.

Hughes entered the room carrying a large tray of food. "I thought you might like to eat in here since the game's on."

Kerry smiled at the butler. "That will be perfect."

As Hughes handed out napkins and plates, Kerry asked Sandor, "Anything else I need to know about?"

"Nope, I'm still waiting on responses to a couple of emails I sent out. When I know more, I'll fill you in."

As he bit into his sandwich, his attention was

drawn to the television when the fans jumped to their feet and started cheering. He was pleased to see that the Mariners now had a three-run lead and it was only the second inning. Kerry, a longtime fan, cheered as well. Good friends and baseball—it couldn't get better than that.

As the mystery man pulled out of Kerry Thorsen's driveway, Lena wrote down his license plate number. Then she called McCabe, who promised her that a friend would run the plates without asking too many questions. Satisfied that she'd done all she could for the moment, she headed back to her hotel. Once McCabe called back with the information she needed, she'd know who the guy was and might be able to figure out why he spent his evenings cruising downtown Seattle. Somehow, she doubted he did it for exercise.

Her cell rang just as she was pulling into the hotel parking lot.

"Hey, McCabe, that was quick."

His laugh rumbled over the line. "Hey, babe, I know people who know people."

"I'd tell you how amazing you are, but your ego is already bigger than is healthy for all concerned."

His booming laugh had her holding the receiver a couple of inches from her ear.

"Coop always did say you had a smart mouth. I think he liked that about you."

The memory made her smile. "So what did you find out, my brilliant friend?" She parked the car and dug out her notebook and a pen.

McCabe rattled off the name Sandor Kearn, along with his address. When she was done, he added, "I had my buddy run his name for priors. He's clean. Not even a parking ticket."

A clean record didn't mean he was harmless, though. Only that he'd never been caught. They both knew that.

"Thank your friend for me. This is a big help."

"Why are you interested in this guy, anyway? Is he a suspect?"

"No, not yet, anyway. He was at Kerry Thorsen's house the day I was there, but he never introduced himself. I'm checking into anyone connected with her."

"Okay, sounds good. Keep me posted."

"Will do."

She disconnected the call. Sandor Kearn. An unusual first name, but it suited him. What drove him to walk the streets at night?

He was clearly hunting. Who was he looking for? And what would he do if he realized that he wasn't alone? He struck her as a solitary hunter, likely to strike out if crowded too much.

The realization made her shiver as she stepped out of the car into the warm afternoon sun. She'd done her fair share of hunting, too. But somehow, this time it was different.

"Can we go out again tonight?"

Kenny was working hard to sound nonchalant, but Sean knew better. There was a good reason Kenny was keeping his eyes averted. The flames flickering in their depths revealed how badly the boy needed to take down another zebra or two. It was very risky to go trolling for victims again so soon, but both prey and predator would be in greater danger if Kenny's tank was running on empty. Far better to top it off regularly than to let desperation drive the hunt.

"Sure. We'll hit the streets about an hour after dark."

Kenny's mouth dropped open in shock.

Sean got up to get a can of pop out of the fridge. "You'll learn better control if you're not starving for it."

As the boy pondered that, Sean picked up the pillowcase filled with dirty clothes. "Until it's time, we'll hit the laundry room."

Kenny's sneer was predictable. "That's women's work. My old man wouldn't have been caught dead washing clothes."

"Yeah, and remember where his rules got him. Around here, you wear 'em, you can help wash 'em. Tara does enough as it is." Sean tossed the bottle of detergent at Kenny. "The sooner we get this done, the sooner we can go on safari. Come on, Great White Hunter, haul ass."

"Very funny." Kenny rolled his eyes, but he was smiling. "Hey, does this mean I get to wear one of those funny helmets and carry a big gun, in case we run into a herd of irate elephants?"

Sean followed him out the door. When Kenny was like this, it was easier to remember why he and Tara had made the boy a part of their small family. Kenny rarely mentioned his life before they'd found him, but there was no doubt it had been a tough one. His mother had disappeared one day, leaving Kenny alone with a father who had been a mean drunk. That temper had landed the bastard in prison doing twenty to life. After a couple of bad experiences in foster homes, Kenny had found living on the streets preferable.

Hell, change the names and you'd have Sean's own story—and Tara's as well. Sometimes life sucked, but the three of them were doing okay together. They looked out for each other, and no one had to sleep with one eye open to watch out for a drunk's fist coming at you just because you were there.

Shifting the bag of laundry to his other shoulder, Sean caught up with his partner in crime. Like he'd said, the sooner they got their chores done, the sooner they could have a little fun.

The sunset behind the Olympic Mountains to the west was stunning. The intense colors, all different shades of reds and oranges and pinks, lit up the Seattle skyline with a warm glow. Sandor stood on the pier near the ferry terminal, enjoying the show and breathing in the saltwater scent of the air. It was almost time to start his patrol.

Reluctantly, he turned away from the fading light. There were bad guys out there, human and otherwise. The familiar tingle of energy burned in his fingers. He flexed his hands and rolled his shoulders as all of his hunting instincts moved to the forefront. He used to be a civilized ambassador serving the Dame and the Kyth, known more for his charm and sophistication than for his ability to strip bad guys down to dust.

And now here he was, patrolling the streets and turning into the barbarian warrior he'd always thought Ranulf to be. Sandor had not been born a real Viking, but evidently time hadn't weakened the warrior blood that ran in his veins. Rather than a shield and sword, he fought with the inborn weapons nature had given his kind. Failing that, the Glock tucked inside his shoulder harness would do nicely.

He strolled down the sidewalk, enjoying the early evening bustle of the piers that lined the Seattle waterfront. Maybe luck would be with him and he'd find the renegade tonight. Even more, he wondered if his shadow would be haunting his footsteps again. He hoped so.

He turned down Denny Way, heading toward Seattle Center. If he were on the prowl looking for easy marks, that's where he'd start. There were plenty of nooks and crannies where a predator could lurk as he waited for the right victim to meander by. After a quick snatch and feed, the renegade could disappear back into the crowd— especially on a night when there was a rock concert and various other scheduled events scattered across the Center.

Sandor circled around the Science Center and headed toward the large grassy area surrounded by the ring of buildings. As usual, people were out in number, some sitting on the benches and low walls scattered around the place. Others walked with more purpose as they headed to one event or another. It was hard not to envy so many people having fun plans for the evening.

Then a familiar sensation warned him he was no longer alone. Good! Rather than whip around to catch a glimpse of his mysterious companion, Sandor took a slow turn along the sidewalk that circled the huge fountain at the heart of the Center. The person ghosting his steps would have to follow, helping him to eliminate the majority of the people in the area. Halfway around, he stopped ostensibly to retie his shoe. Propping his foot on the edge of a bench, he glanced around as he tied the laces. It didn't take long to spot his stalker.

Well, I'll be damned! He stood upright, immediately deciding on a plan of action. This would be fun.

Okay, Ms. Wilson, two can play cat and mouse. Let's see how you like it when the mouse goes on the attack.

He cut across the grass toward the street that bordered the Center on the north, maintaining a leisurely pace until he turned the corner. After a quick glance to make sure she was still following, he picked up speed. He wanted enough distance between them to set a trap, but not so much that she'd lose sight of him before he wanted her to.

He couldn't wait to get his hands on her and find out why she was tracking him. Well, that and because he'd been wanting to get his hands on her since he'd laid eyes on her. Considering that long-legged stride of hers and pretty sun-bright hair, how had he missed picking her out of the crowd before now? Thanks to the combined rush of adrenaline and testosterone, he had some serious regrets that this was all about business and not pleasure.

Though a guy could always hope.

Around the next corner, he broke into a lope until he reached the entrance to a small neighborhood bar two doors up from an alley. He slipped inside and positioned himself at the side of the front window, where he could watch for Lena without her being able to easily spot him.

"Hey, mister, we're not a bus stop. Order something or take a hike." Ham-fisted and built like a linebacker, the bartender had a face that had survived more than a few barroom brawls. A couple of bikers at the far end of the bar looked up with interest, probably hoping to see their buddy in action.

Sandor knew he could take the guy, but now wasn't the time to prove it.

"I'll take a scotch on the rocks." He pulled out two five-dollar bills and tossed them on the bar. "Hold the scotch and the rocks. Keep the change."

The bartender and the other two looked at him like he was crazy. Finally, the bartender grinned.

"Turns out we're having a special on that tonight." He pushed a five back across the counter.

Sandor chuckled and accepted the bill. "Thanks."

Back to business. Lena was walking by the window, looking puzzled as she searched for him, clearly unsure how he could have disappeared so quickly. It was time to make his move before his prey could escape.

Grinning, he slipped outside and pounced.

The door she'd passed a few seconds ago opened with a soft whoosh. That was all the warning Lena had that Sandor Kearn had turned the tables on her. Before she could react, he had his forearm across her mouth, dragging her into the nearby alley. She should've fought him off, but her only coherent thought was wondering how a man his size could move so fast and so silently.

He half-dragged her down the narrow passageway until they'd passed a Dumpster big enough to hide them from anyone out on the street. If any other man had treated her this way, she would have kneed him or screamed for help as soon as he loosened his hold. She glared up into his gleaming eyes with a mixture of fury and embarrassment over being so easily captured.

"Let go of me. Now."

Instead Sandor moved in closer, deliberately crowding her. Was it temper, or something else causing his dark eyes to glitter in the fading light?

"I'm not touching you." He held up his hands to prove his point.

"Then you won't mind if I leave." She stepped to the side to do just that.

"Actually, I do mind." He kept her cornered between himself, the Dumpster, and the wall behind her. "So tell me, Lena Wilson: why have you been following me the past couple of days?"

How did he know it had been her? She was sure he hadn't seen her before tonight. "I wasn't—"

He gently placed his gloved finger across her lips. Shaking his head, he sighed as if sorely disappointed in her. "Tsk, tsk, Ms. Wilson. Want to try that again?"

"Let me go now, and we can both pretend this didn't happen." Although it would be a long time before she could forget the rich smell of his aftershave, combined with the scent of his leather coat. A powerful urge to bury her face against his chest and simply breathe him in washed over her.

He smiled slowly, and she realized he knew it, the big jerk. She stiffened her shoulders and her resolve.

"So why were you hunting me, Lena?" he whispered from close by her ear.

She shivered from the sensation of his breath on her skin. "Hunting? What makes you think I was?"

"You're not ready to hear what I think, little girl." His smile continued to taunt her.

"I'm no little girl." And the way he was making her feel right now was very adult. She really needed to put some distance between them.

But his gaze was fixed on her mouth, and he slowly leaned in so close that once again his warm breath teased her skin. What was he doing? Was he going to kiss her . . . or not?

Her world rocked on its axis the second his lips settled over hers. As her ability to think short-circuited, she grabbed on to him to anchor herself. Her fingers clutched his arms, the buttery soft leather of his duster doing nothing to disguise his muscular strength.

This had to stop! Her protest might have been more effective if it hadn't come out sounding like a moan. She managed to keep her mouth closed, preventing the kiss from becoming too intimate. That worked right up until he nipped her lower lip with his teeth, hard enough to sting. When she opened her mouth to protest, he slipped his tongue inside. He was careful with her, but he still tasted of temptation and male anger. She tingled from head to toe, as if he'd been bathing her with heat stolen from the sun.

Sandor murmured to her between kisses, but her mind was too far gone to understand him. His words finally began to make sense as he asked the same question over and over again.

"Why are you after me, Lena?"

He was temptation itself, but she managed to hold back the information he was trying so hard to coax out of her.

She pulled back enough to smile up into those dark chocolate eyes of his. She slowly slid her hands down his arms, then dropped them to her sides, ending the connection between them. "It's simple, if somewhat embarrassing. I like the way you look walking around town in that duster. I swear, if you could bottle that, you'd make us both rich."

It was the truth, just not the truth he was looking for. And . . . it was hard to tell in the dim light in the alley, but his cheeks looked flushed. Was he actually *blushing*?

"Now, if you'll excuse me, I—"

Once again, he stopped her by putting his hand over her mouth. Who the hell did he think he was? She kicked him in the shin, taking satisfaction in his curse as he jumped back.

"Now if you'll get out of my way?"

But he wasn't listening to her; his attention was

focused on the far end of the alley. She strained to hear what had put such a fierce expression on his face.

There. She heard it. A soft moan, laced with desperation and pain. Someone nearby—a woman or girl by the sound of it—was hurting.

"Stay here."

Sandor changed from sexy to lethal in one second as he stalked away, a gun appearing in his hand. Yeah, well, maybe his commands worked on other women in his life, but not her.

She waited until he'd gone several feet before pulling her own weapon and fanning out to his left. At the sound of her steps, he shot her a hard look. When he spied her automatic, he frowned but gave her a quick nod.

They slowly worked their way down the alley, moving in tandem, as if they'd partnered together for years. He stopped every few steps to listen again. Finally, he motioned for Lena to stop while he eased around another cluster of trash cans to kneel by a pile of broken-up cardboard boxes.

Lena eased closer, trying to see what had caught Sandor's attention. A shoe lay on its side in a puddle that looked too dark to be water. Then the shoe moved. Holy shit, there was a foot in the shoe, and a nylon-clad leg sticking out from under the pile of boxes.

Sandor holstered his gun and lifted the pile of cardboard to reveal an injured woman. He stripped off his driving gloves, then reached out to push the woman's hair off her face. There was a good-sized lump on her forehead. As he ran his fingers down the side of her face, checking for other injuries, the woman moaned and stirred restlessly before lapsing into silence.

Lena put away her gun and joined Sandor on the ground. "How badly is she hurt?"

"Bad enough." He gave Lena an enigmatic look. "While I look her over, check out the rest of the alley in case the bastard who did this is lurking around back there."

His suggestion made sense, so why did it feel as if he was trying to get rid of her?

"Okay. I'll be right back."

"I never expected otherwise."

There was a hint of a smile in his voice. She glanced back at him, but he was running his hands down the woman's arms, looking for the source of what Lena now realized was a pool of blood. Pulling her gun again, she slowly made her way down the alley, wishing she could see better. Other than the occasional beam of light from a window, the alley was bathed in night shadows.

The empty passage gradually narrowed down and came to a dead end. She rose up on her toes to look in a couple of large trash bins, then started back toward Sandor, checking out other possible locations where the attacker might be lurking.

As she peeked into an industrial-sized recycling bin, she caught a flash of light out of the corner of her eye. Whipping around, she brought up her gun. Odd. There was nothing moving, only Sandor rising to his feet.

"Did you see a flash of light?" she asked.

"Maybe you saw my cell phone. I was getting ready to call nine-one-one when I heard you coming back."

Again, his explanation made sense but didn't feel right. "How soon will they be here?"

He held up his phone. "My reception sucks here; I'm going to the street. Can you stay with her?"

"Will do."

Before he got to the end of the alley, she called after him, "And don't sneak up on me. I wouldn't want to mistake you for one of the bad guys."

His teeth gleamed in the darkness as he grinned at her. "If you promise to kiss where it hurts, I might just let you shoot me."

He was still laughing as he disappeared down the alley. If she wasn't convinced that he and his friends were covering up what they knew about Coop's death, she'd be sorely tempted to drag him back to her hotel room to see if he looked as good out of his clothes as he did in them.

The injured woman stirred, her eyes slowly opening. She met Lena's gaze with a confused look.

"What happened to me?" she whispered fearfully.

"It's okay; you're safe now. My friend is calling the police and the EMTs."

When the woman didn't seem to understand her, Lena dropped her guard, hoping her heightened senses would help her find a way to soothe the woman's agitation. Lena grasped her hands, hoping touch would get through where words of comfort hadn't.

As soon as their hands met, Lena was yanked out of the present and thrown back in time. With a tearing pain in her head, she was no longer kneeling in the alley, no longer herself. She'd become the injured woman, Mary Dubois, reliving her experiences.

Trapped in Mary's mind, Lena found herself walking along the street, hurrying to get home to her family after a tough day at work. She was focused on the bus stop up ahead, hoping to catch the early bus. The people gathered there began lining up, warning her it had pulled into sight.

Running in heels was never easy, but she was

making good time, when out of nowhere, an arm snaked around her neck and jerked her backwards. Her assailant dragged her into the mouth of the alley, gradually increasing the pressure on her throat until she could barely breathe, much less scream for help.

Oh, God! Oh, God! Oh, God! She was going to die! Her mind filled with the images of her children—a boy and a girl. Then there was a man, her husband, the one she'd been mad at this morning. How could she die, knowing the last words she'd said to him had been so angry?

Her attacker was taller than she was. That's all she knew. He wasn't alone, for another set of footsteps scuffled through the filthy alley. Then a hand covered her eyes and her oxygen-starved body panicked. Flailing her arms, she tried to get her hands on the arm that was slowly killing her. But her mind was growing hazy and strangely calm.

All sensation faded as the strength in her muscles faded away. Her last memory was pain as her head hit something hard, and then for a short time there was nothing.

"Damn it, Lena, let go of her!"

Strong fingers worked to break her hold on the injured woman's hands. When they succeeded, Lena's own consciousness came flooding back, identifying the hands pulling her away as Sandor's.

"What the hell were you doing?"

She still couldn't open her eyes yet. He was angry because he was worried about her. It was there in the gentle way he helped her to her feet.

"Come on, Lena. Open your eyes and tell me you're all right."

There was a new note in his voice, intense and hot. She was trying to do as he asked, wanting to allay his worries. Before she could manage it, though, he cupped her face with both of his hands. Normally she would have basked in the warmth of his touch, but she hadn't yet raised her guards to shut out all the sensations that were bombarding her. For a brief second, she flashed back to the dance club fire and the shadow man who'd killed Coop.

Her stomach lurched at the wave of sick glee that washed through her, leaving her more bewildered than ever. Finally her eyes popped open. Where had that image come from?

"What the hell?" Sandor dropped his hands away from her face.

As soon as he stepped back, her mind cleared and she stared at Sandor in horror. For a single instant, the man she had kissed a few minutes ago tasted just like the bastard who had killed Coop.

Then Sandor caught her face in his hands and stared down into her eyes—and suddenly, all the fear faded away.

Chapter 5

*T*he approaching sirens made it impossible for Sandor to do more than a down-and-dirty invasion of Lena's mind. It took far more power than he expected, to break through her shields and adjust her memories of the past few minutes. As strong as she was, he'd be lucky if his tinkering held long enough for him to get her somewhere safe to try again.

And he would, even though he knew that if she ever found out, she'd come after him with everything she had. It was too much to hope that she'd understand, or be willing to turn that temper into something equally hot but far more satisfying for the both of them. The flicker of blue lights and screeching tires warned him that now wasn't the time for such thoughts. Too bad.

The police, weapons drawn, were cautious in their approach. Sandor eased his arm around Lena, hoping that they looked like a couple out for an evening stroll. She stiffened briefly, then relaxed against him. Good girl. The closest officer gave Sandor and Lena a quick once-over before speaking. He kept his gun aimed at Sandor, identifying him as the greater threat.

"Where's the victim?"

"There." Sandor pointed toward the woman who sat blinking up at them.

The cop knelt by her side, while his partner kept an eye—and his gun—trained on Sandor and Lena. "Was she conscious when you found her?"

"Not really. She was buried under that pile of cardboard. We never would've known she was there if she hadn't made a sound."

"Do you know her?"

Lena answered, "No, but her name is Mary Dubois. I stayed here while my friend called for help. While he was gone, she woke up enough to tell me her name, but that was all. I don't know how much she remembers of the attack."

Damn it, when had Lena planned on telling him that she'd actually spoken with the woman? When he'd sent Lena down the alley, he'd been able to read only a bit of the woman's memories, but her thoughts had been too chaotic for him to glean much. He did know her attackers had definitely been Kyth renegades, but she'd given him nothing more to go on. The flash of energy Lena had seen had been his failed attempt to use some of his own store of energy to help stabilize the injured woman.

As worried as he was about Mary Dubois, he was even more concerned about Lena. What had been going on when he'd found Lena frozen, her hands locked onto Mary's with such desperate strength? It had been all he could do to break the connection between them. For now he'd blocked Lena's memories of the event, but he needed to get her to Kerry and Ranulf. They should be able to get past the powerful barriers around Lena's thoughts.

Studying her out of the corner of his eye, Sandor liked what he saw. She was athletic, but he was also drawn to her intelligence and the obvious power of her mind. Until he'd met Lena, Kerry Thorsen and the late Dame Judith were the only two women he'd met with such strength.

If she was Kyth, it was such a faint trace that he couldn't read it. But there was definitely something different about Lena, something that the average human being lacked.

He was jerked out of his thoughts when Lena pulled him out of the way of the EMTs. The cops left the Dubois woman in their care and motioned for Sandor and Lena to follow them out of the alley.

"We need to take your statements." The senior partner got out a form and pen. "Can I see your driver's licenses, please?"

While the officer copied down the information, Sandor kept his arm around Lena's shoulder, projecting a sense of calm to help them pass the cop's scrutiny.

"Are you in town for long?" the officer asked as he handed Lena her license.

"A couple of weeks. I used to live here, and came back to visit some friends who work for the fire department."

That caught his attention. "Anyone I know?"

"Possibly. I had coffee with McCabe today." She smiled. "Other than a few more pounds and less hair, he hasn't changed a bit. I've really missed that laugh of his."

Just that quickly, the interview turned from cautious to a little more friendly. "Did he make you pay? He always does me."

Lena grinned. "No, I think he decided to be nice since I was visiting. Even so, I almost fell over from the shock of seeing him open his wallet."

The cop smiled. "I figure he owes me about

ten years' worth of coffee." Then he got back to the business at hand. "So what were you two doing in that alley?"

Sandor was surprised when Lena eased closer into his embrace. "Well, we were looking for . . . a little privacy. We'd made plans to meet over at the Center. We . . . uh, haven't seen each other in a while." She ducked her head, injecting just the right amount of embarrassment to make her statement ring true.

If she'd told the real truth, he could soon be on his way to jail—especially if the cops decided that he'd also been responsible for the attack on Mary Dubois.

He owed Lena one. And if he was right, she would collect.

A few minutes later, the police told them they could go. As he and Lena walked away, Sandor watched the flashing ambulance lights fade into the distance. The attacks had escalated—which meant the renegade's lifespan was now much shorter.

Across the street, Sean moved farther back into the doorway to avoid drawing any attention to himself. He'd ordered Kenny to go straight home and stay there for the rest of the night. Ordinarily the boy would have argued, but Sean had forced him to meet his gaze. One look in Sean's glowing eyes and Kenny had docilely trotted toward home.

Sean didn't like to use compulsion on anyone except when he was hunting, but he had enough to deal with right now. For the first time in God knows how long, he'd lost control while feeding. Once he'd dragged the woman into the alley, he'd stepped back to let Kenny feed first. The boy had taken only enough energy from her to satisfy his body's needs before gently handing her back to Sean.

It was Sean who'd gotten greedy and almost stripped the poor woman of even the minimal amount of energy necessary to keep her heart and lungs pumping. If Kenny hadn't intervened, she would have been *really* dead instead of almost dead.

Sean knew he should've immediately summoned help for her, but 911 calls were recorded and could be traced. Torn between helping her and the need to protect his small family, he'd hidden across the street, immobilized by fear.

Then the scary-looking dude in the black leather coat had appeared. Sean had watched the guy duck into the bar and then reappear to drag the blond woman into the alley. Sean's sense of honor had kicked in, driving him out of hiding. If the guy had intended rape or murder, Sean would have done his best to stop him.

But by the time he'd reached the mouth of the alley, the couple were seriously lip-locked and generating enough heat to light up the night. It was obvious that the man posed no threat to the blonde. From the way she was holding on to him, she was ready for whatever the guy had to offer. As Sean quietly faded back the way he'd come, something caught their attention.

He watched in stunned silence as both of them had immediately pulled guns and moved toward the spot where he'd left the woman hidden under cardboard. He'd taken advantage of their distraction to return to his hiding place, then he'd watched the rest of the drama from the darkened doorway across the street.

It wasn't long before the cops and aid car came roaring down the street. Within a few minutes he'd known the woman was safe, because the EMTs would have been moving faster if they thought she was in imminent danger. The good news was that the cops had little or nothing to go on. Despite his screwup tonight, he'd made sure of that.

They didn't worry him nearly as much as the guy with the blonde. That dude was flat-out scary. The image of him in that black duster, walking down the alley, gun in hand, was enough to terrify anybody. Even now, the guy kept looking around when the cop wouldn't notice, as if he could sense he was being watched.

Sean's gut was tied up in knots. Damn it, he hated being afraid. At the first possible moment, he'd bolt for the safety of home. And tomorrow he'd teach Kenny a lesson that he'd foolishly forgotten: no matter how good a hunter you were, there was always someone bigger and badder out there waiting to pounce. So they'd all lie low for the next few days, then find a different part of town in which to hunt. The last thing he wanted was to poach on another predator's territory.

Lena had firmly told Sandor that it wasn't necessary for him to follow her back to the hotel, but his car had been right behind hers since they'd left Seattle Center. His stubborn insistence shouldn't have surprised her. The evening had spun out of control from the minute she'd recklessly followed him even after she'd realized he'd spotted her.

How on earth had she ended up in an alley kissing a total stranger? Her whole body tingled at the memory. From the first second that his mouth had brushed across hers, it had felt more like a claiming than a simple kiss. She shuddered to think how out of control things could have gotten in that alley.

Having sex up against a brick wall with a mysterious stranger had never been one of her fantasies—but after tonight, it was #1 on her list. Even now, her body insisted on reminding her of how good he had felt holding her, surrounding her with his strength. She ached to be touched gently, to be taken hard, to finish what they'd started.

But she was too smart to get involved with someone with secrets, especially secrets related to Coop's death. Her mission took priority over everything else, no matter how much she regretted it.

She glanced up in the mirror again. Somehow she knew Sandor wouldn't be satisfied to simply watch her disappear inside the building, and she was determined to thwart any plans he might have of going up to her room.

As soon as she turned in to the hotel parking lot, she whipped into a spot near the door, then dashed for the entrance. If she could make it to the elevator before Sandor got into the building, she'd be safe. She would hit the buttons for all the floors so he'd have no way of knowing where she got off, and the hotel staff were trained to never give out room numbers.

As the doors slid closed behind her, she breathed a sigh of relief—or maybe regret. She wasn't sure.

Sandor smiled as he waited for Lena's elevator to return to the lobby. An ordinary man might have been unable to follow her, but his senses were more highly evolved. He stepped into the elevator and punched every number, just as she had. All he had to do was step out onto each floor until he found the one where her scent extended beyond the elevator door.

She was on the fourth floor. He stopped every few feet to test the air, narrowing the possibilities to one of the two end rooms. He leaned close to the door on the right and listened. Nothing but the soft rumble of snoring.

He stepped across the hall and tried again. Success! The room was silent, except for the sound of a rapid pulse and shallow breathing coming from just a few inches behind the door. He raised his hand and knocked.

Lena didn't answer.

He could unlock the door with a carefully controlled energy impulse, but he didn't want to scare her. Besides, that wouldn't work if the door also had a chain. He knocked again.

"Go away, Sandor. You said you wanted to

make sure I got back safe and sound. I'm here; mission accomplished. Now leave."

He smiled at her stubborn refusal. "Lena, we really need to talk."

"Tomorrow." Her pulse was slowing as she convinced herself she was going to win this round.

"No, now."

He pushed at her defenses with a small compulsion, reluctant to mess with her mind any more than he had to. He still needed to smooth out what he'd done to her earlier in the alley.

He heard her hand come to rest on the doorknob. At the click of the lock being turned, he stepped back to give her some space. She was already feeling crowded; this wasn't the time to add to it. He took off his duster, hoping to appear less threatening.

"It's late." She blocked his way, clearly not ready to surrender.

"I know, but we need to talk about what happened."

"If you think we're picking up where we left off back in that alley, you can just forget it."

Despite her obvious reluctance, she moved back. He hadn't been referring to those heated moments back in the alley, but knowing that kissing him was foremost in her mind was a pleasant surprise. He decided to tweak her a bit.

He crowded her a little, watching her eyes widen and then narrow. "Honey, as nice as kissing you was—and I *do* plan to get back to that—that's not why I'm here. You never answered my question about why you've been following me."

If she was disappointed, she hid it well. "I never admitted to following you anytime but tonight."

"Like you said, it's late, so let's not play games. What are you hoping to gain from dogging my footsteps?"

She rubbed her hands up and down her arms, as if cold. The room was chilly from the air-conditioning, but that wasn't what was putting those shadows in her eyes. He fought the urge to offer the comfort of his arms; that would only complicate the situation. He retreated a couple of steps.

"Maynard Cooper was my friend. More than a friend. Someone murdered him, and I intend to see the bastard behind bars for it."

"I got that much. But why follow me?"

She shrugged and turned away. "Kerry Thorsen is the only link I have to the events that led to his death, and you were at her house."

"She wasn't the only person involved in the fire that night; there were lots of other witnesses."

"And I've talked to a few of them personally,

and read all the statements that were taken. No one remembers much except the smell of smoke and how panicky they all were. Kerry Thorsen seems to be the only one who kept a clear head. She's also the only person Coop interviewed. That makes her stand out from the rest of the crowd."

Sandor leaned against the wall and crossed his feet at the ankles, settling in to stay as long as it took to get an explanation out of her. "Okay, I understand why you wanted to talk to Kerry, but I wasn't at the fire that night."

"I never said you were." Lena's chin came up a stubborn notch. "If you'd give me a straight answer as to why you're walking laps around the city, maybe I'd quit following you."

"Only maybe?"

"Oh, yeah." She nodded toward the duster tossed on a chair. "There's not a woman alive who wouldn't walk a few extra blocks to watch a man wearing one of those. Even you."

He couldn't help it; he laughed. "Thank you. I think."

She glared at him. "Don't let it go to your head. It's the coat drawing the attention, not you."

He pushed away from the wall and closed the distance between them. To give her credit, she stood her ground when he crooked his index

finger under her chin and lifted her gaze to his.
"Okay, so you like leather dusters, and you're
checking out all the leads you can find to help you
locate your friend's killer. Let's move on. What
happened when you touched Mary Dubois tonight?"

With a small burst of energy, he removed some
of the haze he'd put around her memories from
the alley.

Lena jerked back as if he'd hit her, and he
watched in horror as her eyes rolled back and
she collapsed, out cold. He scrambled to break
her fall, catching her just before she hit the floor.
Damn it, he hadn't used enough energy to cause
a reaction that strong. Even if she was part Kyth,
she should've been able to absorb it with no damage. What the hell was different about her?

He checked her pulse and her pupils. He had
to get her off the floor and onto the bed. Then
he'd call Kerry and Ranulf to get over here to do
a reading. Maybe among the three of them, they
could figure what made Lena Wilson tick. Kerry's
healing abilities might come in handy, too.

He jerked back the covers on the bed before
picking her up. Ignoring how much he liked the
feel of her cuddled up next to his chest, he laid
her on the mattress. She whimpered and stirred
restlessly, as if caught up in a nightmare. Would

touching her help, or make matters worse?

He decided to risk it. Cupping her cheek with his hand, he whispered softly, hoping that even if she couldn't understand the words, she'd draw some comfort from the warmth of his hand and the gentle reassurance he projected with his voice.

After a few seconds she was resting more easily, but he suspected it wouldn't last. He dialed Kerry on his cell, waiting impatiently for her to answer. When she finally picked up, he apologized for waking her before giving her a quick explanation of what had happened. He hung up after her promise to be there as quickly as possible. To make Lena more comfortable, he tugged off her shoes.

Nothing left to do but wait. He pulled a chair closer to the bed and studied Lena's face as she slept. Even in deep slumber, there was tension in the faint lines around her eyes. He was willing to bet that it had been a long time since she'd been genuinely happy, if ever. Being different was never easy, especially when you had to hide what you really were from everyone around you. She had that in common with Kerry. At least he and Ranulf had been surrounded by their own kind.

He brushed her hair back from her face, wishing he could offer her more in the way of comfort.

A few minutes later, Kerry and Ranulf knocked softly on the door. Once inside, the Viking jerked his head toward Lena, who moaned softly and stirred a bit.

"What the hell happened to her?"

"Earlier tonight, I figured out Lena was the one who's been following me, and I set a trap to catch her. Once I managed to get my hands on her, I pulled her into an alley to confront her. A few seconds later, we heard a noise and stumbled across the renegade's latest victim."

He clenched his fists, his eyes lighting up with fury. "This time the bastard damn near drained a woman dry, then left her bleeding and buried in a pile of trash."

Kerry looked horrified. "Will she be all right?"

"I think so. Lena got her name, so I can check with a contact at the hospital later."

His Dame looked grim. "Good, let me know what you find out. If necessary, I'll pay a quiet call on her before she's discharged. Now, back to Lena. What happened to her that caused this?"

Sandor let his frustration show. "I left her alone with the woman while I went for help. When I returned, Lena was kneeling beside the woman, frozen like a statue, with a look of utter horror on her face. I had to forcibly pry their hands apart before I could get through to Lena. I think she was trapped inside the injured woman's mind. I couldn't afford to have the police show up and find me with two injured women, so I put my hands on Lena and used my energy to break her mind free."

"Was she reading the injured woman, or the other way around?" Kerry crossed to Lena's side.

"It had to be Lena reading the injured woman. For one thing, she picked up on the woman's name."

"My money's on Lena," Ranulf said. "After all, she tried to read us that day at the house."

Sandor ran his fingers through his hair in frustration. "Damn, I'd forgotten that. If Lena was picking up on the woman's memories of the attack directly, no wonder she looked shell-shocked. That would have been hell for a sensitive. But she doesn't feel like Kyth to me. Maybe she has enough of our bloodline to give her one of our gifts, but not the whole package."

Kerry turned to her husband. "We should both try to get a reading on her."

When she started to reach down to touch Lena, Sandor stopped her. "There's more. I blocked her memories of her experience in the alley. When she first stood up after letting go of the injured woman, she seemed understandably confused. Then in the blink of an eye, she was

looking at me as if I'd just sprouted horns and a
tail. I don't know what I did to trigger such a powerful reaction from her, but she definitely sensed
something about me that she didn't like."

"Let's try to get past her defenses to figure out
what's going on," Kerry said.

"Let me go first," Ranulf said. "I've got a better
chance of protecting myself if she senses the invasion and goes on the attack."

Kerry stepped back. Although her gifts were
stronger than Ranulf's or Sandor's, she had far less
experience in wielding them.

Ranulf picked up Lena's hand and closed his
eyes. The seconds stretched out as he stood there
in absolute silence, his eyes unfocused and staring down past Lena's face. Then he gently set her
hand back down on the bed and stepped away.

He silently motioned for Kerry to try. As soon
as she touched Lena, the Dame jerked, as if hit
by a jolt of electricity. At the same time, Lena's
eyebrows drew down in a frown and she fought
to yank her hand free. Kerry held on tighter, her
expression turning grim. Sandor wanted to throw
himself between the two women, to stop the pain
they were both feeling.

A second later, Kerry reached down with her
free hand to lay her palm on the sleeping woman's forehead. With that, they both looked more

peaceful, as if Kerry had broken past the ugliness that had Lena tied up in knots.

When Kerry finally relinquished her hold on Lena, she drooped in exhaustion. Ranulf immediately wrapped her in his arms; the energy in his hands flared brightly in the darkened room, then arced back and forth between the two of them as Ranulf fed his wife some of his own supply. When she was replenished and stabilized, Kerry rose up on her toes to give her husband a quick kiss.

"Thank you. That helped."

"So?" Sandor asked impatiently.

"You're right about her lineage," Ranulf said. "There's Kyth somewhere in her distant past, but it's so faint that it should have had little effect on her daily life. Is that how you read her, Kerry?"

"Yes, exactly. She feels different than normal humans, like there's something extra in her makeup. She seems to have connected with the injured woman and experienced the attack almost as vividly as if Lena had been the one who was assaulted. She actually saw it through the other woman's eyes."

Sandor had been afraid of that, and wondered at its implications. If she'd sensed that woman's experience so clearly, what had she felt when she'd touched him right afterward? How much control did she have over this gift of hers? He'd have to be on his guard all the time now. With her ties to the law enforcement community, they couldn't afford for her to read his memories regarding her friend's death.

Kerry yawned loudly. "I need to go home. You're going to stay, aren't you?"

Sandor nodded. "Just long enough to make sure Lena continues to sleep peacefully."

"Sounds like a plan," Kerry said. "Report in when you can, but get some rest first. You're looking pretty ragged."

"Will do." Although it would take more than a good night's sleep to cure what ailed him. He was tired to his soul. After he let his friends out, he locked the door behind them, shutting out the rest of the world.

After pulling up the covers to keep Lena warm, Sandor moved the chair back across the room and settled into his vigil. With luck, she'd rest quietly, so he could doze for an hour or so. He'd be long gone when she woke up—which was a damn shame.

Chapter 6

As she lay hovering in the pleasant zone between slumber and waking, Lena's awareness slowly came into focus. The air conditioner hummed. The ice machine down the hall clanked as someone filled a container. The muted sound of traffic came in from outside the window. And she could swear that from somewhere close by, somebody was . . . snoring? In her *room*?

Lena's eyes flew open. She was alone in the bed, so where . . . In the chair in the corner.

Why had Sandor decided to sleep over?

Now that she thought about it, a *lot* about last night was a complete fog. She seemed to remember talking to Sandor in an alley. And wasn't there something about an injured woman and the police? Yeah, that felt right, though the details were fuzzy. Then he'd followed her back to the hotel to make sure she made it back to her room safely.

Obviously she had. So why was he here?

She sat up, wincing as her head hurt. "Sandor."

He stirred briefly but didn't respond.

She tried again, louder. "Sandor! Wake up!"

When that didn't work, she got out of bed. If she hadn't been so mad at him for being there, she would have thought he looked sort of cute with his hair falling over his face and his clothes all rumpled. The man was definitely too sexy for his own good—or hers.

She shook his shoulder and jumped back out of range. She'd seen his reflexes in action last night, and the last thing she wanted to do was startle him.

"Sandor, come on. Wake *up*."

Nothing.

When she shoved him harder, he mumbled, "Five more minutes." Definitely a move in the right direction.

She gave it one more try before he finally opened his eyes and stared up at her. "Oh, hell."

"Exactly." She put her hands on her hips and glared. "About time you woke up."

He stretched his arms out and groaned. "What time is it?"

"It's after nine, and *definitely* time for you to start explaining yourself." Who knew a grown man could look so grumpy yet attractive?

"Can it wait until after some coffee? I won't be coherent until then."

Despite the fierce image she was going for, Lena caved. Coffee sounded wonderful. "Fine. I'll call down for breakfast, but you're paying for it."

"It's a deal, and you're a saint." Sandor pushed himself out of the chair and lumbered into the bathroom.

She stared at the closed door as she phoned their order to room service, hungry for a lot more than just scrambled eggs and toast. While she had a lot of questions she wanted answers to, there was one that worried her the most. What was she going to do about Sandor Kearn?

Splashing about a gallon of cold water on his face did little to chase away the cobwebs, and he had a crick in his neck from sleeping in that stupid chair all night. He'd screwed up big-time. Lena hadn't been awake long enough to add up all of his sins. But once she got started, he was going to have to do some fast talking.

He used his finger and her toothpaste on his teeth, then ran his fingers through his hair, straightened his collar, and tucked his shirt in. The results were only marginally successful.

Time to face the music. He left the sanctuary of the bathroom. Sure enough, his judge and jury was perched on the edge of the bed, watching him with eagle eyes.

"Afraid I'll make a run for it?" He gave her a cocky grin. "That would reek of cowardice, don't you think? Especially since I promised you breakfast."

A knock at the door prevented further discussion.

"I'll get it."

He opened the door and let the waiter enter with a heavily laden cart. Thank God, Lena had ordered two pots of coffee and lots of food. While he paid the bill, Lena set the cart up next to the bed and pulled the chair up to the other side. Then she perched on the edge of the mattress and waited for him to sit down.

He wrapped his hands around the mug of coffee she'd poured for him. The heat felt good on his hands, and the promise of caffeine soon to be zinging through his veins definitely improved his mood. After a few sips, he lifted the cover off his plate and dug in. The combination of scrambled eggs and hash browns definitely hit the spot.

Lena seemed content to eat in silence, but he knew she was only biding her time to launch an attack. That was okay; he was ready for it.

Finally, she set her fork down and settled back. As he topped off his cup of coffee, he met her gaze. "Ask away, Lena."

"The hard part is figuring out where to start." She leaned forward. "Why did you find it necessary to spend the night in my room?"

"Because you passed out on the floor from exhaustion. After I lifted you onto the bed, I stayed to make sure you were all right."

"Get real, Sandor. I've never passed out in my life, especially around a man I barely know and don't trust."

"There's always a first time. And remember, you're the stalker in this crowd, not me."

She didn't like that remark, not one little bit. "Listen here, buster, *you're* the one who's been prowling the streets of Seattle looking like an Angel wannabe."

He was pretty sure he'd just been insulted, but he didn't get the reference. "Like who?"

"Angel? As in Buffy?"

He shook his head.

"How can you not know who Angel is? A tall, dark vampire who wore a black coat and walked the streets of Los Angeles to keep the world safe from the bad guys who wanted to suck the life out of us poor humans."

Whoa, that struck a little close to home—especially the sucking-the-life-out part.

"What do you remember from last night?" he asked.

His abrupt change in topics had her frowning and looking a bit puzzled. "Bits and pieces. Some of it's clear; the rest is a little hazy. Did I fall and bump my head or something?"

"Not exactly," he hedged.

"How about if I tell you what I remember, and you fill in the blanks?"

Glad for the brief reprieve, he nodded and sat back to enjoy the rest of his coffee. Maybe he could string together enough facts to satisfy her without having to reveal too much.

"I was at Seattle Center near the fountain when you spotted me," she began.

He nodded. "Up until then, you'd done a heck of a job hiding in the crowd."

She ignored the compliment. "Then you led me on a wild-goose chase until you came leaping out of that bar and dragged me into the alley. We argued, but then we heard—what? Something distracted us."

She'd skipped one of the most important parts. Or did she not remember their kiss? That would really piss him off, because every time he thought about it, he got hard all over again. He was about to call her on it, when he noticed how flushed her cheeks were. She remembered all right; she just didn't want to talk about it.

He said, "We heard a moan coming from farther down the alley. That's when we found an injured woman. Remember? She'd been buried under a pile of cardboard."

He waited to see how well his attempt to block her memories had held up. She was frowning as if her head hurt, but then her eyes opened wide.

"Oh, God, that poor woman. Someone mugged her and then left her for dead. She was bleeding from a scalp wound. Her name was . . ."

There was no harm in filling in that blank. "Mary Dubois. And the EMTs seemed to think she'd be fine."

Lena rubbed her forehead as if to ease an ache, then closed her eyes. "She'd been hurrying to a bus, worrying about getting home late to her family. Then someone jerked her backwards and dragged her into that alley. Whoever attacked her had her in a choke hold that kept her from screaming for help." Lena's breath became choppy. "He yanked her purse out of her hands and then threw her to the ground. Mary was terrified she was about to be raped and killed."

Suddenly her description shifted to first person, as if she wasn't sure whose memories she was recalling. "There were hands on me, more than two, but all they did was hold me. The struggle exhausted me, and when he—no, they—dumped me on the ground, I lost consciousness. By then I . . . no, *she* wasn't scared anymore. Just tired . . . so very tired." Lena's voice drifted off in a soft whisper.

So she had relived the experience with horrifying clarity, and was still doing so. She hadn't realized how much of her odd ability she'd revealed to him, and though he wanted to hold her close and chase the bad memories away, he needed to keep her talking before she did notice. "Could you see her attackers? Any details that would help identify them?"

"The bigger one was definitely a guy. Mary thought they both were. I didn't sense their faces, so maybe it was something about their clothes or voices." She frowned. "No, not his voice, because he didn't speak to her at all. That's odd, isn't it?"

"Not necessarily. If he intended to let her live, he wouldn't want to give her anything that would help identify him later on."

"Yeah, that makes sense." Lena fell silent, looking pale and fragile. "You must think I'm crazy, babbling about all of this."

"Not at all. I saw the powerful connection between you and Mary Dubois. I'm positive that she benefited from the comfort you gave her—a gentle touch after such a violent one."

She looked up at him with haunted eyes. "You really believe me, don't you? That I saw and felt what happened to her."

He owed her that much of the truth. "Yes, I do. I think that's one reason you collapsed last night."

She was silent for a moment. "So what's your part in all of this? Who have you been hunting for the past few nights?"

"What happened to Mary Dubois was one in a series of similar attacks over the past several weeks, all in this general area. I'm investigating the incidents to see if I can catch the bastard who's doing it, or get enough evidence to help the police find him."

That was a lie. Once Sandor had made a positive identification, Kerry would issue the execution order.

"Are you connected to a law enforcement agency?"

"No, I'm not."

She clearly didn't like that. "So then, why you?"

"Because the attacks are in several different jurisdictions, and so far the different police forces haven't connected the dots. As crimes go, these aren't all that serious."

Lena snorted. "Tell that to Mary Dubois."

"It was traumatic for her and for the others involved, but no one has been killed or even permanently harmed. After a few days' rest, all of the victims have recovered completely."

"Except for the fact that they're still victims. Some people never get over that kind of violation. A few will get past it, but others will carry that fear with them everywhere they go for the rest of their lives."

There was nothing he could say to that.

"So now that you know what I'm doing has nothing to do with your friend's death, will you quit following me around?"

She stared into her empty coffee cup. "I haven't thought that far ahead. I still have lots of questions and no answers."

Maybe it would be better to have her close by, so he could keep an eye on her and safely away from Kerry.

"Okay, let's try this a different way. Maybe we could partner up and see where it takes us."

Like maybe to that bed she was sitting on . . . He fought to keep his focus on work.

"Sure. What time?"

"I'll pick you up about six. We can have dinner first, to make plans." He knew the perfect restaurant, with intimate lighting, good wine, and great food. The kind of place a man took a woman to tempt her with soft touches and whispers.

"All right, but only if you'll wear that long leather coat." Her smile was a bit wicked.

"It's a deal." Anything to keep that hint of heat in her pretty eyes.

"Okay, that's settled. I'll meet you there, so write down the name and the address for me and then scoot. I've got stuff to do."

He should have been grateful to escape before she remembered whatever she'd sensed about him in the alley that had horrified her. Did it have something to do with the darkness left from Bradan's death? He hoped not; no one else should have to share that burden.

He followed her into the small alcove that led to the door. If he was going to gain her trust, he should walk straight out the door. It was the right thing to do. The smart thing. And it was the last thing he was going to do.

He stepped close enough to feel the sweet heat of her body and to hear her heart kick-start into overdrive. Oh, yeah, she felt the energy shimmering between them.

"One more thing happened in the alley last

night that you forgot to mention." He leaned in closer, gazing at her delectable mouth.

"What . . . what was that?" She licked her lips.

"This."

Then he claimed her, with his lips, with his arms, and a full-body press. Oh, God, she was so sweetly soft, and that made him hard. Painfully hard. Lena's smoothly muscled body fit perfectly against his, making it even more difficult to maintain control. If he unleashed this powerful desire completely he'd lose her for good, because it was too soon. But it was such a temptation, with her breasts crushed against his chest, her scent filling his head, and the taste of her passion on his tongue.

Finally, he managed to pull back, to walk away. But it was damned hard.

Lena threw the dead bolt, then fastened the chain, Sandor's taste still lingering on her lips and her body humming from his touch.

Drat the man—he could have at least finished what he'd started! Instead, he'd left after reminding her that he'd see her at six. How was she supposed to get anything done when all she could think about was seeing him again? She walked away from the door. She wasn't sure how she felt about him spending the night, watching over her after one of her episodes. No one had ever done that before. But he had simply accepted her truth, maybe because he had secrets of his own.

Only time would tell.

"Was that lady all right? The one we fed off of last night?" Kenny asked between bites of cereal. "She didn't look so good when I left, and she was bleeding from where she hit her head."

Sean's head was pounding. Guilt and fear had kept him up most of the night. "Why don't you shut the fuck up, Kenny, and let me eat my breakfast in peace?"

Tara gasped. "Sean! Watch your language!"

More guilt made him grumble an apology. "Sorry, Tara. It was a rough night."

He'd come close to killing someone. He'd made that mistake once before and still had nightmares from it. He set his spoon on the table, unable to eat with his stomach so tied up in knots.

"Look, kid, that woman was alive and doing fine when I left. I hung around to make sure the medics found her." Not that he'd been the one to call them. He picked up the early morning paper he'd snuck out to buy at first light and tossed it across to Kenny. "Didn't even make the front page."

Tara waited until Kenny finished scanning the brief article inside, then held out her hand. "Do you think she was able to give the police a description of either of you?"

"It wasn't mentioned. Besides, the alley was dark, and I'm pretty sure she never got a clear look at our faces. We didn't talk either, at least not while she was conscious."

He reached out to pat Tara's hand, wishing he was better at offering comfort. Stability had been a rare commodity for Tara, and anything that threatened to upset the life they'd built together scared her. It was worse now that she also had Kenny to worry about.

He tried to reassure her. "Look, we fed enough last night to hold us a couple of days, so we'll stay in tonight. If we need to hunt tomorrow, we'll try a different part of town."

She smiled, although he knew she wished they could stop hunting altogether. That wasn't possible, and she knew it. Even if he could find a job to support the three of them, they'd still need the energy he stole from his victims. Tara could go longer without it, but Sean and Kenny burned energy at a much faster rate. Maybe women needed less, or maybe Tara's calmer personality accounted for the difference. There were always more questions than answers when it came to their special needs.

The bottom line was, you played the cards life dealt you. And right now, he was looking at a losing hand.

He needed to get away from the two pairs of eyes looking to him for leadership. "I'm going for a walk down by the waterfront. I'll be back in a couple of hours."

"Do you want me to come with you? Kenny will be all right hanging out here alone." She shot Kenny a look that warned him not to argue.

Maybe that was a good idea. Her company always had a calming effect on him. "Sure. Let's go."

On the way out, he looked back at Kenny. "By the way, kid, you did good last night. You were there for me."

"The whole thing was totally sick." Then Kenny grinned at Sean. "But if you really want to show your gratitude, bring me back some ice cream—chocolate mocha." He held up two fingers. "Two scoops."

"You got it."

Tara was waiting for him out in the hallway. As soon as he closed the apartment door, she took his hand. A small burst of warmth traveled up his arm, and he didn't complain. Right now, he needed all the comfort he could get. They escaped into the warm sunshine outside and headed down toward the waterfront. Tara always liked watching the boats, and he found the scents and sounds near the water soothing. Hand in hand, they walked in silence, soaking up the sun. The quiet wouldn't last for long, but she was giving him time to chill out before they had to talk about what had happened last night.

Finally, he just blurted it out. "It's getting worse."

He tried never to keep things from Tara. What affected him affected her just as much, if not more.

"The need to hunt, or the reason you hunt?"

"I don't know. Both, I think. It's bound to take more energy with three of us using it. But no matter how often I hunt, there never seems to be enough to go around. I hunger for it all the time, to the point I hurt all over. Touching you helps, but not as much as it used to."

He leaned against a low concrete wall and stared at a container ship making its way through the Sound. Sometimes he wished he could sail away on one of those mammoth ships and leave all this behind. But he couldn't outrun himself, and he'd never be able to abandon Tara. He needed her like he needed the energy he stole from strangers. She'd been the one brightness in his life for a long time.

"God, Tara, it was awful. I've never been as out of control as I was last night. It was bad enough that it happened, but to have Kenny see it wasn't good . . . I'm supposed to be teaching him how to survive, not how to screw up big-time."

Tara leaned against him, offering him the comfort of her touch. When she twined her fingers in his, he moaned with relief as her warmth seeped into his soul. It had always been that way between them from the moment they'd met, like calling to like. He forced himself to tell her what was really bothering him.

"If I get to be a danger to you and the kid, you need to get help. I couldn't bear it if I hurt you or Kenny."

"That won't happen," she said with conviction. "You might lose control with a stranger, but never us."

"I wish I believed that, but I don't."

Her smile was so sweet. "Well, then I'll believe it enough for both of us."

Her hug warmed him from the inside out. Maybe his cards were better than he'd thought. He decided to treat them both to a little extra.

"I've got enough money for us to tour the aquarium if you'd like."

Tara launched herself at him for another hug. "I'd like. I'd really like."

"Then let's do it."

He always liked seeing all the brightly colored fish, and Tara could spend hours watching the otters play. As he passed the ticket seller the cash, a wave of darkness washed through him. Was this the last time he'd get to do this with Tara? God, he hoped not. But if his problems worsened to the point that he was a threat to her safety, he'd be gone.

"Sean, is something wrong?"

He had to work harder to hide his fears. "No, I'm fine, Tara. Let's go see if the otters have missed you."

She laughed, just as he'd hoped, and dragged him through the door and into the soothing darkness inside. Maybe on the way out, they'd stop at the gift shop to pick up a couple of cheap souvenirs. Something with an otter for Tara, and something for him to take with him if he had to leave her and Kenny behind. He'd need all the good memories he could scrounge.

Three hours later, they finally left the aquarium. Tara was still smiling at the postcards they'd picked out in the gift shop.

"We'd better get that ice cream and get back to Kenny," Sean said. "He's on his best behavior right now, but it won't last—especially if we keep him penned up too long."

She smiled. "Make mine a double scoop of chocolate."

"It's a deal."

Chapter 7

Ranulf glanced up with a frown. "About time you reported in, Kearn. We expected you long before this."

"Stuff it, Viking." Sandor poured himself a cup of coffee and snagged the apple off Ranulf's plate, then dropped into his usual seat.

Ranulf glared at him. "If you had any manners, you'd wait until Hughes brought you your own food."

Sandor glared right back at him. "You're a fine one to talk about manners, considering you were born before forks were invented. I'm surprised you still don't slurp your soup straight from the bowl."

"Boys, boys," Kerry chided as she sat between them. "Hughes will be in with more food in a minute."

She eyed her husband's plate and took some grapes for herself. "I'm sure you won't starve before he gets here."

Ranulf pushed his plate toward the middle of the table, where Sandor and Kerry could both reach it.

"So, Sandor, I tried calling your house early this morning." Kerry eyed him with curiosity. "There was no answer, and evidently your cell was turned off."

"I stayed with Lena to make sure she was all right, meaning to leave once she was resting comfortably. However, I didn't take into consideration how tired I was. I conked out and stayed that way until she woke me up this morning."

Ranulf laughed. "She struck me as the kind of woman who wouldn't take kindly to finding an uninvited guest in her bed." He gave Sandor the once-over. "You don't look all bruised up."

Sandor gave him a scathing look. "Unlike some people I could mention, I'm a gentleman," he said, referring to the night Ranulf had watched over Kerry and ended up doing far more than making sure she slept well. "I spent the night in a chair, and have the stiff neck to prove it."

Kerry asked, "So did you two talk about what happened in the alley last night?"

He nodded. "She remembered me capturing

her and dragging her into the alley to talk. Then she told me what she saw through Mary Dubois's eyes about the renegade's attack. She's pretty sure there were two attackers, not one. I don't think Lena's ever told anyone about her ability to read scenes before. She was sure I wouldn't believe her."

Ranulf nodded. "That's probably true; she'd have been afraid they'd think she was crazy. But, if she can read people that easily, you'd think it would interfere with her daily life more."

"You don't read everyone you get near. Maybe she's like you—except she's much prettier and easier to get along with."

Ranulf's response was predictable. "Go to hell."

"Been there. Done that." Sandor took another bite of apple as he thought about Lena's reactions. "I think her gift is keyed more to acts of violence. If that's the case, she was able to read Mary's experience so clearly only because of the nature of the attack."

Uncomfortable, he got up and walked over to the window. "And I think she might have briefly read me, too, though she didn't say anything this morning. When I pulled her away from Mary Dubois last night, she looked up at me with such . . . horror."

The scrape of a chair warned him that Kerry was coming to join him. He moved away, avoiding her attempt to comfort him.

Despite his rejection, she stayed close by. "How do you know it wasn't Mary she was thinking about?"

"Because I could sense her revulsion. What she felt for Mary's attack had a different taste to it. She hated what she learned about me."

"What happened to Bradan wasn't your fault, Sandor. I know he was your friend, but he'd turned into a monster and deserved to die. You only did what was necessary for the good of everyone."

He knew Bradan deserved to die, and his death wasn't what haunted Sandor's dreams—it was the brief flash of pleasure at making Bradan suffer as much as possible while Sandor sucked the life force from his former friend. Maybe Kerry didn't think less of him for the lapse, but he hated himself for it.

He moved on. "I've invited Lena to join me for dinner tonight and then on my hunt for the renegades."

"Why?" Kerry merely sounded curious.

"Because she'd follow me anyway, and her gift might come in handy." And he really, really wanted to spend more time with her.

Ranulf wasn't quite so accepting. "I've read this woman, Sandor. She's a real law-and-order type. Doesn't she wonder why you're hunting down these renegades instead of leaving it to the police?"

"She asked, but she didn't press for details when I pointed out that the attacks happened in several jurisdictions and the police haven't been able to connect the dots. I ascribed that to how badly shaken she'd been, but I'm going to have to come up with something believable by tonight, because she's bound to ask at some point."

Kerry nodded. "I've been thinking that we should get you licensed as a private investigator. A real one."

"I'll give it some thought." Time to leave. But before he could make good his escape, Hughes finally showed up with a huge lunch for all of them. Giving in to the inevitable, Sandor sat back down and dug in. At least eating would help pass the time until his date with Lena. He couldn't wait.

Lena looked at herself in the fitting room mirror and did a slow turn.

This is just plain stupid. She had a perfectly good skirt back in her hotel room. Why did she feel compelled to buy something new for a business dinner with a man she barely knew?

Even on sale, the cost of the dress and shoes made her wince, but she'd known the minute she'd slipped the dress over her head that she had to have it. The silken material brushed across her skin with a gentle touch, and the soft blue emphasized her eyes and set off her tan to perfection. The sandals made her legs look good, but they'd also hold up for long walks. She didn't have many occasions for such an outfit, but the styles were classic and would last for years.

But really, all she truly cared about was wearing something wonderful for Sandor Kearn. Even in jeans and a casual shirt, he looked like he belonged in a fashion magazine. If they were going to pass for a couple out for the evening, she couldn't look like his poor relation.

She had also bought a new lacy bra and panties. She wasn't sure she wanted Sandor to know about those, but after that kiss in her hotel room, she might be willing to let him in on the secret.

"That dress was *so* made with you in mind." The clerk, a matronly woman in her early sixties, motioned for Lena to do another turn. "I'm supposed to say that no matter what the outfit looks like, but in this case it's true. Whoever the lucky guy is, I'd like to be a mouse in the corner when he sees you in that." She fanned her face with her hand. "I bet he goes into a serious meltdown."

Lena blushed. "Thank you."

"I don't know if you're going to thank me when you see this." The woman brought out a shawl from behind her back, settled it over Lena's shoulders, and smiled at Lena's reflection in the mirror. "This isn't on sale, but I'll give you the same discount on it as the dress. They look like they were made for each other, but the shawl is also practical. Summer evenings can be chilly here in Seattle, and you'll be glad you have it if you spend any time outside."

Lena decided she must have Soft Touch branded on her forehead, but the woman was right. The shawl set the dress off to perfection. "Add it onto the bill. I'll be living on tuna and cold cereal for a month, but it's worth it."

"Honey, I'd live on cat food if I looked that good in it." The woman laughed as she left the fitting room.

Lena took one last twirl, then reluctantly turned herself back into a pumpkin with her jeans and T-shirt.

Sandor wore the duster because Lena had asked him to. The supple leather billowed and swirled around his legs as he strode down the sidewalk. He'd originally bought it because it hid his weapons, but if he'd known it would put that look in an attractive woman's eyes, he'd have bought one much sooner.

Lena was taking a cab to the restaurant. Maybe she had other business to tend to first, but more likely she wanted to avoid another heated encounter in her hotel room. Well, he planned to kiss her again as soon as possible, then see where the evening led from there.

How long was she going to be in Seattle? He was in no hurry for her to leave, with this passion simmering between them, but he didn't want her here long enough to find out that he was a professional killer. Considering her career, he seriously doubted she'd find that attractive in a potential lover.

He reached the restaurant early and leaned against a railing to wait outside. As some other patrons went by, he noticed they gave him a wide berth.

Maybe his warrior nature showed more than he thought, but it could also be the coat. He'd never noticed that reaction when he'd worn a suit. Unless the changes inside him were showing on the outside—maybe in his eyes?

A cab turned into the parking lot, and he could

tell that the passenger had golden blond hair. He stayed were he was and watched. When the cab pulled up to the sidewalk, the driver actually got out and came around to open the passenger door.

Hot damn! One look at those long legs stepping out of the cab made one important part of his body stand at full attention, giving him another reason to be glad for the coat. The woman was drop-dead gorgeous. He hoped his tongue wasn't hanging out when he stepped out of the shadows.

For a brief instant she looked unsure of herself, then her shoulders went back as she started toward him. He could have spent hours watching her dress swirl around her legs as she walked. He managed to jerk his eyes up to look her in the eye, admiring the curve of her waist and the way the fabric clung to her body along the way.

"You look beautiful."

"Thank you." Lena gave him the once-over right back. "So do you. I *do* like that coat."

Her impudent grin was adorable. He held out his hand, and when she took it, he tugged her into his arms for a quick kiss.

"I've missed you."

Damn, he hadn't meant to let that slip out. He led her toward the restaurant. "I hope you like seafood. The chef here specializes in it."

"I love any and all of it. When I left Seattle, I

chose the East Coast to be near fresh seafood. I've seriously missed Dungeness crab, though."

The maître d' led them to the corner table that Sandor had requested so that Lena could look out at Lake Union. A scattering of sailboats out on the water added to the picturesque view.

"Have you ever eaten here before?" he asked once they were alone.

"Years ago, but I think it's been remodeled since then. The view is certainly lovely."

She slipped off the shawl, revealing even more of her lovely skin. He closed his eyes and imagined nibbling his way from her shoulder up to her jawline and beyond. The direction his thoughts had taken must have been a bit too obvious, because Lena's cheeks flushed pink.

Even so, she met his gaze head-on. "So where are we going to patrol tonight?"

For now, business was probably a safer topic. "I thought we'd wander the piers and along the waterfront shops. Whoever's behind the attacks doesn't always strike two nights in a row, though, so I'm not convinced we'll see any action."

Of that kind, anyway. He was hoping for some far more pleasurable action before the evening was over. His place or hers, it didn't matter as long as there was a lock on the door to keep out the world.

Over the course of the meal, they discovered they had similar tastes in movies, but not in music. Although Sandor could appreciate some country and western, he much preferred classic rock and blues.

Lena passed on dessert but cheerfully demanded bites of the wickedly rich chocolate cake that Sandor ordered. The way she savored each and every crumb, her eyes half shut in bliss, nearly drove him over the edge. When they ran out of excuses to linger any longer they had a good-natured squabble over the bill, but Sandor snagged the check and paid it while Lena stepped into the ladies' room.

"You can buy next time," he promised, fingers crossed, as they walked out to his sports car.

He unlocked it with his remote, and Lena sighed with pleasure as she settled into the soft leather seat. When he turned the key and the engine roared to life, she grinned.

"Oooh, I bet this baby really rips up the highway."

"I suppose it would, but the speed limit is only sixty or seventy miles an hour, depending whether you're in town or out in the boonies."

Lena snorted. "Yeah, right. You've got all those horses corralled under the hood and you drive like an old lady? Tell me another one."

He gave her an innocent look. "I'll have you know I'm a law-abiding citizen."

That cracked her up big-time. "Sandor Kearn, 'fess up. What'll she do?"

He winked at her. "Rumor has it that she'll top out at one-seventy in the straightaway, but I'm only telling you what I've heard on the streets."

"And I bet those rumors started right after you blasted by someone who happened to have a stopwatch or a radar gun." She trailed her fingers along the dashboard. "She's a real beauty."

"Thank you." He slowed to a stop when the light changed. "So what do you drive?"

"Give it your best guess."

"Let's see. You probably drive your vehicle in your job. Since you have ties to the fire department, I would assume that you're in the same line of work. Am I right?"

She nodded.

"And you're a pragmatic person who thinks that as long as something works, why spend money for something new? Buy quality and it will last." It was getting harder to keep a straight face. "Am I doing okay so far?"

She nodded again, but she wasn't smiling quite as much. "Go on."

"I think you drive a four-year-old SUV with all-wheel drive." He shot her a gleeful smirk. "And it's blue to match your eyes."

She punched him on the arm. "You ran my records, didn't you?"

"Maybe I'm just extra perceptive."

"And maybe you're full of sh—"

He cut her off midword with his hand over her mouth. "Okay, I confess. I checked you out, just like you did me. Are we even on that score?"

When she nodded, he removed his hand. "I needed to know who I'd be working with. It's only sensible."

"Then let me ask you a sensible question. What exactly do you do for a living?"

He didn't even hesitate. "I'm a security consultant for a private firm."

"What's the name of the company?"

"That's privileged information. My employers prefer to maintain a low profile." He hoped she heard the regret in his voice. He hated all the lies between them.

"Privileged information, as in if you told me, then you'd have to kill me?" she said snippily.

He had to laugh at that. "That's a tad extreme. Why do you care who signs my paycheck?"

"Because I'm guessing that person is Kerry Thorsen—or maybe her husband."

"You can guess all you want to. But again, why do you care?"

Her expression turned sad. "Because I still believe one or both of them know something about Coop's death that they're not telling me. If you work for them, then you probably know what it is. And I'm giving you fair warning: I plan to get to the truth."

He hated holding out on her. "Lena, I swear I had nothing to do with your friend's death. Neither did Kerry or Ranulf."

They rode in silence for several blocks. He was about to give up and offer to drive her back to her hotel when she finally spoke.

"Okay, I'll take your word for it." She offered him a halfhearted smile. "Truce?"

"Truce."

Once they agreed to quit talking about touchy subjects, Sandor proved to be an entertaining companion. Despite his incredible good looks, he didn't take himself too seriously. Didn't the man realize how many women gave him second and even third looks? He gave no sign of it. With seemingly no effort, he made her feel as if she was the only woman on his radar. It was flattering, if a bit unnerving, to be the focus of such intense interest.

Was he thinking about getting naked together? *She* could hardly think about anything else.

As they strolled along the waterfront, it was far too easy to forget they were there on business. The sidewalks were crowded with other couples out for an evening stroll and with families on vacation intent on packing in every second of entertainment they could with their limited time in the city.

She didn't blame them. She hadn't realized how much she missed the Seattle area. There was no denying the East Coast had its own beauty, and she'd enjoyed the opportunity to explore cities that she'd only read about before. But the Pacific Northwest felt like home and probably always would. She'd always meant to move back, but not until she'd built up enough courage to face Coop. She shivered. It was too late for that, now.

"Cold?" Sandor asked.

"Not because of the weather."

He let the matter drop but wrapped his arm around her shoulders and snuggled her in close to his side. Normally, being surrounded by that much male strength made her feel claustrophobic, but Sandor's touch only made her feel . . . well . . . warm. Inside and out. Actually, *hot*. Oh, boy, she was in real trouble here.

Did she really want more than a friendly good-night from this man? She was worried the answer was a resounding yes.

It had been way too long since she'd invited a man past her front door, and taking a man like Sandor to her bed would be like going from a forty-yard dash to suddenly competing in a marathon.

Sandor suddenly came to an abrupt halt. His arm dropped away from her shoulder as he backtracked a step to run his hands along a low concrete wall. Tracing a series of circular motions, he gradually narrowed the motion down to one particular spot and stopped.

Lena couldn't read the expression on his face. "Sandor? What's going on?"

"Put your hands right where mine are."

Okay, that was weird, but she did as he asked. As soon as she touched the rough wall, her hands tingled. A few inches either way and the sensation quickly faded.

"You want to explain what this is that I'm feeling here?"

Sounding as grim as death, Sandor asked, "Just feeling? You're not seeing anything, like you did with Mary Dubois?"

She shook her head. "No, all I get is a mild tingling, no pictures. Should I sense more than that?"

"I guess not." He looked disappointed, though,

and started walking back in the direction of the parking lot.

She had to hustle to keep up with him. "So what happened back there? How did you know to stop at that particular spot?"

"Can this discussion wait until we're in the car?"

His sudden mood change made her even more curious. "Sure, that's fine."

He surprised her by giving her hand a quick squeeze before entwining his fingers through hers. The small touch did a lot to ease the tension between them. When they reached the car, he held her door open for her. But before she got in, he caught her face with his hand and pressed a quick kiss on her lips. When he pulled back, she reached up to trace his lips with her fingertip. He smiled and nipped at her finger. The playful bite affected her far more powerfully than it should have, making her ache in all the right places.

When he joined her inside the car, he stared into the gathering darkness for several seconds. Whatever had him tied up in knots had to be pretty serious.

Finally, he spoke. "The reason I wasn't shocked by your ability to read Mary Dubois's experience so clearly is that I have a variation of that same kind of ability. It's not as strong as yours, I'd guess, but sometimes I can follow scents that other people don't notice. I kept getting an occasional whiff of something that reminded me of the alley where we found her, but I didn't think much of it, since city streets all have similar scents."

She nodded. "I can see that."

"Well, at that one spot back there, the scent was almost overwhelming. I think our guy was there, and recently. Like he stopped there for a while before moving on."

"And you hoped I would be able to see him, the way I experienced what Mary saw and felt."

"Yes." He started the car.

"I'm sorry to disappoint you."

He turned those beautiful dark eyes on her with such intensity that it was as if he'd caressed her. "I don't think you could ever disappoint me." The sensual purr in his voice rivaled the power surging in the car's engine.

They rode in silence for several blocks until they reached a stoplight. As they waited for it to change, Sandor gave her a long, considering look.

"Sandor, whatever it is that you want to say, just spit it out."

But she had a suspicion about what was on his mind, because it was also on hers. Butterflies started fluttering in her chest as she tried to make a rational decision about how she wanted this evening to end. Or if she wanted it to end at all.

"I know that it's way too soon to be thinking this way, Lena, but I don't want to take you back to your hotel. I want you to come home with me."

His hand captured hers, then he planted a warm kiss in the center of her palm. She melted. Simply melted. The words she could ignore or refute. But a kiss like that? It would take a far stronger woman than her to say no to that.

"Got a spare toothbrush?"

"It just so happens that I do, because the dentist gave me a new one last week." He let go of her hand to shift gears.

His explanation pleased her. It was his way of saying that he didn't often have surprise overnight guests. She hoped his home was close by, because those butterflies were multiplying fast.

Sandor turned into the narrow alley that ran behind his house and parked next to his second car.

When Lena spotted the beige four-door, she grinned. "I bet that sedan hates being parked next to this beauty. Do you only drive the poor thing when you want to fade into the crowd?"

He laughed. "Sometimes I need a car that carries more than two people. Besides, it was cheap."

"I would have been sorely disappointed if that had been your only car." She ran her hand down the soft leather of his sleeve. "This coat and that car definitely do not go together."

"Which image do you prefer?" he asked, although his smug smile warned her he already knew the answer.

"Definitely the duster." She leaned closer to him. "But if there wasn't a lot more to you than good taste in clothing, we wouldn't be sitting here right now."

His smile widened. "Thanks. Can we go inside now? I'm a little old to be making out in a car."

"Where's your sense of adventure?" she teased.

His gaze turned hot and a little predatory. "Come inside and I'll show you, and anything else you're interested in."

Gulp. Okay.

After he unlocked the back door, he stood back and allowed Lena to enter the house. She was instantly enthralled by the simple lines of his Arts and Crafts bungalow. Sandor Kearn was obviously far more complicated than she'd guessed.

Oh boy, was she in trouble now.

Chapter 8

*L*etting Lena roam from room to room, Sandor banked the burning urge to drag her upstairs to his bed. As much as he wanted her naked and in his arms, he couldn't rush her—not with that soft smile on her face as she admired the home he'd made for himself.

Her fingers trailed over the smooth oak paneling he'd nearly killed himself refinishing. She stopped to admire the narrow stained-glass windows that flanked the door and the much larger one over the fireplace. He already knew that Lena was a sensuous woman, one who savored the feel and textures of her surroundings. Look at the way she'd all but purred at the feel of his leather coat.

Watching her caress this and that was driving him crazy. It was as if he could feel the soft slide of her fingers on his own skin as they lightly grazed the smooth oak side table. He'd never had such a visceral reaction to a woman. Would she bring the same sense of wonder to making love? Gods above, he hoped so.

She stopped to read the titles in the overflowing bookcase beside his favorite chair. "I see we have some favorites in common."

Needing to touch her, he eased up behind her and slid his arms around her waist, resting his chin on her shoulder. "Does that surprise you?"

She leaned back into his chest. "No. Actually, the bungalow surprises me more."

"Why's that?"

"It feels like home . . . I mean, it feels like a home." She turned to look up at him. "I expected more of a bachelor pad."

He kissed the side of her neck and was pleased when she arched her head to the side to encourage him to continue. Her skin smelled warm, inviting, intoxicating. "I got tired of living in apartments. Besides, I needed something to do with my spare time."

She looked around the room in wonder. "You did all of this restoration work yourself?"

"Most of it, although I subcontracted out the plumbing and electrical. Otherwise, I'm really good with my hands." He let his hands wander to prove the point, learning her curves and the fit of her body to his.

"It's lovely."

He turned her to face him. "So are you."

Her eyes searched his face with such intensity. What was she looking for? Unable to bear the thought she might not find it, he distracted her with a slow, hot kiss.

"You haven't seen the upstairs yet," he whispered near her ear, letting his breath sweep across her skin. "I spent a lot of extra effort on it."

"Will I like it?"

He pressed against her so there was no mistaking what he had in mind. "Oh, yeah. I promise to make sure you like it a lot."

"Show me the way."

He led her around the corner to the staircase. At the top, he stepped aside to watch her reaction.

Her eyes were wide in wonder as she looked around. "Sandor Kearn, this is positively decadent! I'm seriously jealous."

He laughed, pleased. When he'd bought the house, the second floor had been a rabbit warren of small rooms. With an architect's help, he'd converted the upstairs into one large bedroom and a luxurious master bath. He'd haunted antique stores and auctions for months to buy the perfect period pieces for his private space. The only concession he'd made to modern design had been the king-sized bed that dominated the room.

And if he didn't get this woman into that bed in the next few seconds, his sanity would be in serious jeopardy. He swung Lena up in his arms, capturing her laughing protest with his mouth.

Then they were both falling onto the bed, and the full-bodied contact flamed the fire between them even brighter. He kissed her hard and growled his approval when she gave back as much as he demanded, their tongues swirling and dancing together.

Craving bare skin against bare skin, he captured the hem of her dress with his hands and pulled it up to her waist. He almost lost it completely at the sight of her pretty blue panties, not to mention the garter belt and nylons.

"Lena, honey, I can't be slow about this."

"Good! Because I'm not in the mood to wait." Her eyes dropped to half mast in invitation.

Swiftly getting a packet of protection out of the bedside drawer, he gently slid her panties down her legs, leaving the garter belt and nylons in place. Then he lowered his zipper, letting his erection spring free of the confinement of his jeans.

Lena propped herself up on her elbows, smiling her approval. "I hope all of that's for me."

"It sure is," he said, flattered by how pleased she looked at that idea.

"Then come take me, lover." The passionate huskiness in her voice drew him like a siren. "We've waited too long for this already."

Kneeling between her thighs, he pushed his pants down and gently caressed her. To his delight, her passage was slick and inviting. "I don't want to hurt you by rushing things."

She tugged him down for a kiss. "You won't."

His body was screaming with the need to get inside her. He tried to go easy even if it killed him, but Lena dug her nails into his shoulders and arched beneath him. In one sharp thrust, he completed the joining.

When Lena gasped at the sudden invasion, Sandor froze. He fought hard not to lose control, telling himself not to move, to give her all the time she needed to adjust.

"Are you all right?" He could barely get the words out.

She took a deep breath and then another as her body gradually relaxed enough to accept him more fully. "Sorry, it's been a while since I've done this."

"There's no rush. We have all night." If his heart didn't explode in the next few seconds. Worse, his control over his Kyth nature was slipping. Glowing eyes and energy crackling along his skin would certainly put a damper on things. He eased down closer to kiss her, giving them both something else to think about.

She tasted so sweet, as intoxicating as the finest wine. Then she smiled against his mouth and feathered her fingertips down his sides to grab his ass. Never let it be said he couldn't take a hint. He flexed his hips, and Lena murmured her approval. He repeated the motion, harder and at a sharper angle. She moaned and wrapped her nylon-clad legs around his waist.

He levered himself back up, supporting himself with his outstretched arms to pump his hips hard and fast, withdrawing almost completely before surging forward again and again. This time, when Lena gasped, it was with pleasure. Her inner muscles kneaded the full length of his cock, creating a slight resistance as he tried to pull back again. She was killing him.

"I'm not going to last long," he warned, driving them both toward the edge. His world narrowed down, as the place where their bodies joined together became the fulcrum of his entire existence.

He broke rhythm long enough to ease a hand between them to slide a finger over the spot guaranteed to drive Lena over the top. She was slick and swollen, and shuddered at his touch.

When he started to withdraw his fingers, she

captured his hand with her own, forcing him right back. He loved that she wasn't shy about demanding what she wanted from him. Her climax was building. It was there in her fierce expression and the way her body moved against his. This was going to be so good for both of them.

When he felt the first tremors deep inside her, he drove them both hard toward the finish line. The second she cried out in release, he exploded in hot, shuddering pulses deep inside her. When the tremors finally stopped he withdrew from her, rolling onto his back but holding her close.

"Are you all right?"

"Do you even need to ask, or are you fishing for a compliment?" She smiled as she cuddled closer. "One question, though. Do you think we could muster up the strength to get naked before we try this again?"

A new burst of energy flowed over him. "I think that can be arranged."

And it was.

Sean was darned tired of arguing. "I'm sorry, Tara, I know I promised I'd stay in, but that's not happening. I've got to go out. Now." He snatched his jacket from the hook by the door and yanked it on. "I won't be gone long."

Tara, clearly distressed, tried to get between him and the door. "No, Sean. I can't let you go out like this. Remember, you're the one who made me promise to stop you whenever your control was this bad."

"Oh, yeah, I was really thinking clearly when I said that." He tried an end run around her, but she anticipated the move and blocked him again. She knew he'd never in his right mind raise a hand against her. Trouble was, right now he wasn't even close to being in his right mind.

"Tara, I need to feed! How the hell am I supposed to get what I need if I stay in here?"

"Feed from me." She tried to cup his face between her hands, but he ducked out of reach.

"Fuck that. I know you only want to help, but it's not *enough*, Tara. Not anymore."

He backed away, putting some breathing room between them. "It used to work, but now it's like offering a starving man a handful of crumbs. I'd strip your supply completely, and I won't risk that happening."

She flinched, as if his words had been a physical blow. He'd hurt her feelings, but right then he couldn't care. His body was screaming so loudly that there was no room for anything but the need to survive, no matter what the cost or who he hurt. He had to feed off somebody, to the point of almost draining them dry, and the threat to Tara and Kenny increased with each second he was caged up inside.

He forced his next words out through gritted teeth, breathing hard as if he was running for his life. "I've got . . . to go . . . before . . . I hurt . . . one of you."

Tara's sweet eyes filled with grief. "Go, then. But come back to us as soon as you can."

He couldn't lie to her. "Can't promise. If I kill . . ."

His throat choked closed. He pressed a rough kiss to Tara's cheek, knowing it might be the last time he saw her.

He tasted her salty tears on his lips as he turned toward the poorer part of town, sure he'd find a donor there.

Victim was what he really meant. His fingers curled up as if they were claws ready to rip out some poor bastard's throat. Relishing the thought of it, he knew he was too far gone. He shoved his hands in his pockets, hoping to hide his true nature until the last possible second.

His hunt didn't take long. The night breeze carried the musty smell of an unwashed human body. Judging by the strength of the scent, his prey was nearby, huddled in the darkest shadows along the building ahead. Sean's muscles cramped from the need to feed, his breath coming in ragged gasps. If he didn't get some energy soon, he'd be reduced to crawling. He paused before crossing the street to where a dark form stretched out along the foundation of a warehouse.

A passed-out drunk wouldn't be much fun, no matter how badly Sean needed a hit of energy. Maybe he could harvest enough to reestablish some control, then prowl the city looking for a victim who'd be more of a challenge.

Wait. What was that noise? Tilting his head from one side to the other, Sean listened hard. Was that a footstep echoing behind him? He'd been so focused on his hunt that he hadn't paid close attention to his surroundings—stupid.

Usually he didn't have much to fear from other predators roaming the streets. Most of the time they sensed their fellow killers and gave them wide berth. But there was always someone out there who could take him out in a heartbeat and smile while they did it.

Although Sean's body screamed in protest, he made an abrupt right turn and walked a hundred feet before stopping with no warning. No sound of nearby footsteps; no movement in the shadows. He cut across the street at a sharp angle that led him to the corner of the warehouse. From there, he'd check all directions one last time for unwanted company before feeding.

All clear.

Kneeling by the pile of old blankets, Sean ignored the stench as he latched on to the back of the sleeping man's neck. The energy was slow in coming, no doubt due to the empty gin bottle nearby. It took considerable effort, but he was finally able to establish a steady flow. Despite the taint of the man's disease and near starvation, Sean harvested enough to soothe the jagged edges of his cravings.

He staggered back to his feet, sick from the crappy quality of his meal, but proud of his control. The snoring bastard didn't realize how lucky he was to be alive. As he walked away, Sean looked back over his shoulder with a shudder. He could very well end up sleeping on the streets himself if his control didn't improve.

Back to the hunt. As he walked along doing his best to look harmless, he imagined the perfect main course, now that he'd had his appetizer. Someone young and strong with the kind of energy that flowed thick and sweet through his muscles and blood, warming everything in its path.

An hour later, he was still hunting. He'd considered and rejected half a dozen candidates. As hungry as he was for their life force, he had enough willpower left to savor his sense of superiority, knowing the choice was his to make. Some stranger's fate was his to decide.

Anticipation was everything, now.

Up ahead he spotted a definite possibility. Male. Young. A big guy, the kind who carried his size like a weapon, confident in his ability to take on all comers. Poor bastard—that was about to change. The target probably had fifty, sixty pounds on Sean, but muscle power didn't always translate as strength against Sean's abilities. One touch, and they'd both know who was the one to be feared.

Sean hurried his footsteps, grateful that his running shoes made next to no noise on the rough concrete sidewalk. He could probably outrun his chosen one, but he wanted a discreet takedown. The last thing he needed was a crowd while he stripped the cocky jerk bare of his ability to swagger home. When Sean was done with him, he wouldn't have the strength left to stand.

Sean narrowed the distance between them, but the timing had to be just right. In this part of town he couldn't risk feeding out on the sidewalk, as he had with the drunk. The attack had to be as close to the mouth of that alley ahead as possible. He sprinted forward, hugging the building, using the shadows to disguise his approach.

But if nature gave predators the skills necessary to survive, she'd also kept the playing field level. Before Sean could make his final approach, his intended victim did an abrupt about-face and stopped. Sean kept moving, knowing that if he even slowed down it would raise suspicions. He nodded at the guy and briefly made eye contact as he kept going until he reached the corner. Ordinarily he would have crossed against the light, but right now he was content to be a law-abiding citizen.

His ploy evidently reassured the guy enough to start walking again, but he was far more attentive to his surroundings than he had been before. Taking him down now would be harder but not impossible, and Sean relished the greater challenge. The guy had almost reached the corner when the light changed and Sean started across the street, looking for another possible site for his feeding. Even an unlighted doorway would do, although the risk of discovery would be higher.

Just ahead was a staircase that led down to some kind of small shop in the basement level. Perfect. He stopped to relieve himself against a wall, a habit common to late-night drunks and the homeless. He deliberately turned around as his target passed by.

The man shot him a disgusted look. "Damn, man, zip it up."

"Sorry, man. I couldn't wait." Sean slurred the words, reinforcing the drunken image. "Hey, buddy, you wouldn't have twenty bucks you could lend me, do ya?"

He hurried after the guy, who predictably did his best to avoid any contact. Sean charged after him, using his momentum to carry the bigger man down and to the right, and they tumbled down the stairs to a small landing.

The guy came up swinging his fists. "Get away from me, you crazy little fucker!"

Sean ducked the blow, glad that the confines of the staircase limited the guy's ability to maneuver. Normally Sean wasn't one to play with his food, but tonight, each time he managed to get a hand on his opponent, he drew off enough energy to gradually leave the guy staggering.

His coordination fading rapidly, the bigger man soon stopped fighting altogether and backed away. For the first time, he looked afraid. "What are you doing to me? What do you want?" He slumped down on the steps, still conscious, but too weak to move.

Sean knelt beside him and ran his fingers across the man's cheek, loving the way his victim shuddered in revulsion. "What's your name?"

"Randall."

Leaning in close, Sean whispered, "Well, Randall, I'll tell you what I want. I want your essence." He closed his eyes, savoring the sweet taste of high-octane fear.

Was this what it felt like to get stoned? If so,

he could understand the appeal. His new buddy Randall had fallen silent, his body folding in on itself as his strength rapidly faded. Sean snickered. Randall had strutted through town like he owned the whole fucking place; now he was just a pile of nothing.

All of a sudden, they were no longer alone. A pair of familiar feet appeared at Sean's eye level. Son of a bitch, why was Kenny running loose at this hour of the night?

"Go home, kid—this is none of your business. And Tara won't like your being here." God, his stomach was churning. Maybe he should have eaten some real food before hunting.

"Tara doesn't know. After you left, she went to bed looking scared and upset. I waited until she cried herself to sleep before sneaking out to find you." Kenny knew better than to touch Sean's skin directly, but he got a grip on the back of Sean's jacket and gave it a strong yank. "Come on, Sean. Let go of him. You've had enough. Leave some for him. Remember? Like you told me the other night—dazed but not dead."

Sean tried to bat the kid away. "Go away. My business. Not yours."

"I'm *making* it my business. You kill that guy, and the police will be all over us." Kenny struggled to get Sean up onto his feet. "Come on, it's time to go home. We both know how much Tara will worry until she knows you're okay."

"Can't go home. Too dangerous for her. You, too. Want to kill somebody." Sean staggered to his feet to face Kenny.

For a skinny kid, Kenny was proving to be hard to evade. It didn't help that the whole world had decided to rock and roll beneath Sean's feet as he pulled himself up the stairs with Kenny still holding on to his collar.

"Come on, Sean. We need to get out of here. The cops cruise this area a lot."

The situation suddenly hit Sean as funny. His laughter sounded odd, out of control and shrill, but he couldn't seem to stop. Kenny pulled Sean's arm up around his shoulders and helped to keep him steady as they trudged down the street.

"Uh, Sean? Could you pipe down a bit? We don't want to draw attention to ourselves right now."

"Okay, shhhhh," Sean muttered, holding up his finger across his lips. "I'll be quiet. Just put me down so I can sleep."

"When we get home."

Why wasn't the kid listening? "Can't go there, Kenny. Not safe. Don't want to hurt you or Tara."

Kenny let out a long-suffering sigh. "Yeah, I know, you're the badass killer. But you still have a lot left to teach me, and you promised. Besides,

I'm not going to take on all your chores just because you want to go on a rampage. So shut up and keep walking."

Sean had left something important behind. What was it? Oh, yeah—not what. Who. He tried to turn back toward the staircase. "What about my friend Randall? He tasted so good. You should try him."

Kenny jerked Sean back around. "Thanks for the offer, but you've had enough for both of us. Now keep moving. We need to get home before someone finds him."

"Okay." Sean started laughing again. God, he wished he could stop. "We could go back and wrap him in plastic wrap like we do leftovers. You know, save him for later."

Kenny laughed, but kept hauling Sean in the direction of their apartment. "Gee, Sean, that's a great idea. When we get back to the apartment, I'll see if we have enough plastic wrap."

Sean smiled. "That'll be good. Tara will like not having to fix dinner."

"Sure, she's going to be real happy about all this. She'll be dancing in the streets when I tell her what happened."

For the first time since plugging into Randall's flow of energy, Sean's mind started to clear. What the hell had happened?

He asked the first question that popped into his head. "How did you find me, Kenny?"

"I followed your scent. It wasn't hard to do."

"You're too young to be wandering around the city this late at night. I should kick your ass for sneaking out." He would, too, as soon as he could walk without Kenny's help. "Remind me to do that first thing tomorrow."

"Sure, that'll be right at the top of my To Do list. Keep walking—we're almost there."

They finally turned onto their street and entered their apartment building. As they staggered down the dim hallway, Sean blinked several times. There was definitely a feminine form outlined in the doorway. Crap, this couldn't be good.

"Uh-oh, Kenny. Looks like Tara's up."

"Looks like." Kenny chuckled. "And for once, she's going to be more upset with you than with me. I can't wait to hear what she has to say to you."

Sean frowned. There had to be other options. "Maybe we can sleep outside tonight. Tell her we're having a campout."

"Ain't gonna happen. Time to face the music, killer. You might kick my butt tomorrow, but tonight *you're* going to be the one with bruises."

There was no escaping the inevitable. Sean pulled himself free of Kenny's grip. If he had to come crawling home, he was going to do it standing on his own two feet.

The dream started well enough. Lena was hanging with the guys at the fire station, waiting for the next call to come in. None of them liked paperwork and used any excuse to avoid it. Right then, they were taking turns flipping playing cards into Coop's boot. She'd just had a run of five in a row. Ha! Let them beat that.

Coop's worn face was creased in a smile. The pencil pushing would get done eventually, but he was the first to admit that sometimes they needed to play. Once they blew off some steam, they'd get back to business.

Suddenly the clock on the wall started spinning and spinning. Then random images flashed in front of her eyes, fading as fast as they came. They started with the fire, the big one where three people died. She'd tried so hard to solve that case without using her secret talent. Sometimes peeking at a scene with it helped, but she couldn't solve cases with knowledge that she couldn't document or explain.

With the big fire, though, temptation had proved too strong, and she'd cheated. Because of her weakness, more people had died. *Her fault.*

Her fault. Her fault. The refrain of blame would end if she could wake up, but when she was awake, Coop was dead and buried, draining her life of joy.

Yet this time, her awakening was different. When she stirred, a strong arm shifted, pulling her closer to a banked fire, where she was warm, safe, and protected. She surfaced long enough to recognize the source: Sandor. Her lips curved in a contented smile. Her lover had been amazing in his determination to please her.

He'd kissed her long and hard and in places she'd never been kissed with such focused intensity. The sex had been way better than good, from that first hurried coupling when they'd barely shoved clothing out of their way, until the last time, when they'd been too tired to do more than move slowly and savor the experience.

She cuddled closer against Sandor's side, hovering in the world between dreams and reality. She breathed in his scent and smiled at the tattoo on his bicep. She'd seen something like it once before, but she was too sleepy to remember where. Why had he chosen such an odd design? She softly traced its outline with a fingertip and felt a slight buzz. How strange. Curious, she tried it again, this time covering the incredibly detailed tattoo with the palm of her hand.

As soon as her skin flattened against his, a terrible darkness, roiling and blacker than black, roared up to suck her down into a nightmare world. Tentacles of pain and fear with a touch of madness plucked at her, pinning her down and holding her prisoner. She couldn't move, couldn't run, couldn't breathe; couldn't even close her eyes as a horror show played out in her head. Animals suffered. Fires flamed hot and then faded, each bigger than the last.

People dancing, dancing, frantic and terrified as the walls around them dissolved into flame. One bright light, cool and soothing, led the dance. The fire screamed out its fury at being cheated of its due as one by one the dancers disappeared into the light.

The fire finally burned out, leaving only the skeleton of a building. A single man wandered through the bones, jotting down notes, taking pictures, reading the story carved into the remains by the heat and the hatred. Coop. God, she knew what happened next. She'd watched it all play out when she visited the arson site, but this time she wasn't a mere observer. Now she was seeing Coop through the eyes of his killer.

She tried to scream out a warning, but she could only whimper as the killer's hand—no, her hand—lashed out to knife her friend. The sick sat-

isfaction from watching Coop die in the ashes horrified her soul, while the arsonist soaked it in with
such joy.

It got worse. A woman's agonizing death, then
a boy's. She screamed in her sleep. Their spirits remained trapped in the hell of their torment, because
their killer swallowed their pain as he used them as
test subjects to prepare for his real targets. Finally,
gloating and bloated with darkness, he stood ready
to fight. His opponents filed into a small room, one
by one. People she recognized. Kerry Thorsen.
Ranulf Thorsen. And Sandor Kearn.

She ached to scream, to warn them of the
monster they faced, but they already knew. The
terrible knowledge was written in their grim ex-
pressions and their determination to fight. An old
woman appeared at Lena's feet, more dead than
alive, yet she still burned with the same blue light
that had fought the flames in the dance club.

The battle began, instantly raging out of control. Through the killer's mind, she felt each blow,
tasted the pain, fighting on three fronts until they
slipped past his defenses. Pain, pain, and more
pain. Must not let Ranulf get his hands on him—
not if he wanted to survive. Then Sandor, his old
friend and new enemy, latched on to his mind,
digging his fingers into the killer's face and holding on with mindless fury.

No! No! The darkness was his, not Sandor's! He fought to hold on to his treasure. But starting as a trickle, then building to a roaring flood, the sweet blackness he'd worked so hard to gather poured out of his mind, out of his body, and into Sandor. Ranulf stole some, too, but it was Sandor who sucked the well dry, draining it all away. Slowly, painfully, he felt himself shrinking, disappearing. He died in agony as he crumbled to the floor.

Then there was nothing left but dust, and someone screaming a name. Lena's name. Over and over, until the insistent noise pulled her back into her own mind.

"Damn it, Lena. Wake up and open your eyes!"

She blinked and shivered. She'd never been so cold, so scared. What had just happened? The nightmare had been worse than anything else she'd ever experienced.

"Come on, honey, talk to me," Sandor coaxed. "Wake up, Lena. Please wake up."

She wanted to tell him that she wasn't really asleep, but she couldn't speak. Because if she put words to what had just happened, she'd have to admit the nightmare hadn't been a dream at all, but real. The details might not make sense yet, but what she'd seen had really happened.

Which meant she'd spent the night in the arms of a killer.

Chapter 9

*W*hat the hell had just happened? One minute he and Lena had been cocooned in the blankets, then in an instant she'd gone from calm and cuddly to terrified and thrashing about. Her skin had a blue cast to it and she was freezing cold; her teeth chattered as she stayed snared in a nightmare.

And it was all his damn fault. He'd let his guard down. She'd been almost purring with contentment when she'd first touched the Thor's hammer branded on his right bicep. The symbol contained its own powers, which the average human wouldn't have been able to tap into, but Lena was anything but average.

Her face was contorted by horror and fear. What was she seeing? He wasn't sure he wanted to know, but he had his suspicions. He had to do something to snap her out of the nightmare. Even with the heavy pile of blankets, she shook with cold.

Maybe a hot bath. He left long enough to turn on the water in the oversized claw-foot tub and throw in some lavender bath salts, hoping the calming scent would help. When the water was the right temperature, he hurried back to the bed and wrestled the still-thrashing woman up into his arms.

He did his best to cushion Lena's descent into the tub. He climbed in behind her, wrapping his arms around her and pulling her back against his chest. Gradually she stopped moving, although her muscles and joints still thrummed with an overload of energy. Every so often he turned on the faucet to keep the temperature of the water hot enough.

If she didn't snap out of it soon, he'd have to force his way into her mind and break the connection, though he wasn't sure what the consequences would be. Murmuring soft words of comfort and stroking her arms and back with his hands, he gradually drew off small jolts of energy from her until at last she sighed and sank back against him in a boneless heap.

His relief didn't last long, because as soon as Lena recovered she was going to start asking questions. And there was no telling what she'd do if she didn't like his answers.

Finally, Lena struggled to sit up. Against his better judgment, he let go of her and tried not to let it hurt so much when she immediately scooted to the far end of the tub. When she turned to face him, her eyes went from foggy and unfocused to eagle sharp in a heartbeat. There was no warmth, no understanding, just cold revulsion and fury.

"Just what in the hell are you?" Lena snarled. "I saw what you did." She scrambled out of the tub. Pain blossomed deep in his chest, making it impossible to draw a full breath. Once she was out of the room, he went after her.

He found her snatching up her scattered clothing. Without a word, he opened a dresser drawer and pulled out two pairs of sweats. He tossed one set to her.

"Here, put these on. They'll be too big for you, but they're warmer than your dress will be. I'll be downstairs." Knowing she wouldn't be happy until he was out of sight, he waited until he reached the landing before getting dressed.

After he ground some coffee beans and filled the coffeemaker with fresh water, he reached for the phone. He hesitated over which number to dial and quickly decided on the Viking's.

He didn't even wait for Ranulf to speak. "I'm

in the middle of a major cluster fuck. Get over here." Then he hung up.

What was taking Lena so long? Even if she'd refused his offer of warmer clothing, she should've been dressed by now. He fought the need to go back upstairs to check on her, not wanting her to feel cornered. He'd already hurt her enough.

If he lived to be a million years old, he'd never forget the pure loathing in her eyes. His gut ached with the need to comfort her, even though he knew she'd throw the offer right back in his face.

The stairs creaked. Good. She was coming down. He headed for the living room, not wanting her to escape without talking to him. He had to know what she was going to do with the knowledge she'd absorbed directly from his soul. It was too much to hope that she would merely take satisfaction in knowing Coop's killer had died and let the matter lie.

He hovered near the front door as she reached the last step. "I set a bag there for your clothing." He pointed to a nearby table. "Coffee is almost ready."

She shook her head, refusing to look at him. "I'm leaving now. And I don't want you following me."

"I understand that you're upset, but at least let me fix you some breakfast."

Her laugh was nasty. "Upset? That's putting it mildly. I'm furious."

"Okay, I get that." He crossed his arms over his chest. "But we still need to talk about what happened up there. Afterward, you can drive my sedan back to your hotel. You can leave the keys at the front desk if you don't want to see me when I pick it up later."

He tossed her the keys, hoping they'd give her some sense of control over the situation.

She hesitated briefly, then nodded. "You talk. I'll listen. If I don't like what I'm hearing, I'm out of here."

"Come on into the kitchen. I make more sense when I've eaten." He walked through the dining room, feeling relieved when he heard her footsteps behind him.

He went to the fridge and began pulling out ingredients for omelets, then reached for a couple of mugs and poured coffee. After setting Lena's within easy reach for her, he began chopping veggies. As long as she was staring at the blur of his knife, she wasn't looking at him with those pain-filled eyes or running for the door.

"That's an awful lot of eggs for two people. How soon are they getting here?"

He should've expected that. This woman investigated crimes for a living, and had a knack for deciphering clues and body language. "Soon enough."

"Why did you call Kerry? To have her kill my memory like you did the other night?"

That one he *hadn't* expected. "I won't apologize for that, Lena. The cops were coming, and the last thing either of us needed was for you to start talking weirdness in front of them."

He started juicing oranges.

"But you admit that you messed with my mind."

He slowly turned to face her. "Yes, damn it, I did."

She glared from across the counter. "So tell me, Sandor—how much did you mess with my mind to get me to go to bed with you last night?"

Okay, now she'd gone too damn far! "Don't you dare cheapen what happened between us! That's an insult to both of us and to what we shared."

She held her ground as he rounded the corner and stood toe-to-toe with her, his hands fisted at his sides to keep from touching her.

"Let's get this straight, Lena Wilson. You ended up naked in my bed because that's right where you wanted to be. And for the record, I wasn't the only one screaming for more, and I've got your scratches on my ass to prove it!"

She gasped with outrage. "That just proves my

point. I've never acted that way with anyone else."

"And you think my life's been filled with mind-blowing sex like that? Do you have any idea how rare a night like that is?"

"But if it wasn't real—"

"Believe me, babe, this is as real as it gets!" He swooped down to capture her lips with his, holding her prisoner between his body and the counter. She opened her mouth to protest, but he immediately deepened the kiss and cupped her bottom, lifting her against his erection.

Hell's fire, was there anything more seductive than a strong woman in full temper? Damned if it didn't make him want her even more. At first she struggled to break free, but then she growled—growled!—in frustration and wrapped her leg around his, increasing the pressure between his cock and the juncture of her thighs.

He rocked against her, increasing the rhythm. Closer; he had to get closer. His sweats fit her loosely enough to tug down easily, especially when she cooperated. After she kicked them off, he boosted her up onto the counter, smiling against her mouth when she protested the shock of the cold tile on her luscious backside.

That was all right; he was going to warm her up from the inside out. She pushed his hands out of the way to tug his own pants down. There was still a lot of anger simmering in her, but she cupped his balls with exquisite care and stroked the full length of his cock with obvious relish. The combined sensations had him throwing his head back and begging for the strength to survive the onslaught.

God, he was going down in flames. If he didn't wrest control back soon, he was going to finish before they ever really got started. He captured her wrists, then gave her a heated look and slowly licked his lips.

"Lean back on the counter, honey."

Her eyes widened in shock at what he was proposing to do. "Sandor, I don't think—"

"Don't think, just feel. Let me do this for you, for us."

She leaned back on her elbows as he slowly kissed his way up the inside of her thighs. Oh, yeah, this was going to be good. He loved the small noise she made when he spread her legs wider. This was no time for going slow and coaxing. He worked his lips and tongue hard and fast, driving her up to the edge.

Then he raised up and positioned his cock against the entrance to her body, frustrating them both by gently rocking forward, careful not to penetrate.

"Don't be a tease, Sandor!"

"Not until you admit you want this, Lena. Just like you did last night."

She didn't want to admit a darn thing; defiance burned in her bright blue eyes. Then she jerked her head in a quick nod. "Yes, you big jerk, I want this. Now!"

"Damn straight you do!" Then he plunged inside her, staking his claim. It didn't take much to have both of them straining toward each other, seeking that right touch to end this battle once and for all.

One, two, three more strokes was all it took. As Lena spun out of control, she clutched him tight and took him flying with her. Together they soared for the heavens, taking their fill of each other in hot pulses of pure pleasure.

Their flight crash-landed as the front door slammed open. Damn! The cavalry was charging in, and Sandor stood with his pants down around his knees and an angry, half-naked woman in his arms.

"Ranulf! Stay where you are. I'll be right there."

He reluctantly withdrew from Lena's body and her arms, the sensation of loss almost killing him. He picked up her sweats and handed them back to her, then yanked his own up into place. The heat they'd generated was already dissipating, leaving a pain-filled chill between them.

"I'll be right back," he promised, risking another quick kiss on her lips. He had to forestall his other guests long enough for Lena to collect herself.

In the living room, Kerry said, "Sorry to barge in, but it sounded like an emergency. Are you okay?"

"I don't know." Unless he was mistaken, the back door had just opened and closed. He should've known better than to leave her alone. His shoulders slumped in defeat.

"What happened?" Ranulf stepped around his wife.

"Come on in and I'll explain over breakfast." He had to do something to keep from charging out the door after Lena.

The pair followed him into the kitchen, where they all stood at the window and watched his car disappear down the alley.

Lena slunk into the hotel in the oversized sweats, with last night's makeup smeared under her eyes. She looked like a raccoon from hell, and felt even worse.

In her room, all she wanted to do was jump into bed, pull the covers over her head, and hide from everything and everyone, including herself. She hadn't gotten much rest last night, and the morning had been . . . She couldn't think about that right now. Not until she'd had something to eat and washed Sandor off her skin. God, had they actually had sex on the kitchen counter, and without using protection? How stupid was that, even if she was on the pill?

If only soap and hot water would remove the taint of his darkness from her memory. She wanted to believe what he'd said about messing with her mind only one time, but even that scared her. His secret ability made hers pale by comparison. How did he live with those horrific memories?

He was right about one thing, though: she'd been a willing participant in their sexual Olympics. But she wasn't going to think about that right now. She needed food, a quick shower, and then sleep. Later she'd think about what had happened, and what to do about Coop's murder.

Forty-five minutes later, she set her empty tray out in the hallway and closed the door. Her bed beckoned, but what if the nightmare came back when her defenses were down? Who would rescue her this time? Damn Sandor Kearn for making her want him and making her care.

Her goal in returning to Seattle had been so clear: find justice for Coop. Instead, she was tangled with a man who'd lied to her, who'd held back vital information he'd known she needed, and who'd made her feel unbelievably cherished as he'd made love to her.

Her skin tingled with remembered touches and the way it had felt to meet Sandor's demands with her own. She rubbed her hands up and down on her arms, trying to wipe away both the goose bumps and the memories. Now all that shared joy was twisted up and blackened from touching that damned tattoo of his.

When the first tear trickled down her cheek, she gave up and got into bed. With the drapes pulled shut and a Do Not Disturb sign on the door, she closed her eyes and her heart against all thoughts of Sandor and the mess her life had become. Finally sleep claimed her.

Sandor deftly turned the last omelet out onto his plate and joined Ranulf and Kerry at the dining room table. He'd told them to start eating without him so their food wouldn't get cold, and they'd taken him at his word.

"I didn't know you were so handy around the kitchen." Ranulf reached for more bacon. "Next time I need a midnight snack, I'll know who to call."

"Stuff it, Viking," Sandor said with no real rancor. He simply didn't have the energy. "Do either of you need anything else?"

"Coffee, but I'll get it." The big man disappeared into the kitchen.

Kerry placed her hand on Sandor's arm. "Are you all right?"

Hell, no, I'm dying inside. But Kerry had enough on her shoulders without him adding to the burden.

Ranulf returned with the coffeepot and topped off all three cups before sitting down.

"So tell us what happened," Kerry said.

There was no good way to say it. "Lena knows."

Kerry blinked. "And I thought Ranulf was a man of few words. Care to elaborate?"

Lena would hate knowing their night together was a topic of conversation among people she barely knew, and trusted even less. But Sandor saw no way around it.

"Last night, Lena and I had dinner and then walked the waterfront. I was trying to find some sign of the renegades and thought she might be able to help. After that we decided to come back here for the night. To—"

Ranulf interrupted. "We already figured that part out for ourselves. Just fast-forward to what happened this morning."

"Lena and I were still in bed, dozing off and

on. Everything was fine. But then unfortunately she noticed my tattoo of Thor's hammer."

Kerry looked confused. "How can a tattoo cause problems?"

Sandor pulled his arm out of his sleeve to show her. "You know that Ranulf carries some of his power in the Thor's hammer he wears around his neck. It's his direct connection to the Dame, and when Judith bequeathed her talisman to you, you got her power as well. She connected the rest of us Talions to her and to our individual powers through a branding. Mine is on my bicep."

When Kerry nodded, he continued. "I felt a small buzz when Lena first touched it. Before I could wake up enough to stop her, she covered the tattoo with her whole hand. Since her ability to read past events seems to be connected to violence, the dam broke. It would have been bad enough if she'd just read my recent experiences, but I think she might have tapped directly into Bradan's, too. All of them."

Kerry shuddered. "How do you know?"

"Because Lena looked at me as if she were facing all the demons in hell. Because she accused me of knowing all along who had killed Coop and hiding the truth from her."

And because she thought he'd used mind games to seduce her. That one really rankled, but he couldn't blame her for thinking so. Maybe he shouldn't have forced the issue in the kitchen, but he couldn't regret it, either. Right now, all he wanted to know was if she'd made it back to her hotel okay and if she was all right. Stupid question—of course she wasn't all right.

He couldn't sit there any longer. He picked up his tableware and headed into the kitchen. After setting it in the sink, he stared out the window.

Someone punched him on the arm. "Earth to Sandor. Earth to Sandor."

Kerry was looking at him with mild exasperation. "We've still got business to attend to. I *assume* you tried to block her memory."

"No, as a matter of fact, I didn't. I did the other night in the alley because I had no choice. This morning's trip down memory lane also showed her that, too."

"And she didn't take it well." His Dame calmly rinsed and loaded the coffee mugs in the top rack of the dishwasher.

When he didn't immediately respond, she used her energy power to give him a slight shove. Despite her diminutive size, Kerry wasn't afraid to face down irate males several times her size. "Well? Details please."

Irritated, Sandor snapped, "No, Kerry, she didn't. Not only that, she accused me of using my secret abilities to coerce her into bed. This, after a night of mind-blowing sex that I've never experienced before and probably never will again. Is that enough detail for you?"

"Watch it, Sandor. That's my wife you're crowding there."

Ranulf muscled in to get right up in Sandor's face, his eyes blazing with blue fire. "I don't give a rat's ass how upset you are over this mess you've gotten yourself into, Talion. You do NOT talk to my wife like that. Am I making myself clear?"

Sandor had been pushed far enough. "No, we're not clear on that, you low-life berserker. This conversation between me and the Dame does not involve you. Stay the hell out of my business!"

He gave Ranulf a shove, a move guaranteed to unleash the Consort's own need to strike out. But before a single fist connected, an invisible force froze both of them in midswing. Son of a *bitch*, he wished Kerry would quit doing that. He really needed to punch someone, and Ranulf was such a great target.

Kerry slowly eased off the pressure, making them prove they'd regained control of their tempers before she released them completely. Sandor wasn't the only one breathing hard from the strain of trying to break through her hold; sweat dripped off Ranulf's forehead.

The Viking gave his wife a chagrined look. "I hate it more every time you do that."

"The answer is obvious: don't make me have to do it again." Her smile was impish.

Normally Sandor enjoyed watching Kerry run her big warrior husband around in circles, but right now he needed some breathing room.

"I'll be back down in a while." He stalked out of the kitchen without looking back.

Half an hour later he came back downstairs, showered and shaved, and still wired. To his surprise, Ranulf was sitting at the kitchen counter alone with a fresh pot of coffee. Kerry's absence gave Sandor a sense of foreboding.

"Okay, where did she go?" he asked, although he suspected that he knew the answer.

Ranulf turned to face him. "To talk to your woman."

"Lena's not one of our people. Kerry has no jurisdiction over her." Though Lena wouldn't be the first human casualty sacrificed for the greater good of the Kyth people. Sandor headed for the door with his keys in hand.

Ranulf just smiled. "I'll ride along so I can catch a lift home with Kerry."

Without waiting for a response, Sandor

slammed out the back door and headed for the garage. The Viking could ride along if he wanted to. But if he or Kerry raised a finger to harm Lena, there would be hell to pay.

Kerry approached Lena's door slowly. At this point only full honesty would do; that was the only option other than a total mind scrub. Even if Kerry was willing to risk the possible damage that might cause to Lena's mind, she didn't think Sandor would ever forgive her.

Besides, they owed the woman. Thanks to her, Sandor was finally showing signs of moving past the horrific experience of having to execute his lifelong friend. The scary deadness in his eyes had all but disappeared since he'd met Lena.

Sometimes she hated her new role as Grand Dame of the Kyth. The burden seemed to grow heavier all the time. It would have been nice to have time to adjust to the knowledge of what she was before having to take on the full duties as Dame, and she wasn't the only one questioning her ability to do the job. But now wasn't the time to worry about that.

Ignoring the Do Not Disturb sign, Kerry rapped softly on the door, then harder when she didn't get a response. After the third time, footsteps shuffled toward the door and the dead bolt was unlocked.

Lena left the chain on and blinked sleepily through the small crack in the doorway. "What the heck do you want?"

Kerry said soothingly, "I thought you might want to talk. If you've got questions, I probably have answers."

The door closed long enough for Lena to undo the chain. When she swung the door open, she looked far more awake and battle ready. "And how do I know you're not planning to use some kind of Vulcan mind meld on me?"

"Because that would upset Sandor, and he matters a lot to me."

Lena allowed Kerry into her room. "Why would it upset him? He's already used it on me himself."

Kerry let a little of her temper show. "And he's beating himself up over that. Why don't you get off your high horse and cut the man some slack?"

Unless she'd missed her guess, those were Sandor's sweats that Lena was wearing. The question was why? For convenience, or for the connection to him? She'd know more about the strength of their chemistry when she saw them together. Which, knowing Sandor, should be very soon.

"So ask your questions, Lena. I'm sure you must have some doozies."

Lena opened the small fridge in the corner and took out two cans of diet cola, set one down on the table in front of Kerry, then sat cross-legged on the bed and popped open her own.

"Thanks." Kerry took a long drink before setting the can aside. "If you want answers from me, you'd better get started, because I have a feeling Sandor will come charging in here any minute."

Lena choked on her drink. When she could breathe, she sputtered, "Why? Is he afraid I'll drag you into a serious smackdown?"

Kerry prayed for patience. "Not because he's worried about me. It's *you* he'll want to protect."

"I don't need his protection." Lena looked insulted.

This time Kerry smiled. She knew just how the woman felt. Ranulf's overprotective tendencies drove her crazy at times, no matter how well intentioned.

"Yeah, but Sandor won't see it that way. The man's got a protective streak a mile wide. Not only that, I suspect Ranulf will be hot on Sandor's heels to keep him from running roughshod over *me*."

Chapter 10

*L*ena wondered. Would Sandor really side with her against the Thorsens? That didn't make sense—Kerry and her husband were obviously very important to him. Buried in the swirling darkness she'd fallen into that morning was the feeling that Kerry and the older woman she'd seen were different from the other people in Sandor's world. Lena tried to remember how, and Sandor's voice echoed in her head.

Kerry Thorsen was . . . royalty? Lena stared at the petite woman dressed in jeans and a T-shirt with the local baseball team's logo on the front, and tried to bring that picture into focus. Kerry wasn't a queen; she was a dame—with a capital *D*.

She blurted, "What's a Dame, anyway?"

Kerry set her drink aside. "A short history

lesson first. Mind you, I only recently found out about all of this myself. If you want more details, you'll have to ask Ranulf. He's lived through most of the history of our people.

"At some time in the far distant past, a subspecies of humans evolved in northern Europe and Scandinavia. Although they looked like everyone else, they had some different abilities. The important one was that they could absorb life energy from other humans, which helped them thrive in harsh climates, especially when food was scarce. When there got to be too many Kyth, as they came to call themselves, they started migrating to other parts of their world."

She continued, "Some of the Kyth developed other abilities. The strongest of the Kyth became the Talions, the defenders of our people. You've met two of the strongest."

"Sandor and Ranulf." That was a no-brainer—not that she was buying into this fairy tale.

"Exactly. But the Kyth have always been a matriarchal society, ruled by a woman known as the Grand Dame. For the past thousand-plus years, that woman was Grand Dame Judith. We lost her recently, and that's been hard on all of us." A shadow passed over Kerry's expressive face.

"But moving on—to rule the Kyth, the Dame has to be stronger in some ways than even the Talions, which is the reason I can control Ranulf and Sandor when I have to. The Dame has the additional ability to share energy with others and use it to heal. Evidently that combination of talents is incredibly rare. According to my husband, he's known only one other woman besides Dame Judith in his thousand-year-long life with that same combination of abilities. And surprise, surprise—that's me."

"You *do* realize that this sounds like a Movie of the Week feature for the Sci-Fi Channel." Lena laughed even though it didn't do to take wackjobs lightly.

Kerry arched an eyebrow, and suddenly Lena found herself flattened on the bed. She struggled to sit up, but it was as if a heavy, invisible blanket was holding her down.

Kerry walked over to stand by the bed. "It would really help if you believe what I'm trying to tell you."

Then she tugged Lena back up into a sitting position. As soon as she was upright, Lena jerked her hand away.

"If it's any comfort, Sandor and Ranulf really hate it when I do that, too." Her grin was infectious, inviting Lena to enjoy the idea of the two men being controlled by a woman half their size.

Lena gave in and snickered. How much could it hurt to play along? "So, you're telling me that your husband is really, really old?"

"Yes. He's a real Viking, and about a thousand years old, give or take a decade or two."

"So what does all of this have to do with me?"

"We're not sure. Evidently you have your own unusual talent. Sandor said that you were able to read what happened to that poor woman in the alley."

Lena had spent so much of her life hiding that secret that it was difficult to admit to it. "It hit around puberty. Suddenly, I could see and hear things no one else could."

Kerry's sympathetic look was almost Lena's undoing, but she quickly squashed the desire to confess all. "It comes and goes. My guard must have been down when I touched her. I just wanted to see if she was all right."

"And your guard was definitely down this morning when you touched Sandor's tattoo."

Okay, they'd finally gotten to the crux of the matter. "Yes. All hell broke loose."

Even as Lena said it, the darkness swirled in her head, threatening to overwhelm her again. It took every ounce of willpower she could muster to refuse to let it control her. When she was sure the room was no longer spinning, she slowly opened her eyes to find Kerry standing right next to her again.

Kerry looked relieved when she returned to her chair. "Nice job pulling yourself together, Lena. I didn't want to have to interfere."

The immediate surge of anger burned away the last bit of fog clouding Lena's thoughts. "As in, mess with my mind? I'm glad you didn't, because I wouldn't want to have to deck royalty."

God, she needed to put some space between herself and everything Kerry Thorsen represented. A knock at the door gave her the excuse she was looking for. *Please let it be Sandor.* As upset as she was with the big jerk, she needed his help to make sense of all this.

Then she could figure out what she was going to do with the knowledge that he'd murdered someone, with the help of his Grand Dame and a thousand-year-old Viking.

"Sean, are you all right?"

He opened his eyes to find a very worried Tara hovering over him. When he tried to move nausea ripped through him, sending him diving over the edge of the bed to grab the wastebasket. It was a position he'd been in off and on all night.

The pain from spending so many hours retching left him weak, and his head felt on the verge of exploding.

When the latest batch of spasms had passed, Tara helped him back up and wiped his face with a cool rag. God, could he be any more pathetic?

"Water?" he whispered.

"Here, but take it easy. Sip it slowly."

She gently raised his head to take sips from a bottle. The liquid gurgled uneasily in his stomach but eventually settled down.

He couldn't remember ever being this sick. Come to think of it, he didn't remember ever being sick at all. What the heck had happened to him? When he tried to remember the past twenty-four hours, all he could come up with was a vague memory of laughing wildly as he'd walked home with Kenny. No—staggered home, with Kenny fighting to keep him upright.

"Is Kenny okay?"

"Yes, he's fine. I sent him out for some of that sports drink you like and some chicken soup. I've got crackers, too, when you feel up to nibbling on something."

The thought of regular food almost had him diving back for the wastebasket again. "I've never reacted to feeding this way. It's like I've been poisoned."

Tara pulled a chair over to sit beside him. She

brushed his hair back off his face and laid the cool cloth on his forehead. He tried not to moan at how good that felt.

She looked worried. "I don't know what happened, but thank goodness Kenny decided to follow you last night. You were staggering and acting like you were drunk when you got back. I kept trying to hush you so we didn't wake up the neighbors, and all of a sudden you turned pasty white and then honest-to-God green. Before we could prevent it, you hit the floor like a ton of bricks."

She dipped the cloth in water again, wrung it out, and started wiping down his arms and chest with long, soothing strokes. "About five minutes after we got you into bed, the vomiting started."

"I'm sorry." The one person he never wanted to worry was Tara, and right now she looked scared. "I'm starting to feel better."

"You look better—but roadkill would've looked better than you did a few hours ago." She managed a faint smile, but the dark circles under her eyes screamed exhaustion.

"Have you had any sleep?"

Her shoulders slumped. "Not so much."

"Go to bed. I'll be all right now."

"I will when Kenny gets back. He already caught a few z's." She dipped the cloth again. "Sean, we almost called nine-one-one."

Which would have spelled disaster for all of them. He wished Kenny hadn't dragged him back here. Especially because he wasn't sure he'd find the courage to leave Tara behind again.

"I'm glad you didn't make that call. Hard to explain that what I ate was human in origin. I doubt they'd understand." He tried to smile.

"This is no joking matter, Sean. I thought you were going to die last night, and then where would I be? And Kenny, too." Tears tumbled down her cheeks, each one like a stab in his heart.

"Tara, honey, I'm so sorry. I know I'm saying that a lot lately, but I mean it."

Then her expression hardened. "I also know that you weren't planning on coming back at all last night, you bastard. How dare you think you could just walk away from me? From us? You'll stay in tonight, or I'll tie you to the bed." She slopped the rag onto his forehead, sending rivulets of cold water down his face and neck.

"Yes, ma'am." Mostly because he was too weak to stand, much less hunt. Besides, he'd promise her anything if it would make her happy. Even if he had to break those promises later.

Silence settled over them, but it wasn't particularly peaceful.

He was seriously losing it. He'd overfed last night, a first for him. Even so, he should have been able to process the energy or pass it off to Kenny. Had feeding from the sick drunk caused this or had it been the other guy? There was no way to know.

The door to the apartment opened and shut quietly, and Kenny came in with a grocery sack. "I got the stuff you wanted for sicko there, Tara."

"Thanks, Kenny. Would you pour some of the sports drink in a glass? I want to get some of it down Sean before I sleep."

The boy did as she asked, grousing about it the whole time, but Sean could tell Kenny wasn't as upset about having to watch over him as he wanted them to believe.

The lemon-lime flavor tasted good as it trickled down Sean's throat. As tempting as it was to guzzle the whole glass, he forced himself to take it slow while his stomach was still so unsettled.

"Go on and get some sleep, Tara. Nurse Kenny is officially on duty."

Kenny slid into the seat by the bed as soon as Tara left. "And I'd better be getting paid for this."

"You'll get paid exactly what you're worth." Sean hid a smile as he rolled over toward the wall. It would take Kenny a while to realize he'd just been insulted, but that was half the fun.

For the moment his stomach behaved itself,

which was a relief. Maybe when he woke up, he could figure out what had happened and what he was going to do about it. Now that Tara was aware that he'd planned to leave in order to protect her and Kenny, she'd be watching him like a hawk. But at the first hint that he'd become a real danger to Tara and Kenny, he'd find a way to disappear. Even if it killed him.

Lena flung open the door and glared at Sandor, her temper obviously still running at full bore. "Well, are you going to come in, or stand out there in the hallway?"

It wasn't the friendliest greeting he'd ever had, but at least she was willing to let him in.

He held up a paper bag and a tray with four coffee cups in it. "The good news is, I come bearing gifts."

"And the bad news?"

"I come with an angry Viking in tow." He jerked his head toward the redheaded behemoth a short distance away. "He's promised not to stay long, although getting him to leave before he eats a doughnut or two will probably be hard."

"Guess I'll have to take the good with the bad."

She held the door open as the two men filed past. Ranulf leaned against the wall next to Kerry's chair, but Sandor waited to see where Lena sat before choosing his own seat. He wanted to be near her without making her feel crowded. Since the hotel room wasn't all that big to begin with, that wasn't going to be easy.

When she sat cross-legged on the end of the bed, he settled on the floor, leaning back against the wall, and offered her the bag.

"You get first pick since we're imposing on your hospitality."

"As if I had any choice." She rooted through the sack and pulled out a cruller. "Coffee, please."

He held out a cup. "You did have a choice. You still do. Say the word and we'll leave, even me."

Although Lena made a point of not looking directly at him, she was acutely aware of him, judging by her body language. That was only fair, since he couldn't keep his eyes off her. He reached over to snag another doughnut and caught Ranulf watching him. He expected the man to be smirking, but there was a hint of sympathy in his expression.

Then Kerry leaned down and murmured something to him, and Ranulf said to Lena, "Kerry has already told you a lot about us. I suspect it will take some time for you to make sense of it all."

Lena glanced at Sandor, then back to Ranulf. "That's putting it mildly. I also don't like being crowded."

Sandor shifted to put himself more directly between her and his friends. She looked surprised that he was so blatant about which side of the fence he'd come down on if the confrontation grew more heated.

Ranulf continued, "We get that, but do you understand our people's need for secrecy?"

Lena shrugged. "I understand that you think you're above the law. Maybe you have your reasons for that, but I'm going to need some time to think this all through. To figure out what I need to do next." She paused. "But until I make up my mind, I'll keep my mouth shut."

"Fair enough." Ranulf stood and offered his wife a hand up. "It was nice meeting you, Lena. Ask Sandor anything you want to. If you want to talk to us, just stop by or call. We'll do our best to help you understand everything that's happened."

Then he pinned Sandor with a hard stare. "You *will* keep us informed on how this turns out. Kerry has enough to deal with right now without having to hunt you down."

There was no mistaking the implied threat. If Sandor couldn't come to terms with Lena, they'd step in.

The question was, would he let that happen, regardless of her course of action? Sandor might not be able to thwart their efforts completely, but he'd do his damnedest to protect Lena.

After they left, Lena threw the dead bolt and hooked the chain. Then she walked over to him, looking as if she was deciding where to kick him and exactly how hard.

He tried for a little humor. Holding out the bag of doughnuts, he smiled up at her. "A cruller for your thoughts."

She shot him a look of pure disgust, but took the bag and resumed her seat on the bed. "Deep-fried sugar and grease, no matter how tasty, do not make up for bad behavior."

He waved his napkin like a white flag. "What will it take?"

"I'd like the full explanation that your buddy Ranulf promised me. Your Grand Dame Kerry has already told an abridged version of the story. But before you start, you need to know that I believe in upholding the law. Without it, all we'd have is chaos."

Okay, no surprise there. She couldn't prove anything about Bradan's execution. His ashes had been scattered, the evidence destroyed. But Sandor's current investigation was a different matter. With her connections to the law enforcement community, Lena's accusations could draw lots of unwanted attention.

First and foremost, all Talions swore to protect the secrets of their people. If Sandor failed in that duty, Kerry would have no choice but to deal with the problem herself or to send in someone who wouldn't care if Lena was harmed in the process. He wouldn't let that happen—though facing off against his own kind held little appeal.

"Where do you want me to start?" he asked.

"You tell me. All I've got is this nightmare playing out in my head every time I close my eyes. I can't make sense of anything, except that at times, you taste exactly like the man I saw kill Coop." Her fingers were busy shredding her empty coffee cup.

Sandor drew his legs up and crossed his arms on his knees.

"Okay, here goes. I assume Kerry told you that I'm not exactly human, at least not as you would think of them. Neither is she or Ranulf, or the bastard who killed your friend. Although we Kyth, spelled K-y-t-h, act and look and even live like you do, we're physiologically different in some pretty fundamental ways."

"The whole energy thing Kerry mentioned?"

"That's part of it."

"So you're telling me that you're all . . . what? Some kind of real-life vampires?"

He'd always hated that analogy. "No, we're not

vampires. No fangs, see?" He flashed his pearly whites at her. "You'd never miss the energy we take, especially when we're in crowds like sporting events and dance clubs."

The gears were clearly turning in that pretty head of hers. "So was Kerry out hunting humans in the dance club the night of the fire?"

"*Hell* no. We don't hunt—not the way you mean. Besides, that was before Kerry even knew what she was. And trust me, she liked my explanation about who and what we are even less than you do. Since she turned out to be the strongest Kyth that we've found in over ten centuries, though, she had to accept the truth."

"And where does Ranulf fit into this story?"

"Until Kerry took over, Dame Judith was our leader. Ranulf swore fealty to her as a young man, about a thousand years ago. He's aged well, don't you think?"

It was good to hear her laugh. "Kerry already told me that about him. And am I to assume you're the same age?"

"Nope, I'm only hovering around the century mark. If it makes you feel any better, Kerry's only in her twenties."

"So tell me what happened the night of the fire and afterward, when Coop died." She'd evidently had her fill of Kyth history.

Sandor stood up and stretched, then sat on the bed next to Lena.

She moved over to put some room between them, but at least she didn't banish him from her side. He took that as a good sign.

"It all started because Kerry loves to dance. She was adopted and raised by human parents, who obviously had no idea about her special needs. Somehow, though, she figured out that she felt better if she hung out in dance clubs and sporting events. Humans give off a lot of energy in those situations, so she kept herself healthy and balanced without even knowing how it worked.

"Unfortunately, once in a while one of our kind develops a craving for the darker spectra of human energy and emotions—like pain, fear, and terror. When that happens, they turn renegade. And to ice this particular cake, this renegade also liked to play with fire."

"Bradan. His name was Bradan." Lena looked up from her pile of shredded paper. "And he was your friend?"

"I certainly thought so. But it turned out none of us really knew him." The usual stab of pain from Bradan's betrayal ripped through his chest. "I don't know how I missed seeing what he'd become. We grew up together."

The grief and the raw pain of his friend's betrayal was difficult for Lena to hear, and she said, "I'm not surprised that you missed it. Look how many serial killers were handsome and charming on the surface."

She hesitated, then shared some of her own pain. "It takes years of practice to hide something like that so well. Most people who have a secret that profound learn how to hide it early on, because it's a matter of survival."

Sandor immediately put two and two together. "Like your ability."

She nodded. "I keep thinking I should've told Coop about it. At first I didn't know him well enough, but later on I could have said something. Maybe he would've understood—but I never trusted him enough to give him the chance, for fear he'd reject me."

Sandor threaded his fingers through hers. "Maybe he would have. Most people don't like dealing with anything outside of their comfort zone unless circumstances force them into it.

"That's what happened to Kerry. When Bradan set the fire, she was able to lead dozens of people to safety. Ranulf happened to be there that night, and saw her carry much bigger people out of that fire—all because she drew strength from the fear and panic around her."

"She also met Coop that night."

"Yeah. He was in charge of the investigation and interviewed her right after the fire. Then, while Coop was dealing with reporters, Bradan drew Kerry's attention to himself by flicking his lighter in a toast to the fire. She knew instantly that he had to be the arsonist and drew a sketch of his face for Coop."

It was all starting to make horrible sense. "And Bradan killed Coop to get the sketch back?"

"No—more likely, he was looking for information on Kerry. Bradan got all of Coop's other files, but your friend died protecting that sketch. We honor his memory for that act of bravery. Without it, many more people—mine and yours—might have suffered and died at Bradan's hands, until we figured out who was behind the attacks."

Lena blinked back tears. When Sandor put his arm around her shoulders and tried to pull her close, she pushed him away, not ready to accept his comfort.

"Lena, you have to know that Coop would've died anyway. Bradan couldn't afford to let him live—not with what he knew. When Ranulf went to meet Coop at the site of the club, we already knew a Kyth had set the fire. Ranulf discovered Coop's body and the sketch wadded up in his fist. Because of your friend's courageous act, we knew who we needed to hunt down."

"And you killed this Bradan. You and Kerry and Ranulf." She infused her words with her disapproval.

"Don't judge us when you weren't there, Lena. Bradan had killed at least two humans just for practice—his words, not mine. On top of that, he'd kidnapped and tortured our Dame. For that alone, he should have died a hundred times over."

She heard the need for vengeance in Sandor's voice and sympathized with it on one level. But the bottom line was that they'd still taken the law into their own hands. Maybe in their eyes their cause was just, but they were still cold-blooded killers.

"You still should've let the authorities handle it, Sandor. I know it sounds trite to say two wrongs don't make a right, but it's true."

He lurched up off the bed and stood glaring down at her. "Don't go all holier-than-thou on me, Lena. If terrorists captured your president and killed him, your military and law enforcement people would break every rule in the book to catch the bastards. Hell, look what they've done since nine-eleven, all in the name of national security!"

She got up to stand toe-to-toe with him, glaring straight up into his dark eyes. "Are you listening to yourself? *My* president? *My* military?"

She shoved him back a step. "They're *yours,*

too. You're part of this country, subject to its laws like everyone else. You can't live here and pick and choose which laws apply to you and which don't just because your genes are a little different than everybody else's."

He came right back at her. "And ninety-nine percent of the time, I'm a perfectly law-abiding citizen. BUT," he snapped, "that one percent of the time when following those same laws interferes with my duty to my own people, I say fuck them!"

She lost it. Grabbing a fistful of his shirt, she yanked his face down to her level. "And do you know what happens when we pick and choose like that? People die. Innocent people die!"

He jerked himself free, but not before she felt a zing of heat arc between them.

"Damn it, Lena, you're not listening! Innocent people *were* dying, and your precious cops were chasing their own tails. We put a stop to Bradan. I won't apologize, because I don't regret that."

Flickers of blue rippled over his skin. He pointed at the doughnut bag, and a flash of indigo light shot from his fingertips. Instantly, the paper burst into flame. Before it could do any damage to the bedspread, he grabbed the bag and carried it into the bathroom. When he returned, he looked only marginally more in control.

"Let me tell you what would have happened

if we had followed the law instead of going after Bradan ourselves." His voice was cold enough to freeze water. "If ordinary cops had gone after Bradan Owen, he would've killed every one of them before they even got close."

Were those sparks of gold fire in his dark eyes? For the first time, his different nature was all too obvious, too real. Instead of feeling repulsed, she found herself admiring his strength of conviction and his warrior nature, even as his angry tirade continued.

"Worse yet, even if they somehow managed to subdue Bradan, the minute they threw his ass in jail, he would have started feeding on all the despair and anger and pain that permeate a place like that. There's no telling how many would have died then, cops and prisoners alike. You're a smart woman, Lena. Add it all up any way you want to, but the bottom line is Bradan had to die. Humans couldn't achieve that, so I killed him. Deal with it."

Before she could think of a coherent reply, she stepped toward Sandor—or maybe he was the one who moved. All that mattered was that his arms crushed her against his chest as he plundered her mouth. Even as she surrendered, she knew she should fight back. They'd already fallen into bed twice, and look where it had gotten her.

She all but dragged him toward the bed, pushed him onto it, then fell on top of him.

He gave her a wicked grin. "I don't want you thinking I'm easy because of this."

"We both know angry sex isn't smart." She knelt right over the impressive ridge in his pants. "And that sex is no way to settle an argument."

His hands slid up her thighs and around to capture the curve of her bottom. "Lena, honey, you're killing me here."

"Good!"

He peeled off her top and tossed it aside, then she suddenly found herself on her back. Sandor's mouth felt so good nuzzling her breasts as his busy, busy hands were yanking off her pants. When he realized she wasn't wearing panties, he murmured his approval.

"Hot damn, woman, I need this. I need you."

She tangled her fingers in his hair and tugged to get his attention. When that didn't work, she pinched him.

"Ow! Why did you do that?"

"Because this isn't going to work if I'm the only one without clothes. Fix it."

He immediately obeyed.

Chapter 11

*W*ith a heated smile and amber sparks flaring in his eyes, Sandor slowly stripped off his clothes, taking his time and letting her look her fill. She sincerely hoped she wasn't drooling; it was so undignified. But, hey, a girl couldn't help it when looking at something that damn hot. And impressive.

She knelt on the bed and waited for her lover to come back to her. He paused to pull a couple of condoms out of his wallet. One he tossed on the bedside table; the second he handed to her. She smiled her approval, liking a man who allowed a woman some control over when and how things got done.

She crooked her finger and used it to motion him closer. "Come here, lover."

"Bossy woman." He grinned and moved to kneel

right in front of her. She set the foil packet aside to run her hands down his well-sculpted chest and arms. He had a warrior's body, all lean muscles and strength. Her hands tingled even though she carefully skirted his bicep. When he realized what she was doing, he caught her hand, brought it back up, and placed it directly over his tattoo.

"I can protect you from that, now that I know you're sensitive to it." After a few seconds, he brought her hand up to his lips and kissed her fingertips. "I am sorry that happened, Lena. That darkness is my burden to carry. You shouldn't have to share it."

She twined her hands behind his neck and leaned into him, pleasing them both with the press of her breasts against his chest. "We all have darkness that haunts us, Sandor. Yours may be worse than most, but I have a few nightmares of my own."

He sat back on his haunches and lifted her to straddle his lap. "Then share them with me. Maybe I can ease them for you."

She shot him an incredulous look and gave his erection a long, slow stroke. "You want to trade bad memories right now?"

"Actually, no." His chuckle was low and rough. "Remind me later."

"I knew you were smarter than that." She rewarded his brilliance with a kiss.

When she finally retrieved the condom, she took her sweet time sheathing him, interrupting the process with wet kisses, long bouts of touching and teasing, until finally Sandor lost patience.

"Keep that up and we'll be finished before we even start." He lowered her to the bed, ready to take charge. "Turn over, woman."

She did as he ordered, but only reluctantly. Then he reached for the bottle of body lotion on her bedside table and poured some on his hands. Using long, slow strokes, he massaged her neck and shoulders, then worked his way farther down. Judging by the way his lady moaned when he worked the lotion into her skin, she was clearly loving the attention he paid to each curve and line of her elegant back. He moved onward to the firm cheeks of her bottom.

Oh, she liked that all right, murmuring both her approval and directions for which spots needed more attention. Then he moved down to her feet, giving each one plenty of attention. Then he made room for himself between her legs, gradually spreading them as he applied more lotion and smoothed it in, starting from her delicate ankles and working his way upward. The longer he prolonged their foreplay, the more tension thrummed through his body and hers.

When he reached the apex of her thighs, he

was all but shaking with the need to claim her. When he lifted her hips up she arched back, pressing her bottom against his erection.

He fitted himself to her and pressed forward, taking her slowly, inch by inch by inch. She moaned and rocked forward and back. He caught her hips in his hands and held her immobilized, not sure which of them he was torturing with that move.

Finally, he couldn't delay any longer and started to move in earnest. Completion wouldn't be long in coming, not when Lena kept calling his name, urging him on. The slap of his flesh against her bottom made him desperate to get closer, to melt into her welcoming heat.

Then she rotated her hips in just the right way to break the dam, sending a flood of pleasure screaming through them both. As she keened out her release, he rode her hard and fast until they were boneless and completely spent.

His last thought as they dozed off was that they hadn't really settled anything. But he didn't really give a damn.

An hour later, Sandor snapped his cell phone shut with frustration. Back to reality. "I have to meet Ranulf downtown."

Lena turned on her side to face him and propped her head up on her hand. "Any particular reason?"

"Yeah. Earlier, I told him about that spot where I felt the renegade I've been trying to track down. Ranulf has some different abilities than I do, more along the lines of your ability to read scenes. I asked him to check it out in case he picked up something I can't."

Lena frowned. "What are you going to do with this renegade once you've found him?"

"I'm not sure."

He didn't know if they'd execute the culprit on the spot or take him up to some remote area to do the job. Either way, the bastard would die. Rather than risk more questions he didn't want to answer, he rolled out of bed and reached for his clothes.

"I'll have to hustle if I want to catch up with Ranulf."

He hated the uncomfortable silence between them. There was so much said and unsaid that needed resolution.

"Do you want to have dinner tonight?" He kept his eyes down and his hands busy tucking in his shirt.

"Let me think about it."

Lena sat up in the bed and stretched, letting the rumpled sheets pool around her waist. It would have taken a far stronger man than Sandor to resist that temptation. Smart woman that she was, Lena immediately recognized his lust, snatched up the sheet, and shook her head.

"No, Sandor."

Did she have to sound so sure of that? Especially with him standing there with his tongue all but hanging out? Maybe he could change her mind. He inched closer.

"*No*, Sandor!" she repeated with more force. "I do not want an irate Viking pounding on my door because you got distracted."

"How's a man supposed to concentrate on work when he's staring at all that beautiful feminine flesh?" He took another step toward the bed.

"You are so full of it, Kearn. Now get out of here so I can finally take a shower and get dressed. I've never spent so much time in bed in my life." Not that she sounded unhappy about that.

"Okay, but I'll be back. After that little tease, you at least owe me dinner."

She finally smiled. "All right. And afterward I'll patrol with you, if you'd like help looking for your renegade."

That might not be the smartest plan, considering her views on Kyth justice. But in bed or out of it, he wanted as much time with her as he could get.

"I'll let you out."

When she threw back the covers and walked him to the door stark naked, he groaned. With her hair rumpled and a love bite on her shoulder, the sight was enough to bring him to his knees. And she knew it, too. Her smile was all siren, well aware of her feminine power and enjoying it to the fullest.

"Lena Wilson, you are a cruel, cruel woman."

Sandor waited until she got close, and then pounced. His captive didn't put up much of a fight before she sighed and surrendered. Determined to make the most of his victory, Sandor decided Ranulf would just have to wait a little longer.

Sandor was still smiling when he arrived at the meeting spot. It was easy to pick out the irate Viking warrior on the crowded pier: he was the one everyone gave wide berth to. A wise decision, considering the way he radiated bad temper and irritation with every breath. But it would take more than a ticked-off barbarian to spoil Sandor's good mood.

As soon as Ranulf spied him, he crossed his arms over his chest and looked aggravated. "Where the hell have you been?"

Sandor grinned. "I had a few important final details to see to. It took longer than I expected."

"Oh, brother." Ranulf mimed sticking a finger down his throat and gagging. Then he clapped Sandor on the shoulder hard enough to send him staggering back a couple of steps. "Come on and show me this place you want me to read."

It was out of character for Ranulf to get over being mad so quickly. "How come you're not reading me the riot act for keeping you waiting?"

Ranulf's smile was too sly for comfort. "Remember your righteous indignation when you caught me in Kerry's bed, when you thought I should be concentrating more on the mission?"

Shit, he *would* remember that. "Yeah."

"I'm petty enough to enjoy the noble Sandor Kearn being a slave to testosterone, just like all of us other poor mortals."

Sandor liked hearing the other man laugh, even at his own expense. Not so long ago, he had expected to lose Ranulf to all the darkness he'd been forced to consume to protect their people. Kerry was definitely good for the Viking.

"I owe you an apology for that, Ranulf. I had no right to be so judgmental, especially under the circumstances."

They walked along in silence for a minute or two before Ranulf spoke again. "You weren't that far wrong. I was barely holding it together. I hated coming down off the mountain, because my control was nearly shot. If it weren't for Kerry . . ."

"Yeah, she's helped both of us." They were approaching the spot he wanted Ranulf to check now. "Lena and I were walking along here when I first sensed the renegade's signature."

It would be interesting to see what Ranulf could pick up that he hadn't. Meanwhile, he could concentrate on other important things—like where he was going to take Lena for dinner, or if she'd be up for taking carryout to his place after they patrolled. That would be more conducive to other plans he had for the evening—and into the wee hours of the morning.

"Damn it, Sandor, can you keep your mind on Talion business for a few minutes?"

Sandor saw the gleam of excitement in Ranulf's eyes, the look a hunter got when he spotted fresh tracks. "What did you find?"

"He's Kyth all right, and you're right about him standing here more than once." Ranulf's expression turned more grim. "But that buzz you felt was so strong because two Kyth stood there, most likely together."

Sandor's good mood went south. "So we're dealing with a pair of renegades."

"Or possibly more. I'm pretty sure I caught a trace of a third individual, but it's too faint to know for sure. That would account for the widespread attack sites, as well as the varied descriptions from the victims."

"Any more details?"

Ranulf shook his head. "My ability is clearer when there's been violence involved, like Lena's. Since these two were evidently just standing here, we're lucky to pick up even that much. I'd guess at least one of them is a male, but mostly because historically most renegades are."

They started back toward where they'd parked their cars. "We can start keeping an eye on this place. If he or they are fond of that spot, maybe they'll come back again."

As usual, the Viking's 1940 Packard convertible had drawn a crowd. Sandor was always amazed by how much patience Ranulf had with people who insisted on leaving their fingerprints on the car's perfect finish. A couple of men hung around to ask questions, then headed off.

Sandor leaned against the front fender. "Lena and I will be out patrolling again tonight, but finding our target that way is going to be really hit or miss."

Ranulf looked chagrined. "With all of today's

excitement, I forgot to tell you that our guy was out hunting again last night. According to the news this morning, the cops found some poor SOB passed out on a staircase early this morning. Same symptoms as the others, except this time no money was stolen."

"Any description?" So far, the culprit had been careful not to let anyone get a glimpse of him.

"A little better than most. The vic remembers thinking he was being followed. But when he stopped to see, the other guy ran on past. He said the runner was male, average height, with nothing to distinguish him from anyone else on the street. Since the victim was a big guy himself, he didn't perceive the runner as a threat."

"Even if the runner was the renegade, the description is useless."

Ranulf nodded in agreement. "I'll see if I can find out exactly where it happened and give you a call. Maybe Lena and I can give the scene a read tonight."

Hmm—maybe it would help Lena resolve her conflict about Bradan if she spent more time with the Thorsens.

"Any chance you and Kerry could join us for dinner tonight?"

"Sounds good. I'll check with Kerry when I get home and give you a call."

"Great. Since the weather is nice, I can fire up the grill and throw on some steaks."

"Even better. See you around six?"

"Perfect."

Sean sighed with relief. The room had finally stopped spinning whenever he tried to sit up. Still, the effort to get upright left him sweating and shaking. He inched toward the edge of the bed and slowly stood up, leaning against the nearby wall for support. He *would* get to the bathroom on his own this time. It was a matter of pride.

The distance to the bathroom seemed almost insurmountable, as he staggered from one piece of furniture to the next, pausing each time to catch his breath. He'd heard the expression *weak as a kitten*. Right now, the smallest furball could take him out with one swipe of a tiny paw.

The trip back to bed was only marginally better. He collapsed on the pillow and waited for his pulse and breathing to slow down to normal. Even the sheets smelled sour from his sweat. God, what had he done to get this sick? Could the energy he needed to live also kill him? Were Tara and Kenny at risk from the same threat? Maybe if he retraced the evening in his head, he could figure out what had gone wrong.

The front door opened, and he heard Tara set the heavy laundry basket by the front door, then go back down the hallway for another load. He wished he could help her.

Her second trip didn't take as long. When her footsteps headed for him, he sat up again, tired of being an invalid.

She poked her head around the corner and smiled. "You're looking better. Are you hungry?"

Come to think of it, he was. "Soup would be good, but no hurry."

She came into the room. "Why don't I help you into the kitchen? While your soup heats, I can strip your bed and run the sheets down to the laundry."

A vicious surge of anger ripped through him. Before he even realized he'd raised his hand, he sent the mug and book on the bedside table flying across the room. "Quit trying to mother me, damn it! I can make it that far by myself."

Tara stepped back, her eyes widening in shock. She backed out of the room, giving him a wide berth as he slowly made his way to the small table and on into the kitchen.

His temper faded as quickly as it had come, leaving him feeling frustrated and embarrassed. "Look, Tara, I'm sorry. It's like I keep telling you—I have no control whatsoever anymore, especially when it comes to my temper."

"It's okay." Her voice cracked, and she was careful to stay out of reach, with her arms crossed around her waist.

"No, it's not okay, and we both know it. I wish I knew what to do about it, but I don't." He pulled out a chair and watched her open the soup and put it on to heat.

"I'll be right back." She rushed from the room without looking at him.

"All right." He sat in silence, listening to her pull the sheets off his bed. He also heard her sniffle. Damn it, he'd made her cry again. The minute he felt better, he had to get away. He couldn't live with himself if it had been Tara he'd damaged, instead of that stupid mug.

As he waited for Tara to return, he began to feel more in control. In fact, for the first time since Kenny had brought him home, he felt . . . okay. He held up his hand. It wasn't shaking—good. He stood up. His legs supported him without protest—even better.

He sat down before Tara could find out. As long as she thought he was still weak, she wouldn't keep such a close eye on him. He'd have to make sure neither Tara nor Kenny had any idea he was plotting his escape.

When Tara approached the kitchen he was

slumped back in the chair, doing his best to look weak and tired.

"That soup smells good."

"I'm glad. Maybe it will give you some strength back."

As always, she forgave him far too easily. Sometimes he wished she'd scream at him for being such a jerk, but she never did. He loved that about her, but it also made him crazy.

Memorizing her sweet face, he watched as she dished up the soup and set it in front of him with some crackers. He'd need the memories to be clear and bright when he disappeared from her life, something to cling to when he was alone. There was some comfort in knowing at least she'd still have Kenny. She wouldn't see it that way, but it was the best thing for all of them.

He lifted a spoonful of soup to his mouth. When he took to the streets, hot meals would be few and far between. But it was worth any sacrifice if it kept Tara safe from his insanity.

Sandor flipped the steaks, then spread the vegetables out on the grill to cook. Dinner wouldn't be long now.

"Can I get you something to drink?" Lena asked.

He smiled over his shoulder at her. "I'll take one of the dark ales if Ranulf hasn't drunk them all. The man's a bottomless pit when it comes to expensive microbrews, especially when I'm the one paying for them."

The Viking rose to the bait, just as Sandor had probably expected. "If you didn't want me to enjoy myself, you should have said so. Speaking of which, Kerry, can you get me another one?"

His wife didn't stir. "Get it yourself, old man. The last time I checked, the Kyth had outlawed slavery."

Ranulf reached over to touch a strand of her dark hair. "I'm sure the fine print on our marriage certificate says something about love, honor, and obey."

She batted his hand away and snickered. "Yeah, right above the part about a cold day in hell."

When Lena brought Sandor his drink, she stayed close by his side. "Are they always like that?"

He stage-whispered, "Worse, usually. They're putting on their best manners for company."

"Hey, you're supposed to be my loyal subject! You can't bad-mouth your beloved ruler." Kerry tried to look haughty, but couldn't keep a straight face.

"Okay, your royal highness, come to the table,

the steak is done." Sandor piled the meat on a platter and handed it to Lena. "Ranulf, I left yours bloody, just the way you like it."

Lena looked at the steak Sandor forked onto Ranulf's plate and shuddered. "Is it safe to eat something that raw?"

"Remember, he's a barbarian, born and bred. It takes more than raw meat to bring the Viking down."

Ranulf grinned proudly. "Darn straight. Back in my day—"

His wife interrupted him. "We know, we've heard it all before. Back in your day, you either ate your meat raw or it ate you."

Sandor joined right in. "So how did T. rex taste, anyway?"

"As I recall, a lot like chicken." Ranulf speared a big bite of his steak. "And those drumsticks could satisfy even the hungriest Viking!"

Lena couldn't help but laugh with the others, even though she didn't want to get too friendly with Kerry and Ranulf. Her relationship with Sandor was complicated enough.

As if sensing her thoughts, Sandor winked at her. Even that small, shared gesture was enough to send shivers of sexual awareness through her.

And he knew it, too, although he tried to hide his knowing grin as he took a long drink. She stared at his throat and remembered the taste of his skin. God, she had it bad.

"So, Lena, how long will you be in Seattle?"

Kerry's question might have sounded like idle conversation, but Lena wasn't fooled. There was too much intensity in the way the woman looked at her, toward Sandor, then back again. Was she wondering what Lena was going to do about them executing Bradan? Or was the curiosity about Lena's relationship with Sandor? Two could play this game.

"I'm not sure." She sipped her iced tea. "How often are you going to order your boys here to break the law?"

Sandor choked on his drink, and Ranulf went from relaxed to full alert. She ignored them. So did Kerry.

A small smile curved the other woman's mouth. "With all the time you've spent with Sandor, I assume you two have managed to squeeze in a few conversations."

Lena took her time folding her napkin and setting it by her plate. "A few."

Sandor began. "Kerry—"

She cut him off with a wave of her hand. Lena realized he was still straining to speak, but somehow Kerry was preventing that from happening. Boy, she had some kind of weird mental mojo.

"Not now, Sandor. Lena and I are just having a friendly discussion." Kerry's gaze flicked toward her husband, who held up his hands and sat back. "So, during one of those conversations, did he explain exactly what Bradan Owen was capable of?"

Lena nodded.

"I'm sure Sandor also told you that I'm almost as new in my awareness of the Kyth as you are. In some ways it was probably more of a shock to me, because I was faced not only with the existence of a different human species, but also with the indisputable fact that I was a member of that race. However, I'm convinced that somewhere along the line, some Kyth made a contribution to your own gene pool."

That did it. "Like hell I'm one of you! For one thing, I'm a law-abiding citizen, unlike some I could mention."

"Come on, cut us some slack, Lena." Sandor evidently had his voice back.

She rounded on him. "Cut you some slack? You haven't seen me calling the police, have you? At least not yet."

It was time to put some distance between herself and this bunch of crazies. Granted, it was hard to ignore the evidence right in front of her face, but she would not be drawn into their world. She couldn't afford the risk, no matter how hot the chemistry between her and Sandor.

She'd bent the rules once already in her life, and it had cost her everything. It had taken her years to restore her self-esteem and professional pride. They could justify their decision to assassinate Coop's killer, convincing themselves that they'd been the only ones capable of taking the monster out. But how soon would they find another monster, and another and another? Where would they draw the line?

She stood up. "Sandor, thank you; dinner was delicious. Now if you all will excuse me, I think it's best I leave."

She made it to the front door before he caught up with her, a set of keys in his hand.

"I don't need a chauffeur," she informed him when he followed her to the street.

"Well, you've got one."

He sounded thoroughly pissed. Good. It would make it easier for her to walk away, which she had every intention of doing. But when she turned to head down the street, he blocked her way.

"Stop it, Sandor. I want to leave—alone. You do *not* want to try to stop me." She gave him a shove with the palm of her hand. It was like pushing a boulder—a very stubborn, angry boulder.

"I brought you here; I'll take you back. I commandeered Ranulf's Packard." He nodded toward the cream-colored convertible. "Get in."

"Oh, and I *so* love taking orders from autocratic jerks!" She spun and headed the other way, even though it was the wrong direction. Circling the block would be a small price to pay to get away from him.

In a quick maneuver, he was back in front of her. "And I *so* love dealing with shortsighted, judgmental brats!"

A neighbor across the street was unabashedly enjoying the spectacle. She shot him a nasty look and demanded, "What are you looking at?"

He quickly disappeared back inside his house.

Sandor looked disgusted. "Real nice, Lena. Do you make it a habit of being rude to people?"

That hurt. So what if she struck out when she felt cornered and scared? And she was definitely scared—of the Kyth, of Sandor, and worse yet, her reaction to him every time he got near her. Once again their tempers were running high, and all she could think about was kissing him.

"Fine. Take me back to the hotel."

He walked around the front of the car and got in. When he turned the key, the huge engine purred. It didn't take long to realize that they weren't headed for her hotel.

"Where are you taking me? Turn around! My hotel is back that way."

He kept driving straight. "You promised to patrol with me tonight."

As he slowed for a stoplight, he shot her a smug look. "I assumed that someone who was so high and mighty about obeying the law would also be a woman of her word. Pardon me if I was mistaken. So which is it: patrol with me, or slink back to your hotel?"

Her hand itched to smack the snarky smile off his face, but she had more control than that. Barely.

"Fine. I'll patrol for a couple of hours, as promised. Then you can drop me off at the door of my hotel."

Sandor wasn't stupid. He knew exactly what she was telling him, and he didn't like it. Too bad. They both knew what would happen if she weakened and let herself get behind locked doors with him. And that wasn't going to happen again.

Even if it killed her.

Chapter 12

*S*andor stopped midblock and looked up and down the street, tension rolling off him in waves. "How am I supposed to find a renegade when there's no pattern to his attacks?"

Lena understood his frustration. Cases that hit a dead end were the bane of every investigator's existence. She'd had her own fair share of files that had turned cold when the leads failed to pan out. Every one of those failures rankled, but she'd learned the hard way to let them go and move on. If she had it to do over again, she would have preferred to figure out that particular lesson without innocent people dying. Knowing their target was going to strike again only made it worse.

"Let's get a cup of coffee," she suggested.

Sandor let her lead him to one of the coffee

shops found on almost every corner in Seattle. He opted to wait outside while she went in. Since they hadn't quite finished dinner before she'd left, she was a bit hungry, and added a couple of sweet rolls to the order. While she waited, she watched him through the front window of the shop.

Sandor was the handsomest man she'd ever known, much less dated. With dark hair and those even darker eyes, he could easily pass for a male model. But she'd always thought those men were merely pretty faces, worth only a passing glance.

There was so much more depth to Sandor. Sure, he could be charming enough when he wanted to be. And God knows he wore clothes well—and nothing at all, even better. Alpha males were common in her line of work, but the powerful confidence Sandor wore like a second skin made them pale in comparison. He was a warrior through and through, and she really liked that about him.

Probably way more than she should. A little hot sex was one thing, but the emotional connection she was feeling for him was a complication neither of them needed. She lived on the East Coast; he lived on the West. She was human; he wasn't. He'd killed for his Dame; she wished he hadn't.

"Ma'am, your order is ready."

Lena realized it wasn't the first time the woman had tried to get her attention. "I'm sorry. I don't know where my mind was."

The woman grinned and nodded in the direction of the window. "I wouldn't be thinking about coffee, either, if I had someone who looked like that waiting for me."

Back outside, Sandor took his cup and started walking again. He'd been pretty quiet ever since he'd bullied her into the Packard and driven her downtown. Granted, he was focused on hunting down the Kyth renegade, but there was more to his silence than that. He kept watching her out of the corner of his eye and frowning whenever he didn't think she'd notice.

She steered them toward a bench down the street. Most of the nearby businesses were closed for the night, so it was unlikely they'd be bothered by anyone passing by.

After they sat down, she handed Sandor his sweet roll. "You're awfully quiet. Got something on your mind?"

The question jerked him back from wherever his mind had wandered off to. His dark eyes focused on her with an uncomfortable intensity that made her wish she hadn't rattled his cage.

"You don't want to know what I'm thinking."

That snarky attitude was back in full force, but

two could play at that game. "Lose the attitude, buster. If I didn't want to know, I wouldn't have asked."

Too fast for her to track, he grabbed her hand. A burst of fire burned up her arm from where their skin connected. The sensation was more uncomfortable than painful, but she knew better than to try to break free.

When he realized she wasn't going to fight him, he eased back on his grip but still held on.

"So you want to talk about attitude? What about yours? You insult my Dame, you insult my people, and you look at me and Ranulf like we're little better than animals. You do *not* know what it is like for us, yet you feel entitled to judge us. How comfortable is it, sitting up there on that high horse?"

Okay, maybe he had a point, but she had a few of her own. "You're right. Maybe I don't understand what it's like to belong to the Kyth. You've always known there were others like you, people who share those spooky talents you're so proud of. But I grew up with my own special ability and no one to share it with."

His eyebrows drew together in a slight frown. "Yeah, that had to be hard."

His sympathy felt genuine, but after years of secrecy and denial, it was hard to know how to react. "I managed to get by on my own."

He gave her hand a squeeze. As he did, her skin tingled and buzzed. The sensation was odd, but pleasant.

"You're definitely a puzzle, Lena—especially in the effect you have on me."

"How so?"

"I've been living in a fog since this whole mess with Bradan. Before that, I trusted him implicitly and thought Ranulf was poised on the precipice of madness. I ended up executing Bradan and becoming friends with the Viking."

"Sounds like you made the right decision in the end." She hesitated. "Well, except for executing the murdering bastard, instead of turning him over to the authorities to stand trial."

Sandor's eyes immediately flashed hot with those golden sparks. "It's a done deal, Lena, and nothing is going to change that."

"I know, I know." It was important for her to make him understand. "But at least you and Kerry and Ranulf will always have the satisfaction of knowing the bad guy paid the ultimate price for what he did. I'm glad he died for what he did, too.

"But we four are the only ones who are ever going to know that. We'll have a sense of closure, but think of Coop's family, his coworkers, his friends. They all think that Bradan not only got away with killing Coop, but he's still out there planning his next attack. They'll always wonder who's going to die next."

"Okay, you have a valid point." Sandor leaned back and stared up at the sky. "But my first loyalty is to my people. I've sworn to protect them, regardless of the cost. That's the way it's always been for the Kyth, and for good reason."

"Times change, Sandor. No one will accept the Kyth as benign if it ever comes out that you operate as if you're above or outside the law."

"Which is why we can't afford for anyone to find out about us."

So now they were coming to the heart of his problem: her. She now knew enough about the Kyth to bring the wrath of humanity raining down on their heads. From their point of view, there was only one logical conclusion as to what to do next. The whole idea made her hurt.

"When are you going to use your special whammy powers on me again, Sandor? Or will it be Kerry who fixes my memories this time?" She leaned her head against his shoulder, drawing what comfort she could from his strength. "Will I remember anything about you at all? Because I really hate the idea of forgetting everything we've shared."

"I gave you my word we wouldn't mess with your mind, Lena, and I meant—"

Sandor abruptly let go of her hand and stood up, his attention riveted on something down the block. He was watching the mouth of an alley on the other side of the street.

Lena didn't spot anything out of the ordinary. "What did you see?"

"We might have hit it lucky. Come on, but act casual. There may be someone keeping lookout up the street."

As they made their way to the corner he kept his arm draped around her shoulders, giving the impression of just another couple out for a late evening stroll. When the light changed, they crossed the street and turned in the direction of the alley.

She could feel the thrill of the hunt thrumming through his entire body, though she doubted if anyone else would have picked up on it. She kept scanning the street for anyone being a little too observant, but no one stuck out of the crowd.

Sandor waited until they passed the mouth of the alley before he leaned down as if to kiss her cheek. "Up on the corner on the left. That girl can't keep her eyes off the alley. Watch her. Every time she looks up and down the street as if she's waiting for someone, her eyes go right back to the alley."

Lena stepped in front of him, halting their

progress. She ran the palms of her hands up Sandor's chest. "So what's the plan? Do you want to
go after the girl while I check out the alley?"

"Other way around. You're not armed and
I am. I don't want you walking in blind and unable to protect yourself. From everything we've
learned, this renegade is pretty powerful."

"Fair enough. Shall I kiss you good-bye?"

His eyes sparkled with heat. "Honey, you can
kiss me anytime, anyplace."

She took him at his word, loving the slide of
his tongue over hers as the kiss went from sweet
to heat in a single breath. When they finally broke
off the kiss, she had to rest her forehead against
his chest to gather her scattered thoughts.

"You pack quite a punch." And she wanted
much more of it. "We'll pick up where we left off
later."

Sandor gave her another quick kiss. "That's a
deal."

She started up the street while he turned back
the other way. She knew the instant he ducked
into the alley, because her target instantly looked
distressed and unsure of what to do next. Lena
headed straight for her.

Before she could reach the end of the block,
the young woman's cell phone rang. As soon as
she answered it, she snapped it back shut and

took off. By the time Lena reached the corner, her target was out of sight. There were any number of shops and office buildings where she could be hiding. Lena decided to wait a few minutes in hopes the woman reappeared. Failing that, she'd track down Sandor and hope he'd had better luck.

She stopped to admire the window display of a vintage clothing store. A beaded purse drew her eye, but more importantly, the window reflected the street behind her, allowing her to keep watch without being obvious. And unless she was mistaken, her target had reappeared, this time on the opposite corner. Lena eased out of the recessed doorway, not wanting to make any sudden movements that would draw unnecessary attention to herself.

Sure enough, the woman had once again positioned herself where she had a clear view of the alley. Looking worried, she stared down the street. Who or what was she looking for?

Lena's own sense of unease was growing, too. Where was Sandor? Surely he'd had time to check out the alley by now. If he didn't reappear soon, she'd hunt him down.

Then the woman's demeanor changed. She went from worried to relieved as a young teenager quickly crossed the street to join her. They carried on an animated conversation for several seconds,

with the boy shrugging and gesturing back toward
the alley. The woman, who on closer examination
was probably still a teenager herself, clearly wasn't
happy with whatever he had to say. Then they
suddenly ran half a block north.

It didn't take a genius to figure out where they
were headed. One of the big articulated buses
that cruised Seattle streets had just rolled into
sight. With her quarry about to make their get-
away, Lena was torn between the need to find out
where they were headed and learning what had
happened to Sandor.

When she heard sirens headed in her direction, it was no contest. Had Sandor stumbled
across another mugging victim? Or had he been
the victim this time? She noted the bus's route
number, then charged to her lover's rescue.

"Lie still, sir. Help is on the way." Sandor injected
a calming note in his voice.

The older gentleman nodded, then groaned
from the pain of that small motion. A thin stream
of blood trickled down the side of his face. Sandor held the man's handkerchief against the small
wound to stanch the bleeding. The need to chase
down the kid responsible for the attack was rid-
ing him hard, but he couldn't very well abandon

the wounded victim the young renegade had left bleeding in the alley.

The sirens were definitely growing louder. Sandor also heard the sound of a woman's footsteps coming down the alley. He'd wondered how long it would take Lena to come looking for him. He wanted her to stick with her half of the hunt long enough to learn where the renegades went to ground, but he couldn't blame her for choosing to follow him. It was exactly what he would have done in her place. Partners watched out for each other.

When Lena spotted him, the relief in her eyes made him far happier than it should have.

"This feels a bit too familiar," she said with a slight smile.

"Yeah, déjà vu sucks big-time."

He removed the handkerchief to see if the bleeding had finally stopped. The old man blinked up at Sandor in the gathering darkness, suddenly growing more agitated. He tried to sit up but wasn't strong enough to do so.

"That boy! He took my wallet! Do you see it anywhere?"

"I'll look around to see if he might have dropped it," Lena assured him. She checked the ground nearby and then in ever widening circles. Sandor kept his fingers crossed. Although the perp was known to steal money, he often left the actual wallet with credit cards and things behind.

Sure enough, about thirty feet away she spotted something lying near a pile of trash. There was little hope that the police would get usable prints off the wallet, but he noticed she used a tissue to pick it up anyway. Maybe they should have left it where it was, but if it would help calm the injured man, too damn bad if the police didn't like it. He'd take the heat.

"I have it, sir," Lena told him. "How much money did you have in it?"

"About thirty dollars maybe, but that's not important. It's the pictures I'm worried about."

Lena opened the wallet. She held it open to show Sandor the cash was gone, but there was a picture of a couple with their arms around each other and smiling at the camera, vintage World War II.

"You and your wife make a handsome couple, sir." Sandor smiled.

"Please call me George, young man."

He finally succeeded in sitting up with Sandor's help, and Lena handed him back his wallet.

"My Mabel was a real beauty, right up until I lost her last year."

"I'm sorry for your loss," Sandor said.

George managed a ragged smile. "Me, too, but

we had almost sixty good years together. I hope the two of you have it as good as we did."

He and Lena would be lucky to have even a couple of more good days together. The thought hurt far more than it should.

The flash of blue lights indicated that the police had blocked both ends of the alley, and one look at the two heading his way had Sandor cursing under his breath. Of all of Seattle's finest, they had to get the same pair who'd responded the night Mary Dubois had been mugged.

Lena immediately stepped close and took his hand in solidarity. Explaining how they'd chanced upon a second mugging victim in only a couple of days was going to take some fancy footwork. Good deed or not, the cops weren't going to like it one little bit.

Sean watched the minutes tick by on the clock, each one lasting an eternity. Tara had taken the boy out to feed, and he hated the thought of the two of them out on the streets without him. He'd offered to drag someone home for all of them to feed from, but she'd gone all stubborn and self-righteous on him.

They both knew that if they ever brought their food source to their own doorstep, they would have to do a lot more than graze. Disposing of a body would be messy and dangerous, even in a city the size of Seattle. He also knew that if they escalated to killing, the police would be paying a lot more attention to the sudden rash of muggings. Someone would connect the dots and realize there was something odd about the attacks.

So here he was, waiting and wearing the carpet out. He stopped every lap around the small room to listen for footsteps. Tara had tucked him in bed before they'd left, thinking he still needed such care.

The minute she relaxed her guard, he'd be off and running. He had no idea where, as long it was far enough that she couldn't find him. The whole idea of starting over by himself really hurt, but he figured he wasn't long for this world anyway.

Lost in that cheerful thought, he almost missed hearing Kenny's return. Sean made it back to bed with only a second to spare before the kid stuck his head through the door.

"I'm back."

"Where's Tara?"

Kenny shrugged. "She took the money I earned tonight and said she had errands to run. Maybe we're out of milk or something."

The truth was someone else had earned that money. The three of them just stole it.

"So, tell me how it went. Any problems?"

"I'm here, aren't I?" But Kenny's eyes slid to the side as he spoke.

"Tell me how it went," Sean repeated, injecting enough energy into his words to force Kenny to answer.

"Okay, okay, fine." Kenny held his hands up in surrender. "Tara stood watch while I culled an old man out of the herd. I took enough to keep me buzzing for a couple of days. We only got about thirty dollars, but I got away clean. We hopped the bus and walked in the opposite direction of the apartment for several blocks before circling back. Just like you taught us."

"That all sounds real good, Kenny." Sean sat up, aware that his control was starting to slip. "But tell me this, what are you leaving out, Kenny?"

"Nothing."

It took more energy to break through the kid's resistance this time, enough that it left Sean breathing hard before he forced the truth out of the little prick. Kenny grabbed the door frame and dropped to his knees, his face gleaming with sweat as he struggled against Sean's compulsion. The battle between them was brief but hard fought.

"Okay! So one minute I was chowing down, and the next, there's this dude running down the alley straight for us. I dropped my dinner and ran to the other end of the alley. I got away clean while the guy stopped to help the old man."

"So you didn't lead him to Tara?"

"Hell, no, you taught me better than that. I wouldn't risk Tara just to save my own skin."

He looked Sean straight in the eye, his words ringing solid with the truth. Good thing. If he ever did put Tara at risk, the kid would be back on the streets before he knew what hit him.

Sean released his hold on Kenny. "Go eat something. It will help stabilize what you took in."

While he listened to Kenny rummaging around in the kitchen, Sean fought against an increasing panic. Someone had seen Kenny in that alley. He had assumed he'd gotten away cleanly, but Sean wasn't so sure. Just because the intruder had stopped to help the victim didn't mean that he hadn't gotten a clear look at Kenny as he'd escaped.

Their time in Seattle was drawing to a close. Tara and Kenny might no longer be safe, even without him.

This guy charging to the rescue bothered Sean on a lot of levels. First of all, what had Kenny done to attract someone's attention? He'd taught the kid right; he knew how to choose the right kind of victim, as well as a safe time and place for the attack. Kenny had doubtless picked the old man because of his age and because he'd been near the alley.

So what had drawn the other man to the alley? He might have been using it as a shortcut, but it didn't pay to assume anything.

Sean would feel a whole lot better when Tara returned and he got her version of the facts. Maybe everything was fine and the intruder was just a bit of bad luck. But Sean's gut was telling him there was more to it than that.

Maybe his worst nightmare had just come true, and the hunters had suddenly become the hunted.

Lena stood on the sidewalk and watched for Sandor. She was tired and her feet were killing her, so she'd accepted his offer to go get the car and come back for her. It had taken far longer to satisfy the cops than it should have. This time they'd really wanted the two of them to come down to the station to make a statement. Clearly they weren't buying Sandor's explanation that their involvement in a second mugging was simply bad luck.

Only the victim's vehement statement that he'd been attacked by someone far shorter than Sandor had kept them from a ride in the backseat of a cruiser. Bless the old man: despite his bad fright, George had defended them to the police.

Lena was exhausted and ready for bed—alone. The past few days had been chaotic and full of turmoil. After a few hours of solid sleep she'd be better able to sort out of her confusing feelings for Sandor Kearn and the secret world in which he lived.

She finally spotted Ranulf's convertible turning the corner, and every eye turned to watch the old beauty cruise up the street. When Sandor pulled up and she got in, she couldn't help but enjoy all the attention.

She grinned at Sandor. "This gorgeous old girl makes it hard to make a discreet exit, doesn't it?"

Sandor smiled and patted the steering wheel. "Yeah, she's a beauty. I'm surprised that Ranulf hasn't called every fifteen minutes wondering where his baby is. Look, I know you're tired, but we really should get her back. I don't think they've been apart this long since he bought her back in 1940."

She liked the teasing light in his eyes. "That's fine. I'm not sure any of us are ready to deal with a Viking with separation anxiety."

Besides, that would give her more time with

Sandor before she went her way and he went his for the night—and maybe for longer than that. Ignoring a sharp pang in her chest, she focused on their mission. "So do you think our young perp is the same one we've been hunting for?"

"Hard to tell. Mary Dubois had thought there were two attackers, but the reading I got off this kid was different from what I got from her or down at the pier. What did you think?"

She'd wondered if Sandor had picked up the quick read she'd done between returning the old man's wallet and the cops' arrival.

"He didn't remember much except the impression of the perp being short, and therefore maybe young. The attack left him tired and confused, but his thoughts were much clearer than Mary's were. That may be because we interrupted the attack, or because he's not as timid as she was.

"From what I could pick up, the attack had some of the same feel, but it was different enough for me to think we have at least two perps involved. Three, counting the girl who was standing watch up the street."

Sandor shot her a quick glance. "So you're convinced she was definitely involved?"

"I'd say so. She disappeared for a while before I could get near her. When I spotted her again, she got a phone call and then a young teenaged boy approached her. It was obvious she was upset with him about something. Then they took off to catch a bus together. I made note of the bus's route number before heading toward you."

"That's more than we had before. When we get home, I'll print out a map of the route and see what that tells us."

Home? What did he mean by that?

When she didn't say anything, Sandor shot her a questioning look. "Is something wrong?"

"You promised to take me back to my hotel."

"You were mad when you said that, and I was hoping you'd changed your mind. But if you haven't, I'll take you there now before I trade cars with Ranulf." He pulled over to the curb. "So, what's it going to be? Home or the hotel?"

The answer depended on whether she was thinking with her heart or her head. In the end, it was no contest at all.

"Take me home, Sandor."

Chapter 13

*I*n the end, they swung by Lena's hotel long enough for her to pack a few things to take to his house. Sandor thought about suggesting that she check out of the hotel and move in with him, but that would be pushing too hard. It was enough to know that once they reached his place, she was his for another night.

Every inch of his body liked that idea—especially certain inches that were definitely making their demands known right now. If he spent much more time in Lena's company, he was going to have to buy looser jeans to keep from causing permanent damage to himself.

He'd love to see the expression on her face if he were to tell her that one. Maybe he would later, just to hear her laugh.

For now, though, they needed to pool what they'd learned from tonight's mugging so he could report his progress to Kerry in the morning.

Lena led the way into his kitchen, and he hid a smile when she glanced at the counter and blushed. Was she still embarrassed over the wild monkey sex they'd had there? Personally, he was thinking about installing a memorial plaque, but he wisely kept that idea to himself.

He set her bag at the foot of the steps. "I'll be in my office looking at that bus route. Feel free to make yourself at home. There's sandwich makings in the fridge if you're hungry."

"Would you like one, too?"

"Sure. Ham and Swiss, heavy on the mustard."

Business, then pleasure. Business, then pleasure. He booted up the laptop and started hunting for the bus route. After he printed out the map, he studied the neighborhood it encompassed. Although it covered a fair amount of territory, it narrowed down the search parameters considerably.

He compared it to the map he'd made of the sites where the earlier attacks had taken place, then added tonight's to the mix. Eliminating the few outliers, most of the attacks had taken place in a limited area, all of which were within easy walking distance of the bus route.

This was good. With Ranulf's help, they should be able to start closing in on the little bastards. But what then? A frisson of icy anger skittered through him, resulting in the now familiar burn of dark energy playing under his skin. The oily blackness made him sick to his soul as he contemplated having to execute not just one but possibly several renegades so soon after Bradan's death.

How had Ranulf lived with this burden for so long without having it destroy him? Sandor guessed he'd have to figure it out, and soon. Renegades endangered the very existence of the Kyth, and their actions could not be tolerated or forgiven.

Which brought him back to the woman headed his way. The depth of his feelings made it clear that he wanted her far beyond tonight. However, she'd made it clear that she couldn't accept Kyth justice. While he trusted her to keep quiet about Bradan's execution, what did she think was going to happen to the renegades she'd been helping him hunt?

Could she possibly be thinking that this time they were going to turn the information over to the police to handle? She should be smart enough to know that wasn't going to happen.

Lena knocked on the door frame. "Mind if I come in, or would you rather I left you alone?"

Her doubt made him see red. If she didn't

know how he felt about her by now, it was damn well time she figured it out. The burn was back, stronger than ever.

"Here's your sandwich." Lena started to hold it out, then froze as her eyes went wide with shock.

"What?"

She pointed toward the paper in his hand. The smoking paper. The one starting to crumple as the smoke erupted into flames near his fingertips. His control was clearly shot to hell and back.

Sandor cursed and tossed the burning map into the trash can, then carried it into the bathroom to put water on it. When the flames were out, he grabbed on to the sink, soaking up the soothing coolness of the porcelain.

"That's the second time I've seen you do that. Does it always happen that often?"

Although Lena kept the question light, there was real concern in her words. Once again he'd managed to freak her out. His shaky control was largely due to the strain of facing a multiple execution, combined with trying to protect her from that particular reality.

He stared at her reflection in the mirror. "No."

When she didn't reply, he forced himself to say, "Would you like that ride back to your hotel now?"

He could hear her pulse speed up and sense

her momentary indecision. Then her arms slid around his waist and she rested her face against his back. With the simple gift of her touch, the darkness was banished.

After a bit, she gave him a quick squeeze and stepped back. "Come on, let's go look at that map and see what we can learn from it. Meanwhile, I want you to eat that sandwich for two very good reasons."

"Which are?"

"The first is because I went to the trouble to make it and don't want to see it go to waste."

"And the second?" he asked, suddenly really interested in hearing her answer.

With a high-voltage smile, she faced him. Placing her hand gently on his chest, she trailed her fingers down the length of his fly. "The second reason is that I've got serious plans for you tonight, and you'll need to keep up your strength."

Bless the woman. He grinned wickedly. "Then maybe you'd better make me another one."

"Would you mind if I take a bath while you wait for an email back?" Lena asked.

They'd studied the map to figure out where the renegades might have gone to ground. Once they had a better idea of how to narrow their search, Sandor had emailed Ranulf and Kerry with the information.

He looked up from the computer screen, his eyes alight with gold sparks. "Go ahead and take your time. And if you need someone to wash your back, call me."

That's what she'd been hoping for. "Only if I can reciprocate."

"You have a deal."

As she walked out, he called, "By the way, there are candles and matches in the right-hand drawer in the vanity. I keep them for when I get a headache and need to zone out for a while. Most painkillers don't work well for us."

Upstairs, she turned on the water in the big, old-fashioned claw-foot tub, then hunted up the candles. It meant a lot to know he had them there for medicinal reasons. A man as handsome and likable as Sandor had to have other women in his life, but that didn't mean she wanted to imagine it.

She turned down the blankets on the bed and tossed her pale blue nightie on the pillow, right where Sandor would be sure to see it. Then she stripped and eased into the huge tub, moaning at the warmth of the water lapping at her skin. As she relaxed, she hoped Sandor joined her soon. Too many hours had passed since she'd last felt the sweet slide of his skin against hers.

Almost immediately, she heard the creak of the steps. Sandor was on his way. The tips of her nipples budded up and the core of her body turned liquid in anticipation. She listened as he reached the top of the stairs. His steps halted briefly. Had he spotted her gown?

There was a thud as one shoe hit the floor, followed quickly by the other. The rasp of his zipper and the soft hush of clothing hitting the floor made her pulse pound. Then he was at the bathroom door, his nude body illuminated by the flicker of the candles. Each lean muscle and powerful line was defined by the soft light and shadows.

The evidence that he wanted this as badly as she did was most convincing. Impressively so. Overwhelming, in fact. It would be enough to make a lesser woman feel a little nervous, but Lena reveled in the knowledge that this warrior wanted her.

She arched an eyebrow and gave him a slow, sultry smile. "Are you going to preen there in the doorway all night?"

With a look that promised retribution, he asked, "Preening, am I?"

"I wasn't complaining," she hastened to assure him. "I was just worried that the water might get cold."

"Don't worry. We'll heat it up again."

Her lover stalked forward, letting her look her fill. Then he slid into the water behind her, surrounding her with his powerful body. Suddenly the tub didn't feel all that big.

He reached for the soap and worked up a thick lather, then began stroking her body with his soap-slick hands. He started at her shoulders and then pushed her forward so he could continue down the length of her back. Gradually, he made his way down her sides and around to the lower curve of her breasts. She leaned back to give him freer access, sighing with pleasure as he cupped her breasts with a soft squeeze.

The man was certainly thorough. In no time, her body was clean as a whistle and strung as tight as a bow. And boy, did he have a shaft she was really, really interested in. She reversed her position to straddle his lap. Oh, yeah, baby, that was better. Time for a little payback of her own.

This time she was the one with wandering hands and mounds of lather. When she slid further down to fist his erection, he tried to stop her.

"What's the matter? You can dish it out, but you can't take it?" she teased.

His eyes flashed wide with golden heat. "I was just going to suggest that the bed's more comfortable. And it has more room for what I have in mind."

"I still get to be on top."

"It's a deal."

They stood and rinsed off under the shower, kissing long and sweetly. Then Sandor dried her from head to toe, taking extra time at certain stops along the way. She took the same care with him.

Afterward, snuggling under the covers, she reminded him it was her turn to set the pace. He surrendered without a fight, and let her have her wicked, wicked way with him.

Such a prince.

Sandor wasn't sure if he could move a muscle. Hell, he could hardly breathe—not that he was complaining. Lena lay cuddled against his side, her head on his heart. Maybe he should have been sleeping, too, but he could feel their time together slipping away and didn't want to waste a single moment.

How was he ever going to let her go? He remembered all too clearly telling Ranulf he would be a fool not to claim Kerry as his own. The Viking must think it was a hoot that Sandor found himself with the same dilemma so soon afterward. Why was it always easier to give advice than to take it? Of course, their circumstances were different. Kerry needed to be part of the Kyth. Lena would be better off if she'd never heard of them.

"You're thinking too hard." Lena lifted her head briefly to peer up at him. "Can't you sleep?"

"I can't seem to shut off my mind."

"Well, it has been an eventful couple of days." She snuggled back in again. "Maybe you need something to distract you."

A woman after his own heart. "What do you have in mind?"

He felt her smile against his chest as she began lightly tracing patterns on his skin with her fingers. "Well, I was thinking about something hot . . ." She paused to nibble his shoulder.

"That sounds promising."

"With a lot of spice . . ." Her hand trailed lower down his body.

"Even better." He'd thought he was all played out, but he was willing to be proven wrong.

"And with lots of cheese."

"Cheese?" Had he heard that right? Or had all the blood in his body rushing south affected his hearing?

The minx giggled. "Yep, I'm hungry for pizza. Is there a twenty-four-hour delivery place around here? It'll even be my treat."

"Okay, pizza it is, then." His hands did some

sneaky exploring of their own. "But what will we do while we wait for the delivery guy?"

She scooted to the other side of the bed. "After you make the call, we'll see."

Luckily, he had the pizza joint on speed dial.

Kerry watched a couple of squirrels squabbling out in the garden and smiled. It had taken them less than half an hour to conquer her newest squirrel-proof bird feeder, setting a new record. Their previous best had been forty-five minutes.

Some people might find that frustrating, but she appreciated their antics, which were a welcome distraction from the business of mastering her duties as Grand Dame. Most of the time she enjoyed the challenges of learning her new culture and its rich history. And luckily, she'd absorbed a lot of information directly from her predecessor, which had simplified the process to some degree.

However, because Judith had been dying when she'd transferred her memories to Kerry, she'd been unable to filter the content. It was disconcerting to see the world through the eyes of someone who'd witnessed over a millennium of history, to feel that it had been Kerry herself who had met people who'd lived out their lives centuries before she had been born.

But it was the personal memories that were the hardest to incorporate into Kerry's new view of the world. Through Judith's eyes, she'd seen Ranulf as a young man, stricken with grief over the death of his first wife. His pain had been so raw, making her wish she could find some way to reach back through the centuries to comfort him.

At times it was hard to sort out her own feelings and beliefs from that of the late Dame. Now was one of those tough moments. She turned away from the window, resisting the temptation to blow off the lengthy To Do list on her desk.

Sitting back down, she checked the file that Sandor had sent her sometime during the night. It contained the latest information on his investigation into the renegades. Her heart hurt with the burden of what she had to do, what her people expected her to do, what their law required her to do. Kerry had trained to be a graphic artist—not exactly a background conducive to comfortably signing an execution order.

She understood the need for it. She'd seen firsthand the horror that a renegade Kyth could perpetrate. Though these particular renegades hadn't killed anyone yet, Sandor and Ranulf were convinced that it was only a matter of time. The attacks were growing more frequent and more violent.

Kyth law was clear on the matter. If a Kyth deliberately harmed a human, the penalty was death.

She set the pen down, needing more time to come to terms with ordering someone's death. She worried about the effect that carrying out her orders would have on Sandor. Ranulf had offered to step in, to save the younger Talion the heartache of another execution so soon on the heels of his first one. But they both knew that Sandor would insist on doing his job, and her husband had already borne that burden for far too long.

Third on her list of worries was Lena Wilson. The woman was an unknown quantity. Kerry was relatively sure that Lena wouldn't turn Sandor in to the police for executing Coop's killer. There was no evidence.

But what did Lena think was going to happen when they found the renegades? Kerry leaned back and briefly closed her eyes. She *so* didn't want to think about this anymore.

Instead, she picked up the heavy vellum envelope that had been delivered by courier earlier that morning. The letter inside was handwritten in ornate calligraphy, the wording stiff and formal. She was the pinnacle of royalty among the Kyth, and all it took was one letter from the Old World contingent of her people to make her feel like a low-rent upstart.

She scanned the words for the tenth time, looking for some clue as to what they really wanted. All she knew for sure was that they'd sent an emissary to present their greetings to the new Grand Dame, as well as their concerns about ensuring a smooth transition. And he was due to arrive in the next twenty-four hours.

As a strategy, she couldn't fault it. Rather than give her an opportunity to tell them that this wasn't a good time for anyone to visit, they'd waited until their man was already in transit to announce his arrival. She didn't need a stranger sitting in judgment on her actions right now, and she had no doubt that he'd be reporting back to someone on a regular basis. Greyhill Danby: his name reeked of Old World sophistication.

Ranulf picked the perfect moment to stroll through the door, and she immediately deserted her desk in favor of a kiss for her husband. Smart man that he was, he didn't question his good fortune until they came up for air.

His callused hand cupped her cheek gently as he banked the flames in his bright blue eyes. "Not that I mind being swept off my feet by my lovely wife, but what's up?"

"I can't just be glad to see my husband?"

"I've only been gone for an hour, so I repeat: what's up?" He led her toward the chair in the corner, sat down, and tugged her onto his lap.

"I've been reading Sandor's report. He's narrowed the search area down and wants you to help him track down our elusive renegades."

"And?"

"And I need to sign an execution order for the first time, with this Talion from Europe due to land on our doorstep any minute. Which reminds me, I need to make sure Hughes has a guest room prepared."

Ranulf's hand stroked her back in comfort. "I don't suppose there's much chance he'd prefer a hotel."

She shook her head. "We can always hope, but I want to be ready just in case. Besides, until we know who's jerking his strings, we can assume his orders are to keep a close eye on how I operate. He'll do that better from here."

Ranulf held her close against the worn flannel shirt he wore over a plain white T-shirt. Her Viking was a man of simple tastes but rock solid through and through. Surrounded by his strength and scent, her stomach unclenched and she could breathe.

He kissed the top of her head. "I think you're doing a fine job. And if this visiting Talion causes you any problems, leave him to me. I'll tie his strings in knots.

"And as far as the renegades are concerned, just think about the people they've been hurting."

"I know. And I know the degree of violence will start to escalate."

"So what's the problem? Our law is crystal clear on this subject."

"So Judith's memories keep telling me. I find myself wanting to lead the charge for justice, sword in hand and screaming a Viking battle cry." She frowned. "You did have battle cries, didn't you?"

He laughed. "Some of the best. Remind me the next time we're up on the mountain, and I'll teach you a few. I'd do it now, but we'd probably upset the neighbors."

"Do I get my own horned helmet?"

He looked a bit insulted. "My tribe never wore anything like that. But if you want to, you can borrow one of my knives to wave around and menace the local fauna."

He was making fun of her. She just knew it. "A knife? Why not a sword?"

"Because you couldn't lift one of my swords, much less swing it. One of my longer knives would be the perfect size for a little bit like you to brandish while you practice screaming oaths in old

Norse." From the way he chuckled, he obviously found the whole idea hilarious.

She loved making her husband laugh. From Judith's memories and her own, she knew that Ranulf had gone way too many years with no joy in his life. That didn't mean she wouldn't extract a little revenge.

She tweaked a lock of his hair. "Well, I might not be able to lift your sword, my Viking love, but if you keep making fun of me, I'll flatten you against the nearest wall and keep you there. How would you like that?"

The blue flames were back. "I'd like it just fine, if you promise to take advantage of me while I'm at your mercy."

Now *that* was an image to be savored. "Are you sure I can't play with your sword? Right now?" She basked in the warm approval in his eyes.

"Only if you promise to take really good care of it."

She slid down to kneel between his legs. "Believe me, I plan to."

Sean hated making Tara unhappy, but right now he had no choice. Neither did she, though she obviously didn't agree.

"I'm not leaving and neither are you!" She

plopped down on her chair, her arms crossed over her chest as she glared up at him.

Sean prayed for patience, but it was in short supply. Where was the easygoing woman he'd been living with for all this time?

"We have to go. It's not safe here anymore."

"*No!* I won't pack, I won't leave, and you and Kenny aren't going to either. This is our home, the first one any of us have had for years."

"We'll find another place in another city. Portland, or San Francisco maybe. You pick."

She stared at him, defiance coming off her in waves. "Well then, I pick Seattle."

"Damn it, Tara, that isn't an option." He began pacing to maintain control over his temper. Despite having fed heavily the other night, he was already hungry again. Maybe the sickness had caused him to burn up his reserves faster than normal, but he needed to feed again, and soon.

"Make it an option, Sean. I'm tired of running all the time." She looked around their cramped quarters. "Every time we move, we have to start all over again. It takes us weeks, even months, to find jobs and save up enough money for an apartment and all the stuff that we need to live."

She wasn't telling him anything he didn't already know. He thought of all the hours they'd spent haunting thrift shops to find furniture and dishes and everything else in the room. They'd come a long way from living on the streets and existing on what they could beg, borrow, or steal. That way of life had its own dangers, and he couldn't stand the thought of Tara and Kenny back out on the streets and going hungry at night. But if that's what it took to keep them safe, so be it.

Maybe it was time to lay all the cards on the table. He pulled a chair over close to Tara and sat down. He gently took her hands in his, and for the moment he let the skin-to-skin contact soothe them both.

"Tara, I don't think it's an accident that someone has twice come to the rescue of one of our prey. The first time, I'm pretty sure the guy stumbled into that alley by chance. I had sent Kenny home, but I hung around. I went too far when feeding and was going to call for help, when this dude in black leather dragged a woman into the alley.

"I couldn't see what they were up to, but after a few minutes I heard sirens. They must have called the police and EMTs."

"Why didn't you tell me this before?"

"Because I didn't want to scare you. And the guy who interrupted Kenny sounds like the same guy I saw in the alley that night. Tall, dark hair, and major scary."

Tara's voice got real small. "I think there might have been a woman with him that time, too."

She tried to pull her hand back, but he didn't let her. "Neither of you said anything about a woman. How come?"

"Because I wasn't sure. She seemed to be headed straight for me, but when I ducked around the corner and out of sight, she didn't try to follow me. She was still window-shopping when Kenny and I got on the bus."

Sean closed his eyes and counted to ten, then to twenty. "She saw what bus you got on?"

"Maybe. But we didn't come straight here when we got off, just like you've always told us to do. No one followed us home."

Any damage had already been done, so there was no use in making Tara feel worse than she already did. "You and Kenny followed the rules. That was good thinking."

"But who are these people? Why would they be looking for us?"

"I don't know. But I'm going to find out."

He'd hunt closer to home tonight. He wasn't about to lead danger right to their door, but he wanted to end this fast. He'd take the guy out—permanently.

"Sean, what are you thinking?"

Sometimes her ability to read him so well was

a real pain. "I'm going to find this guy and ask what he wants. That's all."

She didn't believe him. "Sean, don't do anything stupid. We don't know for sure it's the same guy."

"And we don't know that it isn't." It was time for this conversation to be over. "Look, why don't we go for a walk? I could use some fresh air."

"I'll tell Kenny where we'll be."

"He can come, too, if he wants. I might even scrape up enough money for ice cream."

As soon as she was out of sight, he thought about the guy who was after them. As he pictured the man in his head, he realized his hands were burning. When he looked down, his blood ran cold as he held his hands up in front of his face and tried to deny what he was seeing. Blue flickers like lightning danced under his skin.

What the *hell* was happening to him? What kind of weird monster had he become? The more he concentrated on the light show, the more intense it got. He touched his face with one fingertip and flinched from the heat. What was he supposed to do now?

Tara was coming back with Kenny, chatting about what flavor of ice cream they were going to have. Sean stood up and shoved his hands in his pockets. No use in scaring Tara. He was terrified enough for both of them.

Chapter 14

"No, I'm not going to stay here while you go out trolling for trouble." Lena sipped her coffee, trying to reason with one very stubborn man.

Sandor sat sprawled on the couch. He might have looked relaxed and unconcerned, but she knew him too well now to be fooled. He probably thought that if he acted as if his proposed outing with Ranulf Thorsen was no big deal, she'd fall for it. Fat chance. He and his buddy were going hunting for humans, plain and simple.

Sandor obviously wanted her to hang around his house. She was welcome to sit on the deck, read a book, and drink wine coolers until he got back. He'd even offered her the use of his washer and dryer if she needed them.

Well, that wasn't going to happen. He just

didn't know it yet, and she certainly wasn't going to tell him. She knew where they would be hunting. There was no law against her going for a drive in Seattle, and if her path happened to cross his, well, what a coincidence that would be.

"What's that look in your eye?" Sandor frowned and sat up straighter. "You're planning something, aren't you?"

"You have your plans for the evening; I have mine. Don't worry. I'll be fine." She picked up her car keys. "I'm going to run back to my hotel for a few things."

"I'm not supposed to meet Ranulf for another hour or so. I could take you."

"No, that's all right."

He followed her outside, clearly not happy that she was leaving. "At least take a house key with you so you can let yourself back in."

Maybe she should resent his assumption that she had nothing better to do than wait for him, but before she could say anything, she noticed the lines of strain framing his mouth. Did he think she was walking out the door for good?

She held her hand out for the key. "Thanks, that will simplify things." Rising up on her toes, she gave him a quick kiss. "Stay safe."

As she drove off, she watched him in the rear-view mirror until she turned the corner.

• • •

It had taken longer than she'd expected to change her rental car for one that Sandor wouldn't recognize. She wasn't sure if he trusted her to go to her hotel and then back to his house. The man had good instincts, and she'd told him that she wasn't going to sit by and do nothing tonight.

He and Ranulf were convinced that the muggers were Kyth renegades, and therefore subject to Kyth justice. He knew how she felt about that, and if he had any feelings for her—and she believed he did—he had to respect her beliefs. She'd compromised her ideals once and had lost everything, and she wouldn't give up her self-respect again, no matter how hot the sex was between them.

If it had been only sex, she'd have picked up the phone and called the cops to blow the whistle on Sandor and company. But it was much more than sex—so somehow, she had to step between Sandor and his intended target. He might never forgive her, but thanks to that tat on his arm, she knew the burden of guilt that he carried from executing Bradan Owen and didn't want to see him add to it.

She slowed the car, scanning both sides of the street for any sign of Sandor or Ranulf. At the end of the block, she moved on, heading back toward where the renegade had been hunting the night before.

"Okay, I'll meet you there in a few. I'm only a couple of blocks away." Sandor snapped his cell closed, ending the call from Ranulf.

Neither of them had had any luck yet in tracking down the renegades. He needed something to eat, so he'd suggested meeting at a local sports bar to regroup, replenish, and then redeploy.

As he reached the door of the bar, he spotted Ranulf rounding the corner. Judging by the Viking's grim expression, he wasn't any happier about their lack of progress.

"I checked out the alley from last night," Ranulf said as he arrived. "It's definitely a different signature than the one down by the pier. That confirms that we're looking for at least three individuals."

"Great. Since when do renegades run in packs?"

Ranulf's eyes flickered in anger. "It's a first for me, too."

"I was afraid of that."

They took a table in the back corner, to keep their backs to the brick wall and give them a clear

view of the room. Sandor waited until the wait-
ress brought their beers, then moved out of ear-
shot before speaking. "Do you prefer fighting with
blades or bullets?"

If his question surprised Ranulf, it didn't show.
"Blades most of the time. I'm more comfortable
with knives and swords, mostly because I grew
up using them. Guns are easier to hide when you
have to carry them in public, but they're noisy."

He took a long drink from his mug. "Since
it's important to keep our business from drawing
outside attention, I pick the weapon best suited
to the circumstances. But most of the time, with
a renegade, my Talion abilities were the most effective if I could get close enough for hands-on
work."

"Makes sense. I'm a good shot with revolvers
and automatics; less so with rifles." Sandor braced
himself and asked, "Would you be up for bringing
me up to speed with knives? As you said, they're
quieter."

Ranulf smiled at him over the top of his glass.
"Sure. I need to teach Kerry, too. Once she's
mastered her Kyth abilities she'll be able to de-
fend herself from a direct physical attack, but not
against bullets or blades. Since she could use a
sparring partner, it'll be easier for me to teach you
together."

Despite their improving relationship, Sandor was surprised by Ranulf's offer. "Thanks, I'd like that. I'd like that a lot."

Back outside, Sandor paused to study the street after they'd only gone a block. Someone was watching them—someone who didn't want to be seen.

"We're not alone," he told Ranulf.

"Yeah, I feel it, too."

"I can't tell where it's coming from. No matter which way I face, I can still feel it."

They started walking more slowly, then Ranulf stopped at the newspaper boxes lined up on the corner.

"I think there's two of them, but I can't pick them out of the crowd. It's hard to know if they're working together or not," he said.

While Ranulf bought a paper, Sandor studied the cars driving by. He hadn't been paying much attention to traffic, but he was pretty sure the dark blue SUV that had just passed them had gone by before. As it turned the corner ahead, he cursed.

Unless he was mistaken, that was Lena, sticking her nose in the middle of Talion business. Changing cars was exactly the kind of trick she'd use to throw him off the track. It would have worked, too, if he hadn't happened to have looked up at the right time.

He should've known better than to trust her to stay out of this hunt, especially since he'd brought her into it in the first place.

"Ranulf, I'm pretty sure I know who one of our spies is. If I'm not mistaken, that was Lena who just drove by in that dark blue SUV."

Ranulf threw back his head and laughed, then clapped one of his big hands on Sandor's shoulder.

"I'd offer you my sympathy, but not too long ago, you were smirking over Kerry putting me through my paces. Turnabout is fair play."

"Yuk it up all you want, but Kerry is Kyth. Lena isn't."

"I don't see that making any difference in how you feel about her. It's written all over your face whenever she's in the room."

Sandor sighed. "What should we do about her?"

Ranulf tucked his newspaper under his arm and started walking again. "Your call. If you think she'll interfere less driving around, leave her be. If you want more control, flag her down and let her know her cover is blown."

"I'll flag her down—Wait a minute. What was that?"

"Did you see something?" Ranulf instantly went on full alert.

"I'm not sure. I thought I felt the same energy signature I picked up in the alley that first night, but it's gone now."

Yet the feeling that they were being watched hadn't faded one iota. Sandor scanned the area ahead, watching for anything unusual. "He's here, and he knows we're hunting."

There—someone was lurking near the mouth of an alley, but he ducked back out of sight when Sandor turned in that direction. Was he trying to lead them into a trap? Whoever he was, he hadn't avoided capture this long by being stupid. The renegade definitely wanted Sandor to see him. The only question was, why?

"Did you see him, Ranulf? Watch the entrance to that alley half a block up on the other side of the street."

"Missed him," Ranulf said, shaking his head. "I was busy watching for Lena."

"I suspect our renegade wants to play games and is daring us to follow him." The dark energy stirred deep inside Sandor, ready to do battle. "I'm definitely in the mood to play. You catch up with Lena and get her out of here. I'll check in after I've cleaned up this mess."

"If he's alone, we need him alive—at least until

we find his partners. Then it'll be open season on renegades." Ranulf's own energy was running high; his blue eyes were hot with flames.

"I'll try, but he might not give me any choice but to take him out."

Sandor's hands were burning now, and Ranulf held out his own fingers to show Sandor they matched. They automatically clasped hands, sharing the dark buzz of their need to hunt.

Sandor placed his other hand on his tat. "With luck, I'll be able to follow him back to his lair. When I find where he goes to ground, I'll find the other two. This will end, I so vow."

Ranulf clasped his own talisman with a solemn nod. "Sounds like a plan. Now go, before Lena gets back around the block. We don't want her following you."

After crossing the street, Sandor walked into a bar hoping it had a back door. That would get him out of Lena's sight, and he also wanted to come at his target from behind. No one in the crowded bar took any notice of him walking straight through to the back. The rear door opened up on a narrow alley barely wide enough for a truck, with the normal clutter of trash cans and stacks of flattened cardboard. Sandor knelt down low, prepared to wait out his prey.

It didn't take long. A head appeared only

long enough to take a quick look up and down the street Sandor had been on before, obviously checking to make sure the coast was clear. He probably planned to lead Sandor on a merry chase and then into a trap. Stupid. Rather than playing games, he should be running fast and hard.

Lena smacked the steering wheel and pulled over to the curb by Ranulf. She'd suspected that her luck had run out on that last drive by, but she'd expected Sandor to be the one waiting for her, not the Viking.

She unlocked the door and sighed as Ranulf got inside.

"What tipped you two off? I thought I was being so darn careful."

Ranulf's laugh was a deep rumble. "You were. I didn't spot you at all until Sandor pointed you out to me. While he wasn't happy to see what you were up to, he did think it was pretty damn clever of you to trade cars."

"A fat lot of good that does me." She looked up and down the street. "So where is he?"

Ranulf ignored her question. "Mind giving me a ride home?"

She knew a brick wall when she was sitting next to one. "I might as well."

"Thanks, I appreciate it. You'd be welcome to wait at the house with us if you'd rather not be alone."

She considered the offer. "Thanks, but I'll wait at Sandor's. I'd appreciate it if you'd tell him when he checks in."

Why had Sandor ditched her this evening, when he'd let her accompany him previously?

There was only one answer that made sense. "He's found the renegade, hasn't he?"

Ranulf turned his powerful gaze in her direction. "Yes. Or to be more precise, the renegade let himself be found."

She whipped the car over to the shoulder and stopped. "You let Sandor go after him alone, knowing what that bastard is capable of?"

Ranulf looked unconcerned. "No, Lena. I let Sandor do his job because I know what *he* is capable of. Even on his best day, that renegade doesn't stand a chance against a Talion warrior—especially one of Sandor's caliber."

Lena wasn't so sanguine. The two Talions probably *were* the Big Bad, but that didn't make them bulletproof. What if this renegade didn't face Sandor in a fair fight?

They rode in silence until she let Ranulf out in front of his driveway.

He hesitated before closing the door. "We'll

call when we hear anything. You do the same."

She smiled and nodded, then drove off in the direction of Sandor's house. But after she turned a corner, she pressed her foot on the accelerator and headed downtown to start a hunt of her own.

Sean eased out of the alley and into a nearby doorway to get a better view of the street, but the tall dark-haired guy was nowhere in sight. The redheaded giant was getting into a car, so now Sean didn't know if he'd actually been with the other guy or just waiting around for his ride.

Sean would bet that the other guy was somewhere close by. The only question was where. He headed back into the alley and hurried to the other end, then eased around the corner to check both directions. The hair on his arms stood up, sending him scooting back to the safety of the alley.

The bastard had been trying to sneak up behind him! Well, two could play that game. With luck, he could lead the would-be hunter into another alley that looked like a dead end. Sean would escape by climbing on top of the fence and then pulling himself up on a fire escape. From there, he'd run back along the roof to drop down behind his prey and confront his enemy. Only one of them would walk out of that alley. He'd make Seattle safe for Tara and Kenny, or die trying.

He deliberately knocked over a stack of boxes, cursed as if it had been an accident, then ran for the street. As he rounded the corner, he glanced back down the alley.

Oh, yeah—the race was on.

Chapter 15

*A*s Sandor pounded down the street, people stopped and stared, some reaching for their cell phones just in case. He'd be lucky to make it three blocks without someone calling the police.

He slowed to catch his breath and give the renegade time to get wherever he was going. The idiot probably didn't realize that Sandor could follow the energy trail he was leaving as clearly as a hunter could follow hoofprints in soft ground.

His target rounded the corner at the bottom of the hill. Sandor picked up the pace, but still moved slowly enough that the others on the street quickly lost interest in him. The air was rife with the renegade's energy, a tangled mess of all the flavors he'd been stealing from humans over the past few weeks. Normally Kyth absorbed energy from the humans around them much more slowly, so their energy signatures read as purely Kyth.

This skinny teenager stank from a sour mix of fear and pain. How many people had suffered in order to keep the renegade running on all that high octane? Well, he wouldn't be running for long—or ever again, once Sandor got his hands on him. He'd get the little prick cornered and subdued. If the spot was private enough, he'd end it there if necessary. Otherwise he'd call for a pickup by Ranulf. The woods around the Viking's mountain home would give them privacy to find out where the renegade's buddies were hiding.

The evidence was clear that this renegade was responsible for most of the recent muggings. And since he was draining far more of his victims' life force each time, it was only a matter of time before he killed. Far better that he die himself, before that happened.

Suddenly the trail turned cold, bringing Sandor to an abrupt halt. Okay, where had the renegade rabbited off to? Turning slowly, he studied his surroundings. The sun had sunk low in the sky. It would be light until well past nine o'clock, but the shadows were thickening between the taller buildings.

Walking back the way he'd come, he tested the air every few steps until he found the spot where the scent weakened and disappeared. Unless the runner had ducked inside somewhere, there was only one place the renegade could have gone to ground. Across the street was a short run of cedar fencing between two boarded-up buildings. The gate had been left open a few inches in invitation.

So the renegade had set his trap. Sandor checked the slide of his gun in the back of his waistband. He carried it as a last-ditch resort, but only a fool entered into combat with only one weapon at his disposal.

Crossing the street, he eased the gate open enough to slip through, then pulled it closed behind him, careful not to latch it. If he was wrong about facing a solitary renegade, he wanted the exit open and unobstructed.

In the narrow alley, there was no use in trying to keep to the shadows. His opponent had to know he was coming, so Sandor made no effort to hide, especially because the passageway was relatively clear of obstacles. That also meant there were few places his quarry could be hiding.

A few seconds later, Sandor stopped. The alley ended a short way ahead, the back end closed off with another stretch of fence. Why would the renegade lead Sandor into a dead end? He'd been there, though; Sandor could sense his energy hanging heavy in the late evening air. Where the hell had he gone?

Then the gate creaked open, and he heard familiar footsteps. How had Lena tracked him? This was *not* what he needed right now, especially with a renegade playing a lethal game of hide-and-seek.

He turned and snarled, "Damn it, Lena, why aren't you back at the house? This is my job. Get out of here before it's—"

"Too late." Another voice finished his sentence, and the renegade dropped from a fire escape right behind Lena. He fisted his hand in her hair and yanked her head back to press a knife against her throat.

Sandor wasn't sure if his heart was still beating; he couldn't draw a breath. If the little bastard drew one drop of blood from her, his death would make Bradan's look like a picnic.

He stepped toward them. "Let her go. I'm the one you want."

The renegade, who didn't look a day over twenty, dragged Lena back a step or two. His laugh was nasty. "I want both of you dead. I'm tired of you screwing with my hunting."

Sandor held his hands out to his sides and palms up. The position looked more harmless, but left him in a position to attack if the opportunity presented itself.

"Look, kid, we don't need to do this. I just wanted to talk to you." Sandor pushed a wave of calming energy toward both Lena and the renegade.

The renegade's eyes narrowed in response. "I'm not a kid, and I have nothing to say."

Sandor had to keep him talking. "I meant no insult, but I don't know your name. What would you like me to call you?"

"These days I go by Sean."

"Okay, Sean, my name is Sandor. Her name is Lena. She's in town on vacation."

That was a lie. But the more details the boy learned about them, the harder it would be for him to go on the attack. Sandor risked another step forward.

"So, Sean, why did you want me to follow you into this alley?"

"What makes you think I did?"

"You left the gate open. Damn fine job of getting behind me. That was clever." And wouldn't have saved his scrawny ass if Lena hadn't intruded on their little party.

Sweat was pouring off Sean's face despite the cool air. His eyes were almost bulging out of his face, with the whites showing all around his irises. Son of a bitch, the kid was on the verge of total meltdown. If Sandor didn't play this exactly right, the renegade would kill Lena. He'd either strip her of all her energy directly, or slash her throat and soak up a hot shot from her pain.

Sandor met Lena's gaze: he was glad to see she remained calm. As long as she could keep her emotions under control, the renegade would only get bland energy from her. It would soothe his ragged edges but not give him the high he was looking for. She blinked her eyes slowly, letting Sandor know that she was in control.

"Sean, you need to ease up on that blade before you hurt her. You've already broken enough of our laws. Don't compound it by drawing first blood."

The kid pulled Lena back another couple of steps. "Fuck the law, and fuck you! No way I'm going to jail. Neither of you are going to walk out of here alive, so don't try to bargain with me. I can make it easy for her, or she can suffer. To tell the truth, I hope you *do* try something. I like it when they struggle."

That changed the game a bit. Sean's skills were an unknown quantity, but he clearly had some, the way energy was flickering in his hands. Hell, the kid had Talion talents—strong ones. But he hadn't been trained to use them, and that would make all the difference.

Sandor slowly blinked back at Lena three

times, trying to warn her that he was about to make his move. He waited a few seconds and repeated the same slow cadence. On the third beat, she stomped hard on the kid's instep and shoved her elbow back into his stomach with all her power. When his hand came away from her neck, she fell and rolled to the side to get clear.

As soon as he had a clear shot, Sandor flung an energy bolt at Sean to bring him down.

But the kid didn't die. Sandor started forward, determined to wrap his hands around Sean's neck and drain him dry. Recognizing death headed straight for him, Sean began backpedaling for the gate behind him. In a last-ditch effort to throw Sandor off the track, he threw the knife.

But instead of aiming at Sandor, he threw it at Lena. The blade flashed through the air to land, quivering, in her upper arm. She stared at the bright gush of blood in stunned silence, the suddenness of the attack likely overriding the initial pain. Having successfully distracted Sandor, Sean took off running as if the mouth of hell had just opened up and threatened to swallow him.

That would come later.

Sandor knelt beside Lena as he stripped off his shirt to wrap around her arm after pulling out the knife. Despite the renewed gush of blood, the wound wasn't fatal, thank the gods. Holding the shirt in place, he pulled out his cell and hit speed dial.

"Kerry, I need your healing skills and a clean shirt. We're a block south and west of where Lena picked Ranulf up earlier. There'll be a cedar fence on your left with a gate standing wide open."

He hung up and shoved the phone back in his pants pocket, ignoring it when it started ringing almost immediately. He was too close to the edge himself to handle any questions.

"Sandor? You're hurting me."

"Sorry," he apologized. He loosened his grip, then helped her to her feet. They walked over to a row of plastic recycle bins, and Sandor flipped two over as seats. "Kerry and Ranulf should be here any minute."

He wrapped his arm around her shoulder and held her close. She might not need the comfort, but he sure as hell did. He could have lost her. Sean's fate was sealed now.

"Do you know anyone who could take care of my arm without asking too many questions? If not, I can call in a favor from an EMT I know." Her voice was rough with pain.

"No need. The ability to heal is one of a Dame's gifts. Kerry will take care of you."

Which he'd failed to do. Guilt bit at him until he wanted to scream. He flexed his fingers, imagining them crushing Sean's neck with a satisfying crunch. Despite the energy he'd burned trying to take out the renegade, he was wired to the gills. His hands crackled with the need to punish the little prick.

"Sandor, calm down."

Lena gave his glowing hands a pointed look. Despite the gray sheen of pain on her face, she sat up straighter and gingerly placed her fingers on his. He fought for control, letting her soothing touch cool his temper.

"I'm fine, or will be soon." She gave him a sharp look. "And this wasn't your fault."

"Like hell it wasn't! I figured the renegade was close by, but I didn't warn you to run." He slumped back against the rough brick wall.

Her smile was a bit ragged. "And I probably wouldn't have listened. I was too mad at you and Ranulf for ditching me."

"And for good reason, as it turns out. I told you that humans have no business hunting our renegades."

She rolled her eyes. "Remind me—was I the only one he managed to get the drop on? I remember a definite look of shock on your face when he came flying out of nowhere."

Before Sandor could respond, the gate banged open and an irate Viking appeared. Kerry ducked around his side, giving her husband a dirty look when he tried to block her way. Sandor should have known better than to laugh at the petite Dame bossing around a man twice her size, but he did it anyway.

Two pairs of angry eyes zeroed in on him. Kerry snapped, "What's so funny, Sandor?"

He held up his hands in surrender. "Sorry. Write it off to exhaustion and hysteria. You know how I hate the sight of blood."

Kerry ran to them as soon as she spotted the blood-soaked shirt around Lena's arm. She set down a first aid kit and opened it. "What happened?

"The renegade dropped down behind us and held his knife to Lena's throat. With some quick thinking, she broke free. But to prevent me from coming after him, he threw his knife and caught her in the arm."

"How did he manage to surprise you like that?" Then Ranulf frowned at Lena. "And I thought *you* were going back to Sandor's house."

"Plans changed." She winced as Kerry not so gently unwrapped her arm. "Damn, that hurts."

The Viking knelt down beside Lena. "I'd point out that if you'd gone back to Sandor's place, this wouldn't have happened. But I guess you've already figured that out for yourself."

"Yeah, and nobody likes a know-it-all." Lena bit down on her lower lip and drew in a sharp breath.

Sandor squeezed her shoulder. "Breathe through it, honey. Deep, slow breaths. Kerry will fix you right up."

By now she should've been used to the way the Kyths' eyes showed their high emotions. Sandor's eyes were sparking gold like crazy, as were Kerry's. Ranulf's flickered with bright blue flames.

"Okay, Lena, I'm going to pour this bottle of water over your cut to clean it before I try to heal it. I don't want to trap the dirt inside." Kerry popped the cap on the bottle. "Let me know when you're ready."

"Go for it."

Using the tepid water and folded gauze, Kerry carefully washed away the dried blood. Fresh blood immediately welled up to drip onto the ground.

"We'll let it bleed clean before I try my mojo on it. I'm still pretty new at this stuff, so if it doesn't work right away, we'll take you for stitches."

Kerry held Lena's gaze as she positioned her hand a hair's breadth above the wound. Lena felt a soft tingle radiating out from deep inside her arm. The pain eased up a little, but the bleeding continued.

Kerry frowned in concentration and spread her fingers wider. The blood slowed to a trickle but didn't stop. The young Dame's hand trembled a bit. Then Ranulf squatted down to wrap his powerful fingers around his wife's wrist. Within seconds, the back of his hand began writhing with those spooky blue sparks under his skin.

Almost immediately, Lena's pain faded completely. Kerry used her other hand to wipe away the drying blood again. When she did, Lena blinked twice. The cut was slowly closing up, leaving only the faintest hint of red where the wound had been. A few seconds later, it was gone completely.

"I'd say that was impossible, except I saw it for myself." Lena looked over at Sandor in total wonder. His smile was definitely a bit smug. "What?" she asked.

"Beats stitches and pain medicine, doesn't it?" He gave her a quick squeeze. "Now, let's get you to your car so I can get back to work."

The pain in her arm was gone; the pain in her backside was still sitting right next to her. "Oh, no you don't, Sandor Kearn. That little jerk stabbed me. I want a piece of him—a *big* piece."

"No, Lena! I can't fight this renegade and protect you at the same time."

As mad as she was at the kid who'd stabbed

her, she didn't want him dead. The only way to prevent that was to be there when Sandor confronted him. She patted her gun. "I can protect myself. Now, either we can work together so you know where I am, or we can risk me stumbling into another situation that endangers both of us."

Sandor stood and glared down at her. "No. And that's final."

And intimidation always worked so well with her. The man was a slow learner. She got on her feet and right up in his face. "We've had this discussion before."

"Fine. If it makes you feel better, I'll take the berserker with me."

"No can do," Ranulf said. "While you and I were out patrolling earlier, Kerry and I got a houseguest. We had a hard time slipping away without him noticing, and I'd like to get back to the house before he realizes we're gone."

"Company. Who is it?"

"Greyhill Danby. That Talion who serves in England."

Lena was beginning to feel as if she were watching a tennis match.

"I've heard good things about him, but what's he doing here?" Sandor asked.

Kerry looked thoroughly disgusted. "I suspect our European cousins have a few qualms about me taking over as Dame. I think Danby is here to give them firsthand information on how ill prepared I am to do the job."

She looked at her husband. "Since Judith served for a thousand-plus years, I assume the Kyth don't have a history of overthrowing their government."

"Not so far." Sandor's dark eyes were back to sparking again. "And they're in for a fight if they're thinking about trying it. They have no idea who they'd be messing with. My money's on you, Grand Dame Kerry."

"Thank you. So while we go make nice with our guest, will you be okay on your own?"

"Yes, I will."

Lena hated being ignored. "He won't *be* on his own."

As Ranulf and Kerry went, leaving her and Sandor to duke it out, he asked, "Why are you doing this? It's not your business."

Idiot. "The renegade is not my main concern here. *You* are."

Sandor looked insulted. "I can handle my job, Lena."

"Your ability to do the job has never been in doubt. The question is, what effect will this have on you long term? That jolt of your history I absorbed showed me that you're still reeling with the pain of executing your friend. This time you might have to kill a kid who's probably not even old enough to vote, much less drink."

"He's a renegade. Our law is clear on what that means."

But his dark eyes were filled with grief and remembered pain, and she couldn't bear to see him hurt more.

"Sandor, I understand that your honor demands that you do what you think is right and damn the consequences. But that kind of thinking can ruin your life."

His face was closed. "I don't want to hear another word, Lena. Go back to the house or to the hotel, and don't interfere in my investigation. I'm leaving. Alone."

He shrugged on the clean shirt Ranulf had brought him and started for the gate.

She sighed, then followed him.

Sean ran until he couldn't go another step. He ducked into a dark doorway to let his lungs catch up. Where the hell could he go where that scary bastard couldn't follow him? He *knew* the guy hadn't seen him duck into the alley. Even though Sean had set the trap, he'd never really expected the guy to find him.

The woman had been a lucky complication, although he regretted the knife thing. She wasn't the one trying to fry his ass with freaky bolts of lightning. The memory made his hands burn with blue flames under his skin again, making him queasy.

What was happening to him? He fought for control of his body and his thoughts. As long as he was in panic mode, he wouldn't be able to think straight.

He looked back, half expecting to see that Sandor guy already sneaking up behind him. It was a relief to see that the street was empty, but it was only a matter of time. Sandor might have been willing to bargain before, but now that Sean had stabbed his woman, he'd come in blasting.

Sean could take care of himself, but what about Tara and Kenny? If Sandor caught their scent like he had Sean's, he'd be after them next. Sean had brought destruction down on all of them. He had to get to the apartment and convince the other two to grab the first bus out of town. Once they were gone, he'd take to the streets to lead Sandor as far from his friends as possible.

His decision made, he started running again. But it was as if a noose was tightening around his neck with each step he took, making it hard to breathe and even harder to think. Breaking his own rule, he took the most direct route home and reached the door just as his energy failed. His hands shaking too hard to get the key in the lock, he pounded on the door.

He concentrated on breathing as he waited for Tara to let him in, but he couldn't fill his lungs enough to talk. Spots danced in front of his eyes, and the world faded to gray around the edges. Was he dying? It sure felt like it. No matter, as long as he lived long enough to warn his friends.

An eternity later, the door swung open and he collapsed on the floor at Kenny's feet. Sean was only dimly aware of the kid yelling for help as darkness clawed at his mind and pulled him under.

Warmth and white light flowed through Sean as he slowly woke up. He knew there was something important he should be doing or saying, but right now he could only lie with his head in Tara's lap and soak up her soothing touch. As she continued to feed him a steady supply of energy, though, a sense of urgency destroyed his peace.

Something had happened—something bad. Real bad. The fog in his mind finally lifted, and he jerked away from Tara, his heart revving up again.

"You have to pack! Take only what you absolutely need. Both of you have to go, right now. When you get to the bus station, buy tickets on the first bus to anywhere. He's coming!"

Tara looked bewildered. "Who's coming? And why did you take off without telling us where you were going? Where were you?"

Sean propped himself up against the couch and used the hem of his shirt to wipe the sweat off his face. Kenny thrust a glass of water into his hands. The cool drink eased Sean's throat, making it easier to talk.

"I went to confront the guy who interrupted Kenny in the alley. He *was* the same one I saw that other time." Even with his eyes closed he kept seeing Sandor coming straight at him, with death in his eyes and those blistering hot bolts shooting from his hands.

"Honey, you and Kenny need to grab what you can and leave. Now! *Please.* Sandor—that's his name—tracked me and tried to kill me."

He held up his hands to show her the blue lines moving under his skin. She gasped, and Kenny backed away, stumbling over the packing crate they used as an end table.

"His hands did this, too, only a hundred times worse. I've never been so scared."

Tara scooted closer to Sean and reached out to take his hands. "How did you get away?"

He hung his head in shame. "I threw my knife at his woman and ran."

"Sean! How *could* you? Tell me she's all right."

"I think so, but I didn't stick around to see. All I could do was run. But if he can find me, he can find you." He pushed at her, trying to make her go. "Pack now. Take all the money and *go!*"

Tara's chin came up in a stubborn tilt. "Not without you. If you stay, we stay."

"Hey—" Kenny protested, but Tara rounded on him.

"We're *family*, Kenny, and family sticks together. Got that?"

Kenny looked from her to Sean and back again. "Fine. We stay."

Sean's eyes burned with tears from the combination of frustration and relief. If they wouldn't leave, though, they needed to make some plans. "Okay, we'll stay—but you'll have to do what I say."

Tara looked to Kenny before answering. "We will."

"This guy is like us, only on major steroids. He can do things we never knew were possible."

"Like what?" Kenny kept glancing at the door, as if he thought Sandor was going to burst in any second.

"He was able to track me wherever I went,

even though he couldn't see me. I figure he must be able to detect our scent, or maybe the way we burn energy or something. And he can use energy like a weapon from a distance, though I don't know how far."

Tara looked so scared that it hurt, but it didn't show in her voice. "Okay, so we stay inside. We have enough food for several days."

He didn't know if that would keep them safe, but at least they were taking the danger seriously. "If we do go out, we go together."

"I've got a knife. I'll get it."

Kenny ran for his room before Sean could tell him that they'd never get close enough to Sandor to do any damage. Besides, it might comfort Kenny to have the weapon.

When the boy returned, the three of them sat in grim silence, waiting for the knock at the door. When it came only a few minutes later, Sean stared at his two friends, wishing he'd been able to do more to protect them. Maybe if he offered himself up, Sandor would let Tara and Kenny go.

He stood and offered Tara a hand up off the floor; then he pulled her into his arms for a long hug. "I love you, you know."

She held on tight. "I know. And Kenny, too."

Sean looked over to the boy. "Yeah, him, too. Like she said, Kenny, we're family. Got that?"

The boy swallowed hard and nodded. "Want me to open the door?"

The kid had guts. So did Tara. They were both handling this situation a lot better than he was—but then, he'd actually seen what Sandor could do.

"Thanks for offering, kid, but that's my job. He's looking for me."

Bracing himself for death, Sean opened the door.

Chapter 16

*S*andor waited in the hallway of the cheap apartment building, which was filled with the stench of despair. Living here was barely a step up from living on the streets.

Only one of them would walk out of this building, most likely him—but at what price? He'd lose another chunk of his soul, but worse yet, it would cost him Lena. There was no way she'd stick around if he killed this kid.

And who could blame her? She'd lost Coop to a murderous Kyth. How could Sandor hope that she'd lose her heart to another one?

Going into battle was a helluva time to realize that he loved her, but delaying any longer wouldn't change a thing. He pounded on the door again, then listened to the heavy silence inside the apartment. The only noise was the pounding of three heartbeats.

At the sound of the door opening, Sandor braced himself for an attack. Though Sean was young, he'd proven himself to be willing to fight. Good. That would make executing the little bastard easier to live with.

"What do you want?"

The scent of fear rolled off the boy in waves, but he met Sandor's gaze head-on. He also made no move to let Sandor in. Too bad. They needed to keep this confrontation out of the sight of humans.

"Let me in."

"Why would I do that?" Sean's eyes flickered to the side, no doubt looking at the other people in the apartment.

Sandor kept his voice calm. "Because if I blow this door off its hinges, one of your friends might get hurt."

Sean didn't budge. "How's your woman?"

"She's fine, no thanks to you. Now let me in, and let's get this over with."

"I want your word that you won't hurt them."

The last thing Sandor wanted to feel right now was admiration for Sean's determination to protect his friends. It was obvious the kid wasn't beyond redemption—but the law was clear. There was no plea-bargaining among their kind.

"I can't promise that, Sean. They are responsible for their actions, just like you are. Our laws—"

"Aren't the only laws that apply here, Sandor."

Keeping an eye on Sean, Sandor prayed for patience as he slowly turned to face Lena. "What are you doing here?"

"We started this hunt together. We finish it together."

"You won't like how it ends, Lena." Neither would he, but his wishes were beside the point.

"Before you go in there, you need to hear why I left Seattle. Why I lost the best friend I ever had."

"This isn't story time, Lena. I have a renegade to take care of."

She stood her ground. "Just hear me out. It won't take long."

"Fine. Start talking." He'd listen, but only because he couldn't stand the pain in her eyes or the way her hands shook before she backed away and finally shoved them in the pockets of her jeans.

"Not here."

Sandor turned back to Sean. "I'll be right out front. Don't think you can escape."

Right now he'd do anything to get Lena away from what he was about to do. Outside, they sat down on a low concrete wall near the door.

Lena stared at her hands, then said quietly, "This is harder than I thought it would be."

He took her hand and gave it a reassuring squeeze. "Don't beat yourself up over it. Remember, you already know the worst about me."

She gave him a faint smile. "You mean the fact that you snore and hog the covers?"

It felt good to laugh, even just a little. "Exactly. Whatever you have to tell me, I've got no right to judge you."

"All right. You already know about my so-called gift, but Coop didn't. No one I worked with did. All they knew was that I had a better-than-average arrest rate on the arson cases I investigated. Even the Feds who handled the big cases sometimes called me in for a consult. That was a huge ego boost—from poor white trash to hero.

"Anyway, we were called to a fire where people died. Those were always the hardest cases. We all wanted the perp, and we wanted him bad. I returned to the scene several times, trying to get a clear read of the fire, but only got bits and pieces. This talent of mine is never predictable about how much I'll get at any particular scene. All we really had to go on was the method used to start the fire, which fit the pattern of a known arsonist."

The words were pouring out almost faster than

she could breathe now. He softly touched her shoulder.

"Take your time, Lena. I'm not going anywhere."

"Once I knew that much, I convinced myself that he'd done it. But Coop had put that guy away on a previous crime and knew him. He kept arguing that this arsonist had never killed anyone. He said even lifelong criminals could have some principles, but I didn't believe him. I wanted justice, not to mention the glory, no matter the price. When I couldn't bring the guy in on the real evidence, I . . ."

She choked as tears streamed down her face. "I made the evidence stronger. He was convicted, denying his guilt the whole time. But who's going to believe a three-time loser?"

"Coop?"

She wiped her face with her sleeve. "Yeah, Coop. He kept working the case until he figured out who the *real* culprit was. Unfortunately, by then the perp had gone on a burning spree and more people were hurt. All because I wanted a conviction more than I wanted the truth. I put my own feelings and needs above the law. I left town, unable to face Coop, because he knew what I'd done. He never pointed a finger or said a word, but he knew."

"From what I know of the man, he would have forgiven you."

"He did. He tried to tell me that we all make mistakes, that what we learn from them was what was important. I did what I thought was the right thing for all the wrong reasons, and I couldn't forgive myself."

She drew herself up and turned to face him. "I understand that you need to protect your people, Sandor. Humans aren't always tolerant of those they see as different or threatening.

"From everything I've heard, you did the right thing when you took Bradan Owen out of the world. He was a stone-cold killer, through and through, yet you still haven't made peace with executing him. And I'm telling you: the memory of Bradan's death will seem like *nothing* compared to what taking out that kid will do to you."

Sandor sat in grim silence, knowing full well she was right. But it didn't change anything. Finally, he stood up and took that first step back toward Sean's apartment.

"What are you going to do, Sandor?"

"My duty."

"But—"

"I don't want to talk about it anymore. You asked me to listen and I did. Now I'm going to do my job."

"Fine—but find out this kid's truth before you do something you'll always regret. If justice is willfully blind, then it's not justice."

Sandor returned to the apartment with Lena right on his heels. The woman was nothing if not stubborn, especially when it came to what she thought was best for him. They were quite the pair—both ready to forgive the other almost anything, but unable to cut themselves any slack. If their relationship survived this evening, they'd have to work on that.

Sean had closed and locked the door again, and Sandor sensed the kid standing right on the other side, his pulse rapid, his breathing shallow. Sandor used a small jolt of energy to unlock the door, then hit it with enough force to pop it open.

Shoving Sean backwards, he dragged Lena into the apartment with him, kicking the door closed behind them.

Sean immediately positioned himself between the other two people in the room, but they didn't stay behind him. A slender young woman, probably no older than Sean, moved up beside him on the right while a younger boy took the left. Sandor liked that about them.

Damn it all, could this get any worse? Here

he was, a highly trained Talion, facing off against three half-starved Kyth kids. From the readings he was getting, they were strong ones, too.

"Sean, where's your family?"

"Why? You want to kill them, too?" he asked defiantly.

"Just answer the damn question."

"You're looking at the only family I have." He took a half step forward, trying again to put himself between them and Sandor.

"How long have you been on your own?"

Sean glanced at the girl. "Five years, give or take."

Sandor tried the girl next. "How did you hook up with him?"

Sean answered, "Tara and I were in the same foster home. We left when the father started giving her problems."

Sandor could imagine exactly what kind of problems they'd been. Once this was settled, he'd track the bastard down. "When did you realize that both of you had abilities that other kids don't?"

"What abilities are you talking about?" Sean asked, but his eyes locked onto Sandor's hands.

"Like this one." Sandor made it easy and held them out, letting the three look their fill at the dark energy surging under his skin.

The younger boy's eyes nearly popped out of his head. "Hot damn, that's so cool. I can't do that."

"I can." Sean held up his own hands. "But not until recently."

"All three of you need energy hits to get by, but you don't know why. Am I right?" Sandor asked.

They looked at each other before nodding.

"I know what's going on with you because, as you can see, I'm like you. And there are more of us out there than you know. We call ourselves the Kyth, and we're a separate species of human beings."

"Are you shittin' me?" Sean's face went from hopeful to incredulous.

"No, I'm not." Sandor pointed to the couch. "So why don't the three of you sit down, while I explain some things to you and answer any questions you might have. Then I'll need to make a phone call."

The girl remained standing and asked, "Would either of you like something to drink? We've only got water and maybe some pop."

"Water would be great."

Lena nodded. "Make it two."

Sandor liked the girl's instincts. By acting as if he and Lena were invited guests, instead of invaders, it gave them all a chance to ratchet down the tension. He waited until she returned before beginning his explanation, which he'd used for years to introduce newly found Kyth to their heritage and culture.

By the time he was done, all three of the kids were staring at him with wonder and disbelief in their eyes. It felt good to be playing ambassador again, instead of judge and jury—although they weren't out of the woods yet.

"Okay, here comes the hard part." He looked directly at Sean. "What I am is a Talion warrior. *Talion* loosely translates as 'an eye for an eye' or 'justice meted out in kind,' which means we're the police force for our people. I serve our ruler, the Grand Dame, and enforce our laws. You should know right up front that we do not allow renegade Kyth to live, because when they harm humans, they endanger all of us."

"What's that got to do with me?" Sean asked, but there was resignation in his eyes.

"Don't play games with me, Sean. You've been hurting the humans you've been feeding from. Not only that, your attacks are getting more frequent and more violent."

"Yes." The boy's voice cracked with fear and shame. "I've tried to control myself, but I can't anymore. But I'm the problem—not Kenny or Tara."

"But they've been feeding, too, haven't they?"

Kenny gulped and nodded, but Tara spoke up. "I know it's no excuse, but we didn't know what else to do."

Sandor smiled at her. "And that's precisely what I'm going to tell our Grand Dame when you meet her."

He pulled out his cell phone and went around the corner into the kitchen, glad for a moment's respite from those desperate young eyes. "Kerry, I know I'm causing you a major problem, and I'm sorry about that. But I'm coming in and bringing company with me." He yanked open the refrigerator, confirming his suspicions. "Do me a favor and order in several pizzas, enough for us plus three extra people." He snapped the phone closed before his ruler could say more than a stunned "Okay."

Lena was waiting right behind him, clearly having eavesdropped.

She gave him an impish smile. "I bet Kerry just loves getting phone calls from you. That's the second one tonight where you've issued orders and then hung up on her."

"I figure Ranulf will come after me if I keep doing that, but right now I've got bigger fish to fry."

As soon as he walked back into the living room, Sean stood between Sandor and his friends. "I heard that. We're not going anywhere to meet anybody."

"Sean, right now I'm not too happy with you and your friends. You've been hurting people all over this city, and that's going to stop, because you're drawing too much attention to yourself. I know you have no reason to trust anyone, much less me, but I'm asking you to try."

"Why should I?"

"Because I just stuck my neck out a long, long way for you. If you'd rather I carry out that death sentence, it would simplify my life. It's your choice, of course, but I'd bet Tara and Kenny here would like some say in how this plays out."

He wasn't supposed to give second chances. But if Kerry wanted him to run the Talions, some changes needed to be made. He couldn't live with himself if he didn't at least try to drag his people into the twenty-first century.

Once again, Tara stood beside Sean. "What do you want us to do?"

"Come with me. No harm will come to any of you tonight." He placed his hand on the brand on his arm. "This I swear."

Sean clearly wasn't convinced. "Tara, we don't really know anything about this guy."

"No, but we *do* know that you need help, Sean. I don't want you to die."

Finally, Sean nodded. "Come on, Kenny. Looks like we're going for a ride."

When Lena slipped her hand in Sandor's, the band of tension around his chest eased up considerably. He might be out of a job after this, but he wouldn't be alone.

When Kerry passed her husband for the fifth time, she couldn't help it. She lost it and started laughing. Maybe it was just hysteria, but it felt good. Ranulf did an about-face.

"What's so funny?"

"Us. This." She waved her hand in the air. "We might as well have a track installed in the living room if we're both going to be walking laps like this."

He glowered at her briefly, then dragged her up for a quick kiss. She showed her approval by deepening it.

The sound of someone clearing his throat derailed that, but she didn't immediately step out of her husband's warm embrace.

"Yes, Mr. Danby?"

"Please call me Grey, and I apologize for intruding. However, I believe your guests have arrived."

Grey's expression was a carefully schooled

blank, probably part of that whole stiff-upper-lip stuff. And as much as she loved his British accent, she was finding him impossible to read.

She would have preferred to keep him in the dark about Sandor's visit, but Danby had been standing beside her when the call had come in. She and Ranulf had planned on taking Grey out to dinner. Instead they were having pizza, evidently with a trio of renegade Kyth.

Sandor had certainly put her in a difficult situation. The imminent executions should make for lovely dinner conversation.

Hughes joined the party, giving Grey a sharp look for stealing his thunder. "I thought you'd like to know that Mr. Kearn has arrived. He has Miss Wilson with him, as well as three other individuals."

He then backed out of the room to usher their unexpected guests in.

Kerry kept her fingers crossed that her Chief Talion had a good reason for his unexpected action. Ever since she signed that execution order, there'd been a lump of regret and pain in her stomach that no amount of rationalization could alleviate.

She retreated to her chair and sat down. Ranulf positioned himself next to her, reassuring her with his presence. Grey crossed to stand next to the fireplace, no doubt wanting an unobstructed view of the proceedings so he could report back to his friends in great detail.

Sandor hesitated in the doorway when he spotted Greyhill Danby in the room. Kerry grimaced slightly but inclined her head, signaling that he should approach her. Sandor stopped directly in front of her and bowed slightly from the waist.

"Kerry Thorsen, Grand Dame of all the Kyth, and Ranulf Thorsen, her Consort, thank you for granting me this audience on such short notice. I have come to inform you that I have failed to carry out my duties as Chief Talion."

She followed his lead, falling back on the formal rituals he'd been teaching her. "Explain yourself, Talion Sandor Kearn. Were your orders somehow unclear?"

He jerked, as if she'd struck him. "No, Grand Dame, I understood them, but I thought I might be allowed to bring extenuating circumstances to your attention. If you find that I have acted in error, I will tender my resignation immediately as Chief Talion and accept the consequences."

"I repeat, Talion Kearn. Explain your actions and the decision that led you to postpone carrying out your orders."

"As ordered, I located the three renegades responsible for the attacks on humans in recent weeks, and confronted them. Kyth justice is clear on the matter of Kyth who choose to go renegade and cause harm. However, I would like to point out that this case is different than any other I'm familiar with."

"How so?"

"The Kyth in this instance didn't consciously make the choice to go renegade. They couldn't." A fleeting hint of a smile softened his solemn expression.

"Are you saying they harmed no humans?"

"No, that much was true. What I am saying is that these three individuals were not aware of being Kyth until I told them this evening. I haven't had time to investigate their pasts, but they were out on the streets at a very young age with no instruction on how to handle their Kyth abilities. They couldn't choose to do the right thing when no one ever gave them the chance to learn what that was."

Kerry reminded him, "I was not aware I was Kyth, but I didn't knowingly harm anyone to maintain my energy needs."

"True, but may I point out that you had a stable family, Dame Kerry. These kids didn't have that. That they not only found each other but also a way to cope at all, is a miracle." His voice had thickened, revealing the powerful emotions he was fighting.

"Tell me more." Her eyes begged him to make his argument convincing.

"The oldest one, Sean, has a Talion's talents. They are close to going out of control, but I believe that proper training will rectify that. I'm pleased to say that the girl, Tara, has some of your own ability to calm, as well as to share healing energy. The youngest is just now coming into his Kyth abilities, so they will require further evaluation, as well as training.

"I believe that it would be wrong to destroy lives that have never been given an opportunity to flourish. And I would like to believe that our concept of justice can be flexible enough to allow for second chances. If not, then I will return them to their home unharmed—I promised them that much. I would then have no choice but to resign from your service."

"And what would you do?" This from Ranulf.

"I would make a new life with Lena." As she entered the room, Sandor held his hand out to the woman he loved. "That is, if she'll have me."

"She will." Lena stood shoulder to shoulder with him, her fingers intertwined with his as she met Kerry's gaze. "Though I don't think we'll be going anywhere."

"You are right," Kerry said, "and I believe your decision has merit. While Dame Judith might not have reached the same decision, she did entrust the care of her people to me. These children are our people, even though they had no way of knowing that before tonight."

Sandor looked toward Grey Danby. If he was reading the Brit correctly, that was approval in his eyes. Good. Sandor had put Kerry in a tough spot, because it had been a toss-up as to whether Grey would view Kerry's rescinding an order of execution as a mercy or a weakness.

"Bring them in," Kerry said.

As soon as she saw the three teenagers, it was clear she wanted to wrap her arms around them and protect them.

"You must be Sean," she said, looking at the older boy.

"Yeah."

"Which makes them . . . ?" she asked, looking first at the girl and then at the younger boy.

"Tara and Kenny."

"Have you all understood what Sandor has been telling me?"

The three looked at each other before nodding. "Yes, we've understood," Sean said on behalf of the group.

Kerry smiled and looked at everyone in the room. "Okay. Here's what we're going to do . . ."

• • •

Sean couldn't remember the last time he'd been so full. Maybe he shouldn't have had that last piece of pizza, but he'd learned never to waste an opportunity. Meals could be few and far between—though if these people were on the up-and-up, that was about to change.

Kenny sat up and rubbed his eyes. "Aren't you coming to bed?"

"In a little while. Go back to sleep. I'm not going anywhere."

Kenny quickly drifted back to sleep.

Not only had Dame Kerry fed them but she'd also given them each a serious jolt of energy. For the first time in months, Sean didn't feel the driving urge to be out hunting. And that monster big husband of hers had promised to teach him how to control his needs. That was one scary dude, but Sean would listen to anyone who could make it safe for him to stay with Tara and Kenny.

Tara was in the next room, on the other side of that giant bathroom. Ranulf had said that it used to be his room but Tara could use it as long as she liked. Sean wasn't sure how he felt about moving in with Kerry and Ranulf, but he was willing to give it a try for Tara and Kenny's sake.

He really hoped that this worked out. Thanks to Sandor sticking his neck out for him, Dame

Kerry had made it clear that she would allow Sean a second chance to control his need for energy, but not a third. One screwup and he'd be facing Sandor or Ranulf—and this time there'd be no walking away.

He'd promised Sandor he'd give it his best shot, and the tall Talion had gravely nodded and said his training would start immediately. There had been another guy in the room who'd also offered to help him, but Sean hadn't caught his name. No matter how it turned out for him, though, at least Tara and Kenny would be looked after.

Suddenly, there was a lump in his throat. Maybe he should try to get some sleep. For the first time, tomorrow held hope.

Lena knew they were both running on pure adrenaline and would crash any minute. Ranulf had promised to drive the three kids back to their apartment tomorrow to pack up their things; no one had wanted to let them go back there tonight. Evidently Kerry had continued Dame Judith's policy of keeping extra clothes and toiletries on hand in case of unexpected guests, and they'd found enough to get their new charges through the night. It was a good first step.

Although Kerry had offered her and Sandor a room, he'd insisted on going back to his bungalow. Lena had convinced him to leave his car at Kerry's and to let her drive. Although everything had turned out for the best, the evening had taken a toll on him.

They still had a few things to settle, then she'd be leaving for the East Coast. The only question was whether she'd be staying there permanently, or only long enough to pack her things to move back to Seattle.

Bracing herself, she left the bathroom to face the man waiting for her in bed. Sandor's dark eyes followed her every step until she got under the blankets.

"Why did Kerry ask you to resign as Chief Talion? That hardly seems fair, after all you've been through."

"It wasn't a punishment. It seems that Grey Danby is here for more than a brief visit. Since he's one of the strongest Talions, he'd make a good candidate for Chief Talion. Kerry figures that will keep him too busy to do much spying for the European branches, if that's really why he's here.

"This will free me up to do more of the work I used to do for Judith, acting as more of an ambassador than an enforcer. Besides, someone needs to take charge of the kids' training."

"That's smart thinking on Kerry's part."

"I thought so." He moved closer. "So, I have a question for you."

She braced herself, knowing he was going to demand the words. She was far better at communicating by direct action. "Okay."

"Did you mean it?"

Her heart fluttered when she saw the gold sparks flickering in his eyes. "Did I mean what?"

"That you'll have me." He moved even closer, stopping just short of touching her.

Feeling as if she were about to charge into a three-alarm fire with no equipment, she said, "Yes, Sandor, I meant it."

"And why is that?"

She could feel the heat of his body seeping into hers, warming her from the inside out. "Because I can't imagine living another day of my life without you in it. You made me fall in love with you."

That last small distance disappeared as his strong arms wrapped around her, pulling her close with achingly gentle care. "I'd say that's only fair. Because you made me love you, first."

"Not true. I loved *you* first, because you're sneaky that way."

He smiled against her hair. "You know, we could argue about this until the day we die."

"If that's how long it takes, so be it."

"I'm up for it."

Her hand trailed below the sheet. "I'm guessing that's not *all* you're up for," she said with a grin.

He laughed. "I'm a born multitasker."

Lena drew him in for a kiss. "It's been a long day. How about we concentrate on one task at a time?"

"Yes, ma'am." Sandor loomed over her, gold flecks twinkling in his eyes. "You will have my undivided attention."

She smile up at her lover. "Smart man."

Epilogue

*G*rey Danby walked out to the far corner of the Dame's rose garden, his bad mood showing in the flickers of blue that danced along his nerves and sparkled brightly in the morning sun. He yanked his cell phone out of his pocket and hit the first number on speed dial, resenting having to make the bloody call at all.

In England, folks were very unhappy with the late Dame's choice of a successor. A few were even out for blood. Judging by the cool reception he'd received from Kerry and Ranulf, they suspected the truth behind his unexpected visit and didn't trust the motives that had landed Grey on their doorstep one bit. Their instincts were right on the money.

He'd been ordered to evaluate the new Dame,

determine her weaknesses, and report back as soon as possible. But Dame Kerry had trumped their move by offering him the position of Chief Talion in exchange for his sworn allegiance. He'd accepted without hesitation. So not only would he not be returning to Europe anytime soon but the Dame would also be keeping him on a short leash.

Kerry Thorsen might be young, but she was obviously no fool. He'd have to work hard to earn her trust. The only question was if he would ever deserve it—or even want to.

His contact answered on the second ring, and Grey wished he could see the look on the man's face when he sprang this news on him.

"Sorry to disturb you at this hour, but I thought you'd like to know there's been a change in plans."

Turn the page
for a sneak peek at
Alexis Morgan's
next exciting Paladin novel!

**Coming Spring 2010
from Pocket Star**

*I*t was obvious her new tenant hated being stared at, but there was no way to avoid it. Considering the quaint nature of Justice Point, Hunter Fitzsimon shouldn't be shocked to find out that watching him tote a handful of boxes up a staircase would draw a crowd.

However, her neighbors had spent more than enough time ogling the newest resident. Tate waited until Hunter was inside the apartment and shooed everyone back around to their own yards. If he was surprised to find himself alone when he came back out, it didn't show. With the same look of grim determination, he returned to his truck for another load of boxes.

His limp was getting more pronounced, clear evidence that he'd made one trip too many up the stairs. She'd seen him carry in a duffel bag and a motley assortment of cardboard boxes but nothing that looked like food.

It would only be neighborly to take him some lunch. Making some extra sandwiches wouldn't be that much more bother than making just one for herself. Add a couple of soft drinks, or better yet a cold beer, one of her fresh blueberry muffins, and an apple. No, make that two apples. He might get hungry later.

She tucked the food into a basket and set the sign in the shop window to say she'd be back in fifteen minutes. Timing her approach was tricky. She waited until he'd carried up another load. Picking up two of his smaller boxes, she followed him up the steps.

He exited the apartment just as she reached the top step. He immediately snagged the top box off her stack and stood glaring down at her. She found herself tangled in the net of his angry gaze, his eyes green and smoky, framed by ridiculously long eyelashes. It took considerable effort to look away. He clearly wasn't thrilled to see her. Fine. He was her tenant, not her best buddy. But he still had to eat.

"I didn't ask for help." He shoved the box inside his apartment and reached for the second.

She hesitated before releasing it. "I know you didn't, Mr. Fitzsimon. I realize you are perfectly capable of hauling all this stuff up here by yourself."

He didn't respond. If anything, Hunter looked even angrier. When he held out his hands again for the box, she surrendered it.

"Thanks," he grumbled.

He started back inside. Before he could close the door, she stepped up on the small landing and blocked the door with her hand.

He prevented her from opening it any farther. "What now, Ms. Justice?"

"It's Tate, and this is yours." She all but shoved the basket at him.

"That's not mine."

"I know. It's lunch . . . for you, I mean. I thought you might be hungry." Rather than wait for him to react, she turned away. "No rush in returning the basket."

"Ms. Justice, I don't need . . ."

Ignoring him, she skipped back down the steps. When she reached the bottom, she looked back and smiled. "Look, I know you've got a lot to do, and I've got to get back to the shop. Let me know if you need anything."

The sound of the door slamming closed was his only response.

Hunter watched his pesky landlady through the window until she disappeared into her behemoth of a house. His first instinct was to go after her and shove the basket right back into her interfering hands, but that was his temper talking.

She'd meant well. Earlier, she'd even run off all the nosy neighbors to afford him some privacy when she thought he wasn't looking. Maybe she *did* understand that he wanted to be left alone. And the truth was he was in no shape to drive anywhere just to eat. If he didn't rest his leg soon, he'd be in for a world of hurt.

After a final trip up the stairs, he limped over

to collapse on the small couch and gingerly lifted his leg up to rest on the coffee table. Shards of pain ripped through his much abused limb with lightning speed. Gritting his teeth, he kicked his head back and waited for the worst of it to pass.

On a scale of one to ten, the pain was an eight. Anything less than a nine didn't warrant a pain pill. His rule, not his Handler's. Doc Crosby had argued that Hunter would heal better if he stayed ahead of the pain rather than wait for the medicine to catch up with it. But popping pills that made him queasy and dulled his brain would be just one more in the long line of concessions he had to make because of his injury. He'd already lost too damn much; better that he grit his teeth and ride out the pain. Eventually it would fade to a manageable level. It always did. Meanwhile, he'd check out what Tate Justice had packed him for lunch.

He snagged the cold beer and popped the top. He didn't want to encourage her good Samaritan act, but he definitely owed her one. The beer was a brand he wasn't familiar with, probably from a local microbrewery, but it tasted damn fine.

Figuring he shouldn't be downing alcohol on an empty stomach, he fished out one of the sandwiches and took a healthy bite. He wasn't much for bean sprouts, but the sliced ham was definitely a cut above the bologna he'd planned on buying for himself. By the time he'd finished the sandwich, an apple, and half the blueberry muffin, he felt a helluva lot better.

For the first time, he took a close look at his new home. It wasn't much space-wise, but he couldn't complain. Whoever had designed the apartment had done a decent job. He'd certainly made do with less in his life. The pillowtop queen-sized bed was a pleasant surprise as was the over-sized tub with spray jets. He planned on trying that out as soon as he unpacked and made a quick trip to the grocery store.

Right now, he was just glad to not be moving. He closed his eyes and let his mind drift. Since his leg had quit throbbing for now, he could use a little shuteye. He'd drive to town later and maybe treat himself to a decent meal before coming back. To-morrow would be soon enough to start learning the lay of the land surrounding Justice Point.

Tate opened the kitchen windows to dispel the smell of burnt muffins and had to admit she was more than a bit distracted. She set the charred remains aside to toss into the woods later. Her usual customers wouldn't appreciate charcoal-flavored pastries, but her four-legged friends weren't nearly as picky.

Once she stuck the replacement batch in the oven and set the timer, she'd sit down at the table and see if she could concentrate long enough to polish off her latest chapter. That she could also keep an eye on the apartment over the garage was beside the point. Tate had no business spying on her new tenant, but she'd never been able to resist a puzzle, and Hunter Fitzsimon was definitely puzzling.

What was he doing here in Justice Point? As much as she loved the place, it didn't have much to offer a man like Hunter. He was obviously recuperating from a major injury, but he didn't seem the type to be drawn to quiet village life. There was too much intensity in his eyes to be satisfied with the slow pace of her boring life.

No! She didn't mean that. Her life was quiet, true, but calm didn't mean boring. Life with her mother had been unpredictable and chaotic. The only respite Tate had ever found had been her summer visits to her uncle's house, which now belonged to her. Bless Uncle Jacob's heart, he'd left her his ramshackle Victorian and enough money to live on for several years as long as she was careful. He'd made it possible for her to pursue her dream of becoming a published author.

Her mother had promptly demanded she sell the place, probably hoping Tate would then share the profits with her. But in case Tate's resolve wavered, Uncle Jacob had staged a preemptive strike against Sandra Justice's greed by stipulating that Tate couldn't sell the house for at least five years or the proceeds would go to charity. When her mother had heard the terms of the will, she'd stormed out of the attorney's office cursing her brother-in-law's idiocy and leaving Tate to find her own way back home.

It had taken Tate less than a week to break her lease, quit her job, and move into the house. Her mother had only spoken to her once since then and that was to ask for money. When Tate had explained she didn't have any, good old mom had hung up in a snit. No doubt, Sandra would get over it eventually and reach out to Tate again, probably about the time her creditors started calling.

Meanwhile, Tate wondered what her mother would think of the newest resident of Justice Point. Sandra always had an eye for a good-looking guy, but she preferred her men old, rich, and malleable. Glancing out the window toward the garage, Tate had to admit that she was strangely relieved her tenant didn't fit those demographics.

The timer on the stove chimed, reminding her that she was there to keep an eye on her baking, not Hunter. As she was setting the muffins out on the rack to cool, a noise outside caught her attention. She moved closer to the window and groaned as soon as she realized what was going on. One of the Auntie M's was standing at the bottom of the garage steps and hollering. If they kept this up, Tate might very well lose her new tenant. However, short of posting No Trespassing signs, she didn't know how to keep people from bothering Hunter.

Besides, it wasn't her job anyway. She'd be better off keeping a wary eye on things and seeing how he handled the situation himself. But after making her decision, she immediately ignored it and went charging to the rescue. The only trouble was that she wasn't sure who needed saving.

Hunter jerked awake, his well-earned nap ending abruptly, leaving him groggy and confused. It took a second or two for him to recognize his surroundings. Someone was raising a ruckus right outside. He carefully lowered his leg to the ground and used the arm of the couch to push himself up to his feet. After grabbing his cane, he started for the door, ready to order Tate Justice to leave him the hell alone.

Only it wasn't Tate. Outside on the landing, he found himself looking down the steps at a tiny old woman banging her own cane on his steps with a surprising amount of determination. There were a lot of things he'd done that he wasn't proud of, but abusing little old ladies wasn't one of them. He choked back his temper and aimed for somewhere close to polite when he spoke.

"Can I help you, ma'am?"

She stopped banging away at the step and peered up at him. "Young man! Come down here right now."

There was no getting around it. It would take an

even harder heart than his to ignore her summons. He started down the steps, taking his time to avoid setting off his leg again. His visitor stood at the bottom and watched him through the thick lenses of her glasses for several seconds before abruptly turning away.

At first he thought she was embarrassed for him as he awkwardly limped his way down the steps, and his anger flared. Then he realized that someone else was headed in their direction. He didn't have to look to know that once again Tate Justice was intruding on his privacy. She was still a few yards away when he reached the bottom. The old lady immediately turned back toward him and thrust a plate of cookies at him.

"My sisters and I wanted to welcome you to Justice Point. We thought Tate would've had the good manners to introduce you around." She shook her head, looking sorely disappointed. "I'm Mabel. My sisters are Madge and Margaret. They would've come along to meet you themselves, but we didn't want to overwhelm you on your first day in town."

It was impossible not to like her feisty spirit. "That was nice of you, Miss Mabel. I'm Hunter Fitzsimon, and I have to admit I do have a sweet tooth. These cookies will be greatly enjoyed, so please thank your sisters for me."

She patted him on the arm. "I'll do that. You have nice manners, young man. Now I'd better get back home."

As she made slow but steady progress back up the driveway, he debated whether to wait for Tate to get up the courage to make her final approach, or go on back upstairs. He decided to wait, figuring she would make a better target for his aggravation.

"Well, have you taken root there or did you want to say something?"

She winced. "I was going to try to head Mabel off at the pass but didn't get here fast enough. She and her sisters like to bake cookies for everybody in town."

"So what's the problem? Did you think I got my kicks being rude to old ladies?"

She shifted from foot to foot. "Not exactly, but I could tell you don't like being bothered."

He couldn't resist tweaking her temper a bit. "Maybe it's only nosy landladies I don't like bothering me."

Her chin came up and her dark eyes narrowed. "I wasn't being nosy. I was being neighborly."

"Obviously my mistake, but then it's hard to tell the difference. At least now you can sleep nights knowing that I don't eat old ladies for dinner."

Tucking his cane under his arm, he held the plate of cookies in his right hand and kept his left on the railing to better support himself going up the steps. When he'd gotten about halfway, he looked back over his shoulder to see Tate still standing right where he'd left her.

"The show's over, sweetheart. You can go back

to whatever it is you do besides stare out your kitchen window."

Ignoring her gasp of outrage, he continued on up, waiting until he was inside before risking another look. She'd almost reached her back porch, righteous indignation clear in every step she took. He set his cane aside and ate a cookie as he watched. Chocolate chip, his favorite. A door slammed across the lawn. Tate Justice definitely had a temper.

For the first time all day, he smiled.

Take romance TO ANOTHER realm WITH paranormal bestsellers FROM POCKET BOOKS!

Nice Girls Don't Have Fangs
MOLLY HARPER

Jane was an unemployed children's librarian before she got turned into a vampire. Now she has a new host of problems—and a really long shelf life.

New in the SHADOWMEN series from USA TODAY bestselling author JENNIFER ST. GILES!

Kiss of Darkness

A man whose inner demons have been released must turn to a woman with magical abilities for help, despite his skepticism—and his irrepressible desire for her.

Bride of the Wolf

When a heroic werewolf is trapped in the twilight realm, only a passionate woman with a spirit as wild as his own can set him free.